G000254426

THE MARIONETTE

JOHN SURDUS

THE
DEEP
PRESS

Published by The Deep Press.

Copyright © 2022 by John Surdus

All rights reserved.

No part of this book may be reproduced in any form or by any
electronic or mechanical means, including information storage and
retrieval systems, without written permission from the author, except for
the use of brief quotations in a book review.

Note

This is a work of fiction. Names, characters, events and incidents are the products of the author's imagination. Any resemblance to actual persons, living or dead, or to actual events is purely coincidental. Certain long-standing institutions, agencies, and public offices are mentioned, but the characters involved are wholly imaginary.

For Mark McGuinness

While lost in these illusions I forgot my destiny - to be one of the hunted.

Jorge Luis Borges.

Contents

A Psychiatrist Speaks

The appointment was a mistake, for the psychiatrist looked more disturbed than he was. He was about his own age, a wiry figure in a pin-striped suit. No tie, but a pink shirt that spilled out from the front. Thick, greying hair and pebble glasses that gave his eyes a fanatic look. Outside, the one-way traffic thundered up Wimpole Street. Inside, the consulting room was bathed in cream light, filtering through venetian blinds.

"How would you describe your state of mind?" asked Dr Adcocke.

"Bored, listless, apathetic..."

"Suicidal?"

"No. Not that."

"Your appetites? Food, sleep, sex...?"

"Normal."

"What would you say was wrong with you?"

Michael had never been exactly sure. Whether it was something he inherited from his mother, a brain abnormality, or the result of too much philosophy. Even now, he was certain that thoughts would find him rather than the other way around.

"That each thing I think, say, or do has been decided in advance. That nothing that comes from me will make any difference."

"The statement you just made: was that, too, decided in advance?"

"Indeed. Rather like the sounds on a vinyl record when you place the needle on it."

The psychiatrist licked his lips and typed some more.

On went the questions. The man loaded the answers into a laptop, unaware that Michael was drifting away.

He looked at the dreamy prints on the walls: mass produced surrealism from eBay. On a polished side table was a hunched figure of a woman embracing a child, although it was hard to tell whether she was nurturing it or suffocating it.

On completion, Adcocke sat down on the leather recliner opposite.

"You have at least five markers for clinical depression," he said.

"I don't feel depressed."

"That is what depression is. An absence of feeling."

Adcocke stretched out his legs. First point to him. Michael met that with more silence.

"There are more unusual markers."

"Such as?"

"The absence of volition, for one thing. That, and the schizoid element in the clinical picture."

"Spare me the jargon. Tell me what that means in your own words."

"No."

"What?"

"The 'jargon', as you call it, is an essential part of the procedure. It carries an exact meaning."

"Tell me what the exact meaning is, then."

"The schizoid personality is locked away in paranoid thoughts and fantasies, with the delusion of having special powers. The problem you have is that your mother shared those delusions. What we call a folie à deux."

"Whereas your delusions are fine, because you share them with other psychiatrists?"

"We have a consensus of scientific opinion, if that's what you mean."

"This schizoid thing you're excited about: should I be concerned?"

"You ought to be. Such people are capable of violence once their rage and despair are unleashed."

"I don't wish anyone any harm."

"Quite so. The rage is often well hidden."

"How do I know it is there?"

Adcocke took off his gold-rimmed spectacles and made a show of polishing the lenses.

"You will need treatment, my friend."

"What did you have in mind?"

"A course of psychotherapy."

"How would that work?"

"An operation to uncover the lineaments of frustrated desire."

Adcocke replaced his spectacles and rebalanced them on his nose. His eyes gleamed from behind them.

"How would you go about uncovering those?"

"Through tracing the objects to which that desire is affixed. I'm particularly interested in the fact your mother brought you up, that you shared her bed as a child, and that she was taken from you when you were sixteen."

"She wasn't taken, she was murdered."

3

"Quite so. Yet the roots of your disorder can be found there."

"If they are there."

"If it is the word 'depression' you dislike, then we can call it something else. 'Anguish', for example. For myself, it is simply a disturbance that began at birth."

"You think birth is a mistake?"

Adcocke shrugged and stretched out his legs some more.

"It's a convenient view to have for a man in your profession," said Michael. "You'll never run short of patients."

"I would put it the other way. Your cynicism means that you will never have to become a patient."

"I'd consider becoming one if I thought I was going to be understood. Seems to me you've already made your mind up about my case before we started."

"You taught philosophy, I believe? At Queen's?"

"What's that got to do with it?"

"Only that your education makes you more resistant. It has become your refuge, has it not? A place where you are safe from the truth."

"The truth I will only find once you have taught me psychoanalysis? And a new vocabulary to go with it?"

Adcocke's moustache twitched. Michael's smile of mockery was unyielding. At length, he gave up.

"I can prescribe an anti-depressant if you prefer."

"Another drug? Don't you have anything apart from indoctrination and chemicals?"

Adcocke's hand patted the armrest while he searched for a retort.

"It seems your visit has been a waste of time," he said at last, getting up.

"Not entirely," said Michael, going over to fetch his

raincoat. "It's always enlightening to see how these cults work."

On his way out, the receptionist stopped him.

"Dr Adcocke has the four-thirty slot on Mondays free. Will you take that? An annual block booking is seven thousand pounds."

"I have decided not to accept that privilege."

The receptionist, a well-groomed woman who looked as if someone had thoroughly analysed her, opened her mouth in surprise.

"You won't find anyone better in London."

"Someone else told me that," said Michael.

Out on the street, the spring shower had cleared; it was warming up again. Michael looked at his watch. The reception at the Bayes Gallery would start about now; he wanted to miss that. He walked up to Cavendish Square and went into *Pret a Manger*. Ordered a macchiato and sat by the window.

His phone buzzed, and a text appeared.

Where are you? Wilf.

He put the phone back on the table and tried to clear his head. What was swirling around inside his skull, waiting for him to open the door on it? It had a feeling of dread attached to it with something like a string.

He thought hard as he stared out the window. Prosperous citizens laden with fresh bags from department stores walked on up towards Marble Arch. Others, not so fortunate, were heading in the other direction towards the Oxford Circus Tube station.

It had something to do with his wife, he guessed. A reasonable assumption, since she occupied his thoughts a lot these days.

Random images came up. Of he and Peggy sitting on a beach in Blackwater the summer before. She in a deck chair and sun hat, dozing, voluptuous in the heat. He staring out at the sunlight flashing off the sea, listening to the cry of the gulls circling above. Connecting nothing with nothing. A smell of rank seaweed in his nostrils. The feeling of something trying to break into his head. With so much force, he had dived off the rocks into the cold, green sea. Shortly after that, he requested leave from his university post. Peggy hadn't been pleased about it, something that had led to their estrangement.

Was it for her he had made the appointment? Knowing in advance that no one could understand his oddity better than he did himself? Now that possibility, too, was closed. Leaving him with little else to go on.

He wondered where Peggy could be now. Would she miss him as much as he missed her? He doubted that. Most likely she was busy at her kiln. Or spending the afternoon with her lover. Unable to bear that last thought, he hurried out of the cafe. A black cab was cruising along by the pavement, its *For Hire* sign showing. On impulse, he got in.

"Where to, mate?"

"The Bayes Gallery. Halfway up the Old Brompton Road."

2

The Art Scene

Forty-five minutes before Michael got in the cab, The Right Hon. Perry Winter addressed a crowd of art-seekers.

"On the occasion of the twentieth anniversary of the Bayes & Bayes Gallery, it gives me great pleasure to unveil Clarice Angel's tribute."

He pulled a cord, and a curtain lifted away from the exhibit. To reveal a steel tripod crowned by an Aztec skull in blue and white acrylic, its teeth set in a ferocious grin.

Cameras flashed, and applause broke out. Two servers clothed in black circulated with trays of champagne and canapés. Press photographers roamed the gallery, taking pictures of dim celebrities in pairs and trios.

A sleek, blonde man in his late-forties, Winter turned to the co-founder of the Gallery beside him. A tall, elegant woman, also blonde, dressed in a white trouser suit that emphasised her straight back.

"Was that all right, Cosima?"

"Yes," she hissed, her grey eyes staring deep into his. "You kept it short."

"Not much to add, really," said Winter, looking up at the tripod.

"Less is more," she said, patting him on the arm. "Gives them something to wonder about."

Her hooded eyes fixed on his in encouragement. Her thin lips creased in a passable imitation of a smile.

Winter turned to a knot of admirers wanting to ask about the incoming government. He had the professional politician's knack of pretending to listen to people as if what they said was of great importance. Replying to them as if he were speaking to a fellow cabinet minister.

"Between you and me, I happen to know that the Prime Minister is of exactly the same opinion as you…"

Cosima Bayes circulated, glass in hand. Her brother, a one-eyed man wearing a cowboy hat and boots, was giving a press conference in the back office. She stopped for a moment to listen. Tristan was leaning back on the edge of the desk, replying to a journalist's question.

"London is the capital of the art scene. More so than New York, I would say. And this gallery is the hub. Walk around and see for yourselves the talent we are gathering here."

He was speaking rather fast, she decided. Taking way too much cocaine. She would speak to him about that.

She caught sight of two of her friends, Angus and Lou Ogilvie-Parkes, standing by the reception desk talking to Abisola, who was showing them a catalogue. Lou lifted her eyes beneath her hat and smiled back at her, mouthing words she did not recognise. Cosima signed to meet back at the house in Onslow Gardens after the party was over. Receiving back an upraised thumb in acknowledgment.

Out of the corner of her eye, another figure raised his glass in appreciation. A low-class man wearing a fake club tie, whom she recognised as the accountant Tristan used to finance some of his flaky deals. A man named Pilcher, who winked at her and prepared to approach. Overcome with horror, she turned about face and, for want of any other refuge, headed for her ex-husband.

Wilf Rising was standing with his arms folded around a green moleskin jacket, talking to a group of artists in his faint New York drawl as she came up. He and Clarice Angel were in the middle of an argument.

"You will admit that your installation is in the nature of an elaborate joke?"

"I might do," said Clarice, a thin, intense woman in red jeans and Dr Martens boots, "if you admit your pictures are reactionary fairy stories."

Wilf stroked his beard. He was about to tease her some more when he noticed Cosima heading fast towards the little group. He stepped aside to accommodate her.

"Wilf, what are you here for?"

Wilf surveyed her for a moment, knowing that Cosima disliked inspections. He pointed to a picture on the far wall.

"You have one of my paintings on show. Right there."

She turned to check, then stared back at him.

"Quite so."

"I like to come by now and then. Check out you and Tristan are doing your job of representing me."

By now, the other artists had separated away to form fresh groups, leaving the two of them alone. Around the gallery, the champagne had done its work and the hubbub rose to a fresh pitch.

"Where's Claudia now?" Wilf asked.

"It's a weekday. Therefore, she's at school," said Cosima, as if she were talking to another child.

"Might have been nice to have her come by. I'd like to see her."

"Look, our agreement was quite clear…"

"Chill out, Cosima. I haven't come here to quarrel. I'm going away for a while. To Lucca, in fact. The Instituto Casiraghi have invited me over."

"Fine. I'll have her call you."

Wilf looked at her with sorrow. Before he could say anything else, Michael appeared at his elbow, in cropped hair and Ray-Bans, behind which he was gazing around in horror at the people in the room.

Cosima recoiled in distaste.

"I'll leave you to your freaky friend," she said, heading back towards Winter, who was surveying the room like a child searching for its mother.

Wilf put his hand on his friend's shoulder in concern.

"Are you alright? I apologise for my ex-wife's disgusting manners."

Michael looked over at Cosima's retreating back. A smile of contempt playing on his mouth.

"I'm ready," he said.

"Ready for what?"

"To meet some middle-class trolls."

Seizing his arm, Wilf made to go.

"Are you a communist, or are you a hermit? Come and look at this."

Michael followed Wilf through a crowd to the back of the room, where three steps led down to a smaller gallery. A darkened, tranquil room with a few isolated pictures on display. In the middle a pedestal, on which stood an ageing faun in bronze. Michael stopped to look at it, then back at Wilf. With its mocking eyes, sensual lips, and thin beard, the satyr might have been Wilf himself. Who was now contemplating a painting on the wall to the left. A canvas about four feet by three, it was a semi-abstract in which an orange-brown cliff appeared to be crumbling into the deep blue sea, held back by a lone, indistinct figure half-submerged in the water. In the bottom right corner was the signature: Fillipo Casiraghi.

"This is the real thing," said Wilf, moving up to inspect the brushwork.

"Explain it to me."

Wilf looked at him with impatience.

"What the picture means, or why I admire it?"

"The latter."

"I saw Fillipo working on this canvas about eighteen years ago. But he hadn't finished when I left."

Wilf raised his fingers and felt the paint, murmuring to himself, then stood back.

"Look at the juxtaposition of these colours on the sea and the rocks, with the contrasting greys in the sky, and this woman in the water. Don't you feel the emotion in that?"

"The melancholy?"

"Yes, but there's danger there, too. As if something were about to overwhelm her."

Wilf shivered.

"Let's go. I've seen all I want to see here."

"Where are we going?"

"The pub, of course. I'll need a few stiff ones after this visit."

The White Devil

An hour later, they sat beneath the lime trees outside *The White Devil*. It was a balmy May evening in Clerkenwell; the first really fine weather of the summer. A festival crowd had come out in airy clothes to eat and drink. On the other side of the square, a mobile unit was filming. A girl in a baseball cap and ponytail held up a clapper board to the camera, which swivelled towards the pub and drank in the scene. Indifferent to those watching, a t-shirted couple at the next table cleaned out each other's mouths.

He stared hard at the intrusion. A head appeared from behind the camera and spoke to the clapper girl, who held up her board again. The crew looked his way before going into a huddle.

Wilf took a deep draught of his beer and pointed to Michael's Ricard and water on the table.

"Do you remember that bar in Viareggio? Where you started drinking that stuff?"

"I do."

The beach bar had been in a piazza with pine trees on

either side of a statue of Shelley. Who had washed up on the shore up the road, minus his face, after his boat sank in the bay. The search party had cremated his body on the beach. The statue didn't look like a romantic with dreams of human progress. Rather, it looked like a man who had just been asked to pay the rent. Most afternoons, he, Wilf, and the others would assemble on the beach to surf the rollers that came in off the bay. Afterwards going to the bar for aperitifs before they headed back to their apartment in Lucca.

He reached into his bag and took out a blister pack. *Sevredol 50 mg.* He popped one in his mouth and washed it down with the Ricard.

Wilf stared at him in surprise.

"What's that you're taking?"

"A pain-killer."

"Why are you taking that?"

"An old wound," said Michael. "But let's not talk about that. Why are you reminiscing about Tuscan places?"

"Because they are better than English places."

"How so?"

"Youth, Love, Art. Some beautiful landscapes, too."

"You forgot irony."

It was an old joke between them. The answer was always the same.

"I never forget irony," said Wilf.

"Good. Because if you forget irony you'll never get the joke."

But Wilf was not smiling. Rather, he was nursing his drink with a troubled air.

"Will we ever get back the intensity we had there?" he said.

"I doubt it," said Michael. "We were twenty-two years

old. What we had then was a brief interval between painful adolescence and disillusioned adulthood."

A look of pain wore over Wilf's face. Silence descended as they contemplated the revellers filling the square. Michael noted with satisfaction that the film crew were patiently transferring their gear into a 4 by 4, its doors open, ready to take them on to fresh spying trips.

"What are you working on?" asked Wilf.

"Translations into English. Some stories by Heinrich von Kleist."

"What sort of stories?"

"The usual thing. A rape on an aristocrat in Italy in the French revolutionary wars, a slave revolt in Santo Domingo, an earthquake followed by a mass lynching in Santiago."

Wilf snorted.

"Why do you like that stuff?"

"Because it's true to life. Moments of illusion broken up by chaos and random violence."

Wilf was about to say something but judged better of it.

"Doesn't seem to be much room for art in those stories," he said, at last.

"The story is the art. Showing us we are insignificant creatures at the mercy of forces we cannot control."

"But what about love, beauty, and human solidarity?"

"You mean lust, sensory delight, and the pack instinct?"

"Is that meant to be ironical?"

"No, for once it means something direct."

"But what about artists and writers who can see beyond the human condition?"

"You mean, improving it?"

"Why not?"

Michael shuddered.

"There's not much chance of that."

"You belong in a monastery. I've always thought so."

"It might suit me if I knew what to pray for. Do you want another drink?"

"In a moment. I have something to ask you."

"Concerning what?"

"Art, funnily enough. And that I'm not doing much of it anymore."

"You've just finished that picture on show in the gallery."

"Journeyman stuff. It's not in the same class as the work I produced in Lucca."

"It pays the bills."

"That's the first commission I've had all year."

Michael didn't know what to say about that. He was half-dreading it would come to this.

"They've invited me to do some teaching at the Casiraghi Institute," Wilf added.

The cricket in Michael's head was clicking in an irregular rhythm. Something wasn't right.

"When do you go?"

"It will have to be soon. Before June, at any rate."

Michael was still listening to the cricket. He picked up their glasses and walked back inside. Ordered more drinks and took a deep breath while he waited. It was still only 7.30; bright and warm. The doors were wide open to let in a breeze and light filled the room. He paid for the drinks with a credit card and took the tray back out. Wilf was leaning back on the seat with his knee between both hands, as he watched him distribute the drinks on the table.

"Something wrong?" asked Wilf.

Michael considered carefully before translating.

"Don't go."

"Why not?"

"Two things. You won't enjoy teaching, and you won't find what you're looking for in Lucca."

"That might be true. But it's a bit like losing your car keys. You've checked every room in the house three times, but there's nothing else to do but keep on searching."

"Maybe it's time to give up art."

"Give up painting?"

"No, just give up being an artist."

"Explain."

"You've become trapped by the Bayes and their art circus. So busy worrying about originality you've forgotten your craft. You remember how Casiraghi used to go around with his sketchbook, drawing the tombs in the Duomo? He was happy to do the journeyman stuff when there was nothing else on."

"I have an idea about that."

"What is it?"

"I want to borrow the carving."

"What do you want with it?"

"I'm planning to make some pictures from it. Using the figurine as a symbol. But first I'm going to make some castings in bronze."

"You want to create your own figures?"

"I want to use your mother's piece as a model. It was an idea I had this morning."

Michael mulled it over. It was hard to let go of something so dear to him, yet Wilf needed it more.

"Can you get it insured?"

"Of course."

"I'll lend it to you then."

"Thanks. You know, you could come over to Lucca yourself. I have an apartment on San Michele. Peggy could come too."

Michael winced.

"Peggy told you?"

Wilf lit up a cigarette and scrutinised him before he spoke.

"She told our mother she was moving out. Renting a place in St. Katherine's Dock."

He could hardly tell Wilf he had caught his sister sleeping with a martial arts instructor. Coming back early one morning, skipping the last day of a philosophy conference in Warwick, to find the man in boxer shorts sitting in the parlour drinking tea, while Peggy washed up, wearing nothing but her knickers. Or the scenes that followed.

"What's gone wrong between you?" asked Wilf.

"It started after we gave up the fertility treatment. She would get angry with me and then the arguments followed. We drove to Blackwater for a fresh start, and that's when I had my trouble."

"I never learned what was wrong with you. What is it exactly?"

"Acedia."

"What's that?"

"A state in which nothing you do makes any difference."

"Why ever not?"

"It's hard to explain."

"Try."

"I'll give you a metaphor. It's like being a marionette, except with consciousness. Knowing that every time you think, say, or do anything, something else is pulling the strings."

"But what about choice?"

"An illusion. The next move in the puppet dance is already decided."

"But Mike, that's only an idea. Isn't that what you're

always telling me about philosophy? That it's just a collection of thoughts?"

"True. But what if those thoughts don't belong to us, either? Like they are pre-programmed?"

"God. That's insane."

"A psychiatrist just told me that," said Michael.

4

Spitalfields

Darkness was falling as Michael came out of Shoreditch High Street and walked through the long, dark tunnel under the railway. He hurried on towards Spitalfields, for this was a dangerous area. The housing estate in Quaker Street was rife with drug-dealers and their clients. The latter, when short, would sometimes go out mugging in the streets for watches, mobiles, and cash to pay for their next baggie. Two thieves with knives had robbed him of his wallet the year before last. Another had killed his mother.

On Commercial Street he breathed easier, for this was a major road with kebab parlours, shops, and supermarkets. Outside *The Blade on the Bone*, crowds of drinkers overflowed onto the street while techno music boomed from within. Strobe lights lit up some dancers on a stage like a scene from hell. Further along was Christ Church, a Hawksmoor creation, its spire soaring above the Tuscan columns that supported it. Not a building Michael liked much. He turned left onto Foulard Street.

The house was halfway up on the left. A plain three-storied Georgian house with shuttered windows and a door with a portico on the right-hand side. A house he had lived in all his life. He let himself in.

The hall light laid bare the stripped stairway which led to the upper rooms. He had spent weeks planing down the oak, but restoration was slow, for there was only himself to do the work now. He stopped to listen. The silence of an empty house. Afar off, he could hear the hum of traffic on Bishopsgate. Some day he would find the money to instal double glazing to keep out the noise. Suppressing his spleen, he went down the narrow stairs at the back into the basement.

In the corner was a five-foot sorrowing angel, her arms reaching to the ceiling. On trestles placed against the wall were graveyard figures: stillborn children with wings; sleeping cats and dogs; effigies of the mature dead. He looked for the carving, placed it on the table and contemplated it.

It was a limestone figure of a woman. Erect with an urn held before her. Her expression half smile, and half sorrow. On the vessel an inscription:

You grieve for those for whom you should not grieve.
The wise grieve neither for the living nor the dead.
Never at any time was I not, nor thou.

Next to it was a photograph of his mother, taken a few days before the robbery. Along with the note she had left for him. Her killer had battered her half to death in this very room; her skull caved in by the laundry iron next to her, lying face down on the ground, still breathing. Dried cannabis strewn over the floor from her struggle to hold on to it. All that was left of the investment bought with the last of their savings. Twelve thousand pounds in cash; street value forty thousand. Enough to pay off the arrears on the mortgage and settle with the bailiffs. Instead, a dealer from the estate had killed her for it.

At that time, the house was dilapidated; damp on the walls and rotting floorboards. Like something out of a Charles Dickens novel. Dust everywhere. The first time Wilf visited, he found it fascinating and made him show him round.

"Is this house haunted?"

He hadn't liked to tell the truth: that from childhood, a woman scared him by walking up and down the stairs, or on the landing outside his room. A few times, he saw the woman descending the stairs to the ground floor. Wearing a shift and holding a burnt-out candle. He could feel a slight breeze as she passed. Sometimes she would enter the front room downstairs, where she appeared to be looking for something.

After a while, he became used to night walkers searching for things they could not find in the other world; just as the many seek for something in this world which cannot be found here. He knew other people found this subject distasteful, so he never talked about it. Just as he never spoke about the cricket in his head.

Wilf picked up the carving that stood on the mantelpiece.

"It's beautiful. But what do the words mean?"

"They are from the *Bhagavad Gita*. The words of Krishna to Arjuna."

"She looks unearthly... serene."

In fact, this was the woman he had seen walking down the stairs. Once he had come across his mother making an effigy of her one afternoon when he came back from school. Sitting at the trestle, smoothing away the imperfections with a wire brush.

"Who is it, Mother?"

"She came to me out of the rock as I was carving. She's been hiding in there, waiting for me to reveal her."

He had known his mother was lying. Later, she put down the carving and hugged him.

"This has to be a secret. You understand?"

"Why can't we tell anyone?"

"Because people like us... they think we're crazy."

The 'shining' she had called it, after her favourite film. An unwanted gift. One that had switched off abruptly the day she died in hospital. All that was left was the whisper from the cricket.

He and Wilf contemplated the faint, sad smile on the woman's face as she held out her offering, giving them the feeling that somewhere, somehow, everything would be alright. Then Wilf got out his sketchbook and started drawing her.

He turned off the light and went back up the two flights to his bedroom. On the walls was a pale yellow paper with a pattern of flowering cherry trees he had found in an eighteenth century catalogue. Beside his bed was a cabinet from the same period, restored by himself. On that was his bedtime reading: *Schopenhauer's Essays*. He folded up his clothes and brushed his teeth in the closet next door. On the landing he stared down the long stairway that led to the front door and listened. Not a sound. Yet the silence was intense.

His final thoughts before falling asleep were of Wilf and Peggy. The day after tomorrow, he would go round and ask Peggy if she would come away with him. If not to Lucca, then to some other place where they could be together. He missed her a lot.

The cricket hummed woefully.

5

San Frediano

In mid-September, at the time of the Luminara, the heat in Tuscany is less oppressive, the nights cooler. Out in the villages on the hills, showers fall, wetting the parched fields and the dusty cypresses strung out in rows along the roads back to Lucca. The shift in seasons was harder to detect inside the walls of the town, for the narrow, claustrophobic streets trap the heat. Now and then dark, crowded thoroughfares open into sleepy squares, each of which features a church, its white walls bleached by the sun.

It was in one such, the Piazza San Frediano, that Wilf was taking his morning coffee in the cafe alongside the twelfth century church of that same name. The sky cloudless and sapphire-blue was just warming up. Next to him sat a woman with her blonde hair tied up in a knot, dressed in a green kaftan, watching him half in suspicion, half in hunger. To his left, high on the wall of the church, was a gold mosaic of Christ rising to the sky, looking down sternly at the slack-jawed sightseers taking photographs below.

It was the last day of the residency. It had been a tiresome few weeks, for the quality was low and perceptions dim. Conceptual art at one extreme; Christmas card stuff at the other. Six artists, all claiming to be established. Except he had found out that the Institute bent the rules for entry. 'Established' might mean anything from an exhibition to an at-home walk-in for friends and neighbours. Or a website with some pictures for sale. He would have preferred to get on with his own stuff were it not for the contract he'd signed, which tied him to yet another residency after this one.

"What are you thinking about?" said the woman next to him, whose name he remembered as Anna. From Stuttgart.

He knew she was naked under that dress, which she had put on in a hurry when she heard him going down the stairs to the street door. Over candlelight in the *Bar Tredici* the night before, it was her face that intrigued him. It was a sensual, ravenous face.

"I was thinking it's your last day," said Wilf.

Anna sipped at her *americano*, a drop of which fell on her open chest. Putting the cup down, she shielded her eyes from the sun with her right hand as if she were stroking her eyebrow.

"No more inspections for you," she said.

He ignored the innuendo and changed the subject.

"Where do you go from here?"

"To Munich. My partner is there."

"Your business partner?"

"No. She is my lover. But she has a business in the city. She is a…"

She searched for the word as if it hid in her dress.

"… A pharmacist."

"I see."

"She does not much like it here. She prefers to go with me to the mountains and lakes."

Wilf did not know what to say to that, so he motioned to the *proprietaria* for two espressos and lit another cigarette.

"I want to ask a question," she said.

"Go ahead."

"Do you think I should go on?"

"Go on with what?"

"My art."

"I don't know. It depends what you want."

"You will tell me the truth. Whether I have enough talent."

"Enough talent for what? There are plenty of artists out there with no talent. They seem happy enough."

"You don't want to answer my question?"

"Not particularly."

"Excuse me, I annoy you."

"I can't answer your question unless I know what it is you want. Money? Fame? Or do you just want to produce original work?"

Wilf stubbed out his cigarette and observed her while she thought it over. He hoped she wouldn't be stupid enough to say, 'all of them'. If she was really bright, she would say 'yes' only to the first one.

"It is the last one."

Wilf thought about the paintings she had shown him. Distorted human figures with extended limbs and garish faces in acrylic. Striking in their way, like a mid-priced wine which hit your taste buds hard, but with a limp finish.

"You can't draw. That is the first thing I noticed. But you have a flair for depicting movement and a good eye for colour. But your style is a derivative of the *Blaue Reiter*, and that's been copied hundreds of times. There is no originality there at all."

She flinched and bit her lip just as the bell in the campanile tolled, followed by another, fainter bell from the square behind. Pigeons fluttered down from the roof tops.

"I think your canvases will sell, if that's any consolation. There's always a market for post-impressionist retro."

"Thank you."

"For what?"

"For telling me the truth."

"You're welcome."

She got up, and he threw her the keys.

"You're not coming?" she asked.

"No. I have to buy some things in the Fillungo."

"Will I see you again?"

"You will tonight. We're all having dinner with Petrulengo in the *Artigianale*. Remember?"

She gave him a conspiratorial smile.

"You could come and stay with me in my hotel when it is over."

Then, turning on her heel, she headed off to the corner of the Via Cesari.

He was not due at the workshop until eleven, so he went through the side door of the little church. Inside, it was cool and shadowy, with Romanesque columns leading up to the altar. He headed for the cinquecento chapel to the left, in which was a carved altarpiece in marble executed by Jacopo della Quercia, showing a Madonna and Child.

Casiraghi would sometimes come to this chapel in his heavy, scruffy denims and sit on a portable canvas stool, contemplating it for an hour or more. On the floor were two exquisite slab tombs on which were carved the effigies of an old merchant and his young wife. Both in the sleep of death with their arms crossed. Casiraghi had made sketches, which he showed to Wilf.

"Look. Michelangelo himself learnt a lot from studying those. What do you see?"

"That these could be paintings, except they are in marble."

"You see these two faces? The man was an old devil, and his wife was tired out. Notice how their heads turn away from each other in death. Della Quercia must have known them well."

Wilf looked up at the Madonna. The artist had carved her as a teenager with a pensive face, holding up the child as if he might break. Burdened by the charge given to her, and half afraid she would fail. He had drawn her from the life, whoever she was. Immortal now. Perhaps that was why Casiraghi had liked these early renaissance masters: their graceful simplicity and human insight.

By a series of associations, Wilf's thoughts turned to Michael. First, he recalled the carving, now lying in a leather hold-all in his bedroom. There was the same mournful expression on it as the Madonna's. Then he recalled Michael's text from the day before:

Have you found what you were looking for?

Wilf looked at his phone and smiled. Dear Michael, always so tactless. For what answer could he give without sounding defeated?

For the first few weeks, he hired a scooter and motored around the hills inland from La Spezia. Surveying those same landscapes he had put into his art twenty years before. The mountains, forests, caves, and bays transformed into a mythical world of maenads running after a stag; the Minotaur lurking in a grotto, yearning for sacrifice; remote figures of Apollo and Dionysus staring down from afar at their worshippers. Serene, cruel figures drawn in hard lines below thunderous skies. Pictures he had created in a frenzy, as if possessed. It was a Faustian pact he wanted back; never had he felt more alive. Some of those pictures had sold for sixty-thousand pounds at his first exhibition.

Yet, no matter how hard he stared, the demon refused to be summoned. When he looked at the hills beyond Carrara now, he saw peaceful villages with houses of cream stucco and red roofs, tall, grey towers, and castle ruins. The little winding streets leading by degrees to the vineyards and olive trees outside on the slopes. He'd sketched them, capturing their charm. He was a good enough draughtsman and, if he wanted to, could always make a soft living producing portraits and landscapes on commission. But could he settle for that?

He peered up at the Madonna holding up the child. There was nothing demonic there, he saw. Yet della Quercia once had to flee Lucca on charges of rape, sodomy, and robbery. Was it only insipid souls that produced savage art?

Taking out his sketchbook and pencil, he drew the faces of the Madonna and that of St. Jerome to her right, whose face staring down into his with a look of intense inquiry, reminded him of Michael. He worked fast, remembering what Casiraghi used to tell him:

"Do not make art out of what is in front of you. Paint what is there behind your eyes."

While he drew a tear rolled down his cheek.

6

Murky Business

The Institute was on two floors in a sixteenth century convent in the Via del Moro. The owners had renovated the ground floor in steel and glass to provide offices and meeting rooms. In the vaulted basement were two studios where classes were held. The Institute's brochure claimed that Casiraghi's studio had been here, but that too was misleading; Filippo had rented the basement only for a few months back in the 1970s, while he was looking for something cheaper. Wilf had only ever seen him in the old warehouse he came to rent near the flea market; a barn of a place with canvases stacked up on the floor and high windows set in the walls that gave all the light required. It was there he had completed his apprenticeship.

As he walked past the reception cubicle, the man behind the glass passed a note to him in silence. He stopped to read it.

The Program Director wishes to speak to you in her office.

He crumpled the note in his hand and walked on into the main office. Putting his bag on a desk, he turned to greet the woman who shared the space, a frumpy textile designer from Minneapolis, who sniffed as if a bad odour had just come into the room. Ignoring his salute, she looked back at the slides she was preparing on her laptop.

Taking that as a cue to explore what this treatment was all about, he walked round to Janice Petrulengo's office. On the door was a brass plate screwed in tight:

Dott. J. Petrulengo. BA (Cantab). MA (Fine Arts). M.Phil (Education). Program Director.

Without knocking, he opened the door to find her listening to her mobile phone. She watched him while motioning him away with her hand. Ignoring that, he sat down opposite her and waited. She had thin mouse-brown hair cropped short over her forehead and protu-berant eyes. He knew she wore contact lenses. After a struggle, she ended the call and placed the phone on her in-tray.

"You wanted to speak to me?" asked Wilf.

"I didn't ask you to butt in while I'm on a conference call."

"If it's any consolation, I can think of a lot more useful things to do than sit here talking to you."

She sighed.

"Have you been sleeping with Anna Hesse?"

"That's none of your business."

"Your contract states otherwise. I assume you read it?"

"No. What does it say?"

She quoted the apposite clause, dwelling on the phrase 'professional integrity'.

"She's a grown woman, not a school-girl," said Wilf.

"We have a duty to protect the vulnerable."

"That doesn't stop you taking their money for fake art courses."

"A course on which you were happy to take part."

"Let me make one thing quite clear, Janice. I will take

no lectures from nonentities like you. So here is what I am going to do..."

Two hours later, Wilf was back in the apartment, packing for the six pm flight from Pisa. His suitcase was on the bed, the balcony windows wide open to let in the breeze. He packed quickly, for there was unfinished business he had to take care of before the taxi arrived.

As if on cue, the buzzer sounded. Going back out into the lobby, he let in Carlo and listened to his heavy tread coming up the stairs. He left open the door and went into the sitting room.

Carlo Casiraghi was a semi-bald man in his fifties who looked as if he were trying in vain to swallow a wasp, his small mouth pursing with the effort. Small, crafty eyes hidden behind grey-tinted spectacles.

"Maestro," he said, holding out a hand to shake. "Va bene?"

"Va bene," said Wilf.

"You are leaving?"

"I go to Doremouth. I'm taking up a position there with the University of Wessex."

"Un peccato. There is to be a party here after the Luminara. They invited you."

"Maybe next year, Carlo."

Wilf motioned to the six pictures propped up against the wall. Carlo goggled his eyes and pointed.

"They are ready?"

"Ready to go."

Carlo grunted, picked up one canvas, and placed it on the easel standing in the middle of the floor. It showed an abstract seascape with strips of low cloud in grey, moving across stormy waves sketched roughly in dark green. To the edge, on the right, a woman with outstretched arms was gesturing at the sky.

Carlo pretended to examine it as if he were a connoisseur. Looking close up at the oils on the canvas, then standing back to view the whole. Then he did the same with two of the others.

"Why have you put this image of the woman in each of the pictures?"

"Artistic inspiration."

"Bah. I asked for pictures in my uncle's style."

"Your uncle was a genius. Nothing can imitate that. These are an homage. You ought to know they are some of the best things I have ever done."

Carlo rubbed his chin and glared at him.

"How much do you want for them?"

"Carlo. We agreed on a price when you commissioned them. Forty thousand euros for each picture."

Carlo's eyes flicked from side to side behind his spectacles while he thought it over.

"In cash?" he asked.

"No. It will have to be a bank transfer. I have no way of disposing of that amount of cash, and my bank won't accept it without proof of origin."

"As you wish."

Carlo pulled out his phone and made to execute the transfer from a Swiss bank account.

"On one condition," Wilf interjected.

"Eh?"

"The pictures are to be kept together in a set and are not to be sold to a third party."

"This was not something we spoke about before. I don't know if I like it when you make extra conditions after I have agreed to pay for them."

"You said you wanted to hang them in your new hotel, right?" said Wilf. "The one are building up at Portofino?"

"What of it?"

"So what does it matter if you keep them there?"

"It does not matter to me. I only think of my wife and children who will inherit after me. Also, I have business partners."

"What have they got to do with it?"

"It is better for you if you don't know about them."

Carlo's lips shrivelled to a sour kiss while he looked at the floor. Then he shrugged.

"They are not signed," he said. "No one can sell them. Let us leave it there."

Carlo sat down and, ten minutes later, invited Wilf to check his own account.

"You will see it in a few moments," said Carlo.

Wilf went over to his laptop and, going online, waited for the money to appear. As if by magic a new entry appeared on his account. Three-hundred-thousand Swiss Francs converted to the sterling equivalent. As he might have expected of Carlo, the net sum was four hundred pounds short of the total. But by now he was in a hurry to leave if he was to get to Pisa in time.

"I will give you a receipt," said Wilf.

"No receipt necessary," said Carlo with a flick of his hand.

"As you wish. Do you want me to pack them up?"

"No. I have the Jeep outside. Help me put them there."

7

A Call to Philosophy

Michael unlocked the front door and looked out into the November darkness. Sheets of rain chuted down on the pavement with a slight roar. Yellow light from the sodium lamp over the door reflected in the puddles. He went to fetch his mac from the peg in the hall, going outside to open the shutters. The latch was stiff, and in the struggle to get it to lift, the rain ran down his neck and into his sweater. Leveraging it open at last, he fixed the doors to their hooks and went back inside.

He took off his mac and dried his neck. Then he opened the shutters from the inside. A ghostly yellow light threw the lathe in the corner and the racks of tools on the walls into relief. He turned on the light. A ceiling rose, a window frame, and some wainscot panels were lying about in disrepair.

He sat down at his bench and examined a damaged spindle from a chair under a spotlight. The crack had gone deep into the wood and it was too fragile to repair; he would have to replace it. He rummaged about in the box beside him and selected a mahogany piece salvaged from another chair. Switching on the lathe, he turned it, slowly, rhythmically, gracefully.

At 9 am sharp, his phone buzzed, a call he'd been half expecting.

"Julia. What can I do for you?"

"It's about your sabbatical. Comes to an end in six months."

"I know."

"Michael, how are you? Do you ever feel like coming back to the Department?"

"I never feel it."

There was a longish pause while Julia waited for some sentences to emerge.

"I may have something for you. There is a position for a Visitor coming up in the department. Would that interest you?"

"It's kind of you to think of me. But I think my academic days are over."

"You wouldn't have to do much teaching."

"I don't want to do *any* teaching."

"Why not?"

"It disgusts me. Recycling stale thoughts to dumb teenagers."

"They're not all dumb."

"True. But the few that can think will find their way without my help."

"Don't count on it."

"I don't. But after sixteen years, I've done my share of youth prospecting. And it's cost me a lot. In personal terms, I mean."

There was another silence.

"Why don't you get Heygate to do it?" he asked. "I heard he's free for hire now they've dropped the charges."

He could almost hear Julia shuddering down the phone.

"Michael, what are you going to do?"

"I have some money put by."

"Yes?"

"This house has caught my interest. I want to see how far I can go restoring it."

"Is Peggy with you?"

"She's back. But the house isn't really her thing."

"It seems like a waste to me."

"There's more utility in rebuilding a staircase than in teaching Kant."

"Doesn't it matter that people want to learn about it?"

"It does if they believe that memorising other people's ideas will teach them how to think."

"Can't you teach them that instead?"

"You can't teach that, Julia. People are either set up for deep conversations or they aren't. The ones who are don't need teaching."

After a few stilted farewells, he switched off and went back upstairs. Peggy was still in bed, a half-consumed mug of tea by her. Her black hair spread over the pillow. The room was warm with her scent.

"Hey you," he said.

Her head turned, as if she never heard his voice before.

"Oh. Come in, honey. Who was that?"

"Julia Citrine. Inviting me back."

She sat up. Her breasts heavy underneath a dark green t-shirt with *Choose Life* on it. He felt a lurch of desire.

"That's wonderful news."

"I told her, no."

"What did you say that for?"

"No sense in giving out false hope. Looks like they're going to give it to Heygate."

"You could at least say you'll think about it. You might feel differently in a few months."

He grunted.

"What are your plans today?" he asked.

"Don't change the subject."

"What is there to say?"

"You could tell me what *your* plan is."

"I don't have a plan."

"You turned down Julia's offer and you don't have any other plans. That's foolishness, right?"

"Don't use Americanisms."

"What?"

"Judgments that end with the word 'right' and a question mark."

"Don't pedanticize me."

He suppressed the urge to laugh, knowing it would annoy her still more. Yet there would be more affection in that laugh than she would ever know.

"If you want a deep conversation, we can talk about our marriage," said Peggy. "What do you think about that?"

"A lot. But not now. Not when you're this angry."

"You got that right. You're really irritating me at the moment."

"Ok. We can talk tonight."

"We will Michael, we will."

She pulled back the bedclothes, revealing her bare legs. When she saw him staring at them, she pouted and stood up. Stretched out her arms behind her shoulders in a way that lifted her breasts.

"I'm having a shower now," she said. "If you're going to the market, you can get us some focaccia for supper tonight."

He went into his own bedroom and changed before an

ornate mirror stand. He always wore the same combinations: a light blue shirt and a dark blue pullover and chinos with black brogue shoes; keeping identical items in his wardrobe so that when one went to the laundry, there was another to replace it.

He stared at his face in the mirror. It was thin and sallow, and his jaw was hard set, which made him seem grimmer than he really was. In the next room, he could hear the sound of hot steam switching on.

Going over to the dresser, he inspected his sunglasses on the rack he made for them. He had several pairs, all in different degrees of smokiness. Some were jet-black, others in shades of green or brown. Ray-bans were his favourites, but he had some other pilots in retro styles. He chose them partly by the weather outside, partly according to the person he was about to meet, partly by the mood he was in. Selecting a pair of green shades, he put them on.

Out on the landing, the framed Casiraghi on the wall was askew and he set it right. He hadn't looked at it for a while. *Girl in a White Dress and a Red Hat.* A figure in profile with a dreamy look, twisted on a chair, contemplating something to the viewer's left.

He thought of Wilf, now in Doremouth. There had been no reply to his text three days before; one he had sent at Peggy's urging, who wanted to know whether he was all right, since Wilf hadn't returned her call. He didn't have a good feeling about that. He breathed on the glass and wiped away a smear.

He walked down the stairs, now carpeted, and took an umbrella from the stand. Closed the front door and headed off towards the market. Surveillance cameras tracked his progress up the street, relaying images to computer screens in secret back offices staffed by government agents. He forced himself not to dwell on that. Instead, he stopped off at a corner store and bought *The Times* and some cigarettes. He didn't much like newspapers, but he liked to complete the crossword. That, too, was part of the morning ritual.

Along Fournier Street were more town houses, similar to his in construction. Some of these houses were run down; others, like his own, were being restored. One of them had a blue heritage plaque on the wall which conveyed the date of construction: 1734. He liked to stop and stare and occasionally took photographs. Most of them had window shutters like his, painted in burgundy, dark green, or royal blue, and two of them displayed the original eighteenth century porticos.

He sometimes wondered whether he was a hypocrite. He, who was secretly proud of his lowly origins, was yet drawn to these houses, and even lived in one himself. Yet it was not bourgeois domesticity that attracted him, but the history of the place. Like the 21st, the 18th had been a century of protest, riot, and violence. But its architecture displayed order, simplicity, and restraint. Whenever he contemplated it, he found repose for his trouble.

Inside the market was an old-fashioned cafe with painted wooden chairs and tablecloths with a red-and-white check of the kind he preferred. The proprietors, an Asian couple, greeted him and the wife came over to hold the door open. She knew him well and forbore to speak. Inside it was nearly full; the heat of the urns behind the counter filled the room with steam. He went to his usual table, and the woman brought him his regular order: orange juice, latte and two eggs with toast. He glanced through the paper. It was full of stories about the hopes of the nation and its new coalition government. Nothing there of interest to him. He started on the crossword. The first clue was '*Attributing human characteristics to something inhuman*. Fifteen letters. The reverse might have been a more interesting clue, he thought.

He had just completed the crossword when the phone buzzed again.

"Hello? Dr Gereon? This is Ralph Schoenman. I'm over here in the UK visiting from Baltimore. I understand you are the owner of two works by Filippo Casiraghi. Is that correct?"

"It might be."

"I'm a collector myself. Would it be possible for me to come over and see them?"

"I don't think I know you well enough to ask you round."

"I have a very particular reason for asking. And some information to share with you."

"What kind of information?"

"It's sensitive material. About some Casiraghi pictures that came on the market a few months ago. But I would have to tell you about it in person."

Michael thought about his itinerary and whether he really wanted to go. After a brief struggle he gave in to curiosity.

"I could meet you in a pub in Wapping about five? It's called *The Execution Dock*. A few minutes' walk from the Tube station."

"I can find it. Look out for a Yank in a blue raincoat with a black briefcase."

8

New Awakenings

Sarah shuffled the Tarot pack over the cramped little table in the back room of her magical emporium in Shoreditch High Street. Opposite her sat Peggy. Behind her was a hand-written sign: *New Awakenings Cafe*. Above that, an occult portrait of the Goddess Diana shooting a stag with her bow.

"What is the question you wish to ask?" said Sarah.

Peggy hesitated, for it was not something she had done before.

"How does it work?"

"You hold the question in your mind while you shuffle the cards, and your guardian angel will do the rest."

Peggy thought of the unsatisfactory scene with Michael that morning. Beyond that, to the turmoil of the past two years. Michael's neglect, the on-off affair with Patrick, her departure to an apartment in St. Katherine's Dock, her guilt over Michael, her return to the impasse in which they were in now. Would it ever reach a conclusion?

"I have one," she said.

Sarah passed the pack over, and closing her eyes, Peggy flipped the cards.

"Keep shuffling them until you feel the Tarot is ready to show you the answer," said Sarah.

Peggy did not know what feeling was meant. Instead, she counted to ten and handed them over.

Greedily, Sarah dealt. Hers was a pale face, framed by long, thin, parted hair. A style that didn't suit her, for it made her nose stick out.

"The first card is the Two of Swords. That is yourself. And here is something that covers you. The Eight of Wands."

"What does that mean?"

"You are in conflict, but events around you are moving swiftly. But here is the Death Card."

Sarah laid out the rest. Cards Peggy did not recognise except for the last one. The Hanged Man swinging in the wind. That she recognised from a story she had once read.

"What does that card mean?"

"Stagnation, I'm afraid. It's the last card, too."

Peggy stared down at the man hanging upside down on a tree, a dreamy look of resignation on his face. His hands tied behind his back.

"It is strange," said Sarah, "I was expecting to see the Sun, or the Wheel of Fortune, out for you. But the cards can be funny that way."

"Is that the answer?"

"It is for now."

"What about that card?" Peggy asked, pointing to Death.

"The end of something. The start of something new?"

Sarah sipped at her camomile tea and waited for her to speak.

"I saw Patrick last week. Maybe that's what it refers to. I can't think of anything new that might happen."

"Does he still want you to go away with him?"

Peggy thought about their last meeting the week before. She had gone round the corner to meet him at the daytime rendezvous; the park next to the churchyard in Bethnal Green that was always damp and dreary. There, sitting on the round bench underneath the dripping willow tree, Patrick had pleaded with her to come away with him. To 'a magical isle' he said. She had smelt the whiskey on his breath and noticed for the first time that his waistband was too tight for him. After that, she got angry. Told him to go back to Carrie, his teenage children, and his big house in Victoria Park. That she was tired of stroking male egos and he should stop playing with her. To her horror, he had cried in a way she had seen no one cry before. Great racking sobs that disgusted her with their self-pity.

"That's over now," said Peggy. "I don't think it was ever anything more than a mirage."

She looked over at the shop. It was obsessively neat. Crystals and stones displayed in a large wooden tea box on the polished table. Behind that on the wall, an antique post rack with packets of incense. On another table, bundles of candles of every colour and size. A few of them placed in ceramic holders Peggy had made herself. In the corner stood a six-foot high wooden Buddha, a scornful smile on his face.

"How are you and Simon getting on?" she asked.

"He. Is. Driving. Me. Crazy," said Sarah, putting down her cup.

"What's happened now?"

"Get this. I arranged weeks ago to spend Christmas in Nuneaton with my parents. Now he tells me he's going to Barbados to play golf."

"Poor you," said Peggy, still looking at the display. "How long has it been now?"

"Eight years and counting," said Sarah, looking at her engagement ring with its zirconium.

"Why do you stay with him?" she said, taking both Sarah's hands in hers.

"I'm going to be thirty-six in a few months, and time's running out. And every time I see Mum and Dad, it's 'when are you going to have children? Your sister's got two and there's another on the way…'"

Sarah put her hand over her mouth.

"I'm sorry. I shouldn't talk about it that way."

"It's ok," Peggy lied. As she always did when people brought up the subject of non-existent children.

The shop door opened, and a couple came in from the rain; twenty-somethings in matching dreadlocks. They stamped about to shake off the wet, before heading for the media section. The woman selected a book on witchcraft and looked through the contents, while her partner fingered a CD on soul clearance. There was something furtive about him, Peggy thought. She raised an eye in Sarah's direction, who shrugged.

"Tell me about you and Michael," said Sarah. "How did you two get married?"

"It was an accident," said Peggy.

She paused, for she had told no one this before.

"Well, not exactly an accident. Just random. The summer we got together, I was going out with another guy, who was coming on to Lucca, after his mountaineering trip in the Alps. That guy met someone else and never showed up. I cried a lot, and Michael was there, and he was kind to me."

"You and Mike have known each other since you were, what, 12 years old?"

44

"That's right. So he was like a brother, except he wasn't my brother. You get me?"

"Sure. He was like a brother, but you could sleep with him if you felt like it."

Peggy recoiled slightly.

"You put it more crudely than I would."

"Sorry. So, what was 'random'?"

"Six weeks later, I passed out one night at the pensione. They took me to the hospital in Pisa and discovered I was having an ectopic pregnancy."

"No!"

"Turns out I might have died if they hadn't got me there in time."

"How awful for you."

"I was sick for a long time, so Michael took me back to London and looked after me in Spitalfields. I didn't want my mother to know about it."

"Your mother being into that whole Catholic thing?"

"Not that so much. She was having a hard time with my father, and I didn't want her to worry about me."

"Do you know who the father of your child was?"

"It could have been either of them."

"Did Mike know that?"

"He told me it didn't matter. We got married eight months later."

"Then what's gone wrong?"

It was a question Peggy often asked herself. Whether it was her fault, or Michael's, or whether the whole thing had been a mistake, was impossible to tell.

"My husband is an extremely intelligent man, but he's not grounded. When he doesn't have a purpose, he gets possessed."

"By what?"

"He won't tell me. But it's something weird that messes with his head."

"I've met Mike a few times, and I've always found him odd. Like he lives on another planet. Why did you ever go back to him?"

Peggy thought some more about her husband. How he would spend weeks in his interior castle, shutting her out. Now and then he would come out and be kind and sexy. Before his demons descended once more, and the gates slammed shut.

Before she could answer the question, Sarah stood up and shouted.

"Hey you! Do you mind putting that book you put in your bag, back on the table right now!"

The woman, who was just going out the door turned, sheepishly, and taking out a book on astral travel, replaced it on the table. Then she fled. Her partner, standing outside the window, gave Sarah the finger before trudging off after her.

"You'd think New Age people would know better," said Peggy.

"New Age, my ass. If they're a fresh start, then we're in real trouble."

After Sarah calmed down, she pointed to Peggy's satchel.

"Show me what you have for me today."

"Just a few things," said Peggy, bringing out some articles wrapped in tissue from the leather bag on the floor.

"O my. They are beautiful," said Sarah, opening up the six tiny incense dishes Peggy had made. "So delicate."

Peggy placed an incense stick in the tiny mount in the middle of one. They both stood back.

"You have a real gift," said Sarah. "You should make more use of it."

"I would if I had more time and space," said Peggy.

"Where are you working them now?"

"I keep the kiln at Mom's house. There is a shed in the garden."

"You know, I've been thinking," said Sarah, standing up. "Maybe you could have a stall here."

Peggy looked around at the tiny cafe with its four rickety tables. The kettle on the table next to the refrigerator stocked with juices. The two cake stands on the sideboard.

"Here?"

"I've been thinking of closing the cafe for a while now. It doesn't make any money and it's fiddly running in and out, making cups of tea and serving cake. It's not like the people who use it buy much, anyway."

"I don't know if I have enough items to sell," said Peggy. "They take a long time to make."

"I was hoping you'd help with the shop. I could pay you? And you'd keep any money you made on selling your own things."

Before she married Michael, after she'd come out of university, Peggy would have thought it a dream move. Now she didn't know whether her heart was in it anymore. It was fine to make beautiful things in her spare time. Going back into business was another matter. Besides, she hated the thought that Sarah felt sorry for her.

"Can I think about it?" she said.

Her phone beeped and played *Twinkle Twinkle Little Star*. Embarrassed, Peggy stared at the screen, wondering how people changed their message tones. She could never work it out.

A text appeared:

Going over to Wapping to meet an art collector. Will be back for dinner. Michael x.

"Anything important?" asked Sarah.

"My husband's going off on a ramble somewhere."

Sarah rolled her eyes.

"Have you ever met a man who wasn't just a fantasist? The things we do for them."

9

The Heart Weakens

"Come through, Michael" said Sophie, from somewhere deep inside the house, "the door is open."

He was standing on the step outside the old house and had been about to go back to Kennington Tube when, thinking his mother-in-law might sit beside the house phone, he had tried that.

He pushed the front door and finding it not locked after all, he went inside.

To the right was the old parlour, which was now a storeroom of sorts. Against the wall was an oak dresser festooned with family photographs: Wilf and Peggy as children; Sophie's wedding day; her two grandchildren by her eldest son, James; faded black-and-white portraits of her Irish parents from the 1940s. On the lower shelf, a pile of neatly folded napkins awaited re-use some day. In one corner was a round-top bureau crammed with papers; in the other was a disconnected electric piano.

He placed his mac over the piano and went down the narrow passage to the back of the house.

Sophie was sitting upright on an old chaise longue listening to the radio. Michael had often looked at that divan, for he had once thought it was Directoire, of the kind on which Madame Recamier might have languished. Some springs were broken, and the buff fabric torn, but with attention it might be restored and sold for a lot of money. He had once told Sophie that, but she had looked alarmed, as if he were threatening to take it away from her.

Behind her was a large cage with a macaw in it. An old, vicious, moulting creature with a huge, black beak that flapped and growled when anyone came near it. Sophie got up and threw a tea towel over the cage, proffering her cheek to Michael to be kissed, before sitting down again. A tray laid out before her on a coffee table. Beside that was a chair placed for him.

"It's only a coffee bag," she said, pouring some hot water and milk into a cup. "It's all the cleaning woman could manage."

Michael sipped: it tasted of mud. He waited for her to speak.

"You know, I've always considered you one of the family. Even before you married Peggy. I remember the day you came round here, the day after your mother was… hurt. You sat downstairs with us at dinner and never said a word. We only discovered by chance that your mother was in hospital, that you were all alone in that house and that you were going to go home without telling us anything about it."

Michael remembered it, too. He had gone straight from the hospital, unable to bear staying indoors on his own that night, to drop in on Wilf. Hearing him wandering around upstairs, Sophie laid another plate for him at dinner. He hadn't known where to start on telling them that his mother had been battered close to death in a drug deal gone wrong. Easier to say nothing, even when Wilf asked him upstairs in his bedroom what was up. Later, when the news showing a photo of his mother came on after *Two Point Four Children*, there had been uproar. They had all looked at him as if he had killed her himself. Even Boyo was shocked. Then Sophie had taken him back upstairs and made him tell her everything he knew. Told him he was a fool for keeping it to himself; that he was to stay there that very night and Boyo would drive him back in the morning. Later, she had gone to the hospital to verify the facts for herself.

"Your mother told me before she passed over, that I should look after you. I hope I kept the promise I made her."

Michael knew that couldn't exactly be true, because his mother was mostly comatose during her final four nights on earth. But he guessed she might have held Sophie's hand for a while.

"I always appreciated what you did for me, Aunt Sophie. I haven't forgotten it."

"Bless you, my dear," she said, suppressing a cough. "But here I am twittering on, and I haven't even told you why I asked you here."

"What did you want to ask me about, Aunt Sophie?"

"Have you spoken to Willy lately?"

"Not for about six weeks. Just a text to say he'd gone to Doremouth and was taking his boat with him."

"Well, I want you to go and see him."

"Has something happened?"

"On Sunday night, he called me, and he was drunk. Stinking drunk."

"I've seen Wilf drunk a few times."

"That's different. This time he was drunk on the phone to *me*."

"I see."

"Do you? Knowing what you know about our family? About Boyo?"

Michael considered for a moment. Then he remembered Wilf had once thrown his father out for coming home drunk and threatening his mother. That being the reason Wilf drank nothing but a glass of wine over dinner while she was around. Boyo's alcoholism was something nobody in the family ever spoke about directly.

"I see now."

Sophie was watching carefully to see that he did. Satisfied, she pulled her waiting palms apart as if releasing a charge.

"Something is driving my son to distraction."

"Has anyone else tried to speak to him? James, perhaps?"

"Wilf and James don't get along. He treats Peggy like his baby sister, so he won't tell her anything. And he keeps things from me because he thinks I'm too old and doddery to hear the truth."

They sat in silence for a minute. From inside the cage, the macaw squawked once, as if checking whether there was anyone still in the room.

"There's something else you should know," she said. "But you mustn't say anything to Peggy about it."

She got up and, leaning on her stick, hobbled over to the bookshelf where she kept her romantic stories and magazines. Coming back, she handed over an envelope with a blue NHS logo on it. Michael took out the letter inside and read a report on an examination Sophie had undergone the month before at Guy's Hospital. Skimming through the medic's yada-yada, he got to the solid matter:

shortness of breath, tiredness, oedema, reduced left ventricular function.

"My heart's worn out," said Sophie.

"People can live for years with a condition like that."

"Some people can."

"Does anyone else know?"

"James knows. Wants me to live with him and Cicely in Walton-on-Thames."

She pronounced the first syllable of her daughter-in-law's name with a slight hiss.

"Why don't you want Peggy to know?"

"Because Peggy is a compulsive helper. She'd fall apart if she found out there's nothing she can do."

"You sound like you've given up hoping."

"Hope is for people who are still young."

"Why do you want me to know all this, Aunt Sophie?"

"Because I can speak to you about this in a way I can't speak to my own children. And because…"

Her jaw dropped as she struggled to say the words.

"Because you want to know the truth about Wilf before things get any worse?"

She cried.

"I know he's in trouble."

He took her dried-up hand in his.

"He's done pretty well so far," said Michael. "Better than most of us."

"He so needs help."

"I'll go and see him. I promise."

She got up and fetched a box of tissues from the sideboard. Dabbed her eyes and checked her face in the mirror. He could see her scrutinising him in reverse, as if waiting to see if he was ready to hear something else.

"How are you and Peggy getting on?" she asked.

"We're working at it."

"She did a terrible thing to you. I told her so."

"We are both to blame for what happened."

"That's what the counsellors always tell the injured party. Well, I don't buy it. If she was unhappy with you, there were other ways of dealing with it."

"You may be right. But blaming each other doesn't help."

Sophie gave him a hard stare, as if he, too, were a problem her daughter couldn't solve.

"Do you still love Peggy?"

"Unreservedly."

"I sometimes wonder whether she married you because she wanted someone to look after. I never would have thought you two would get along."

"Do you think I need looking after?"

"Your mother thought you did. She worried about you."

He knew what she was referring to. For years, the social services had tried to get him placed in a school for disturbed children. His mother had fought them tooth and nail and made his grandfather pay the fees to get him into Lauds. He remembered little about it, other than that he hated other children and that his childhood had been a long boredom.

"Your mother was a remarkable woman. A real saint."

"I know."

There was a flash as the TV turned on and its volume filled the room. The macaw jabbered, shifting uneasily under its blanket.

"My goodness, is that the time? *Home and Away* will be starting. I lose track of the story if I miss one episode."

Michael got up, bending down to kiss her. She held his hand with one eye on the tv.

"Be sure to call me after you've seen Willy. Let me know what you find out."

Mechanically, she gave her full attention to the bubble-gum music that came with the credits. Taking off the tea-towel from the cage, Michael left her to it.

The macaw watched the television and squawked in contentment.

10

Execution Dock

The air was turning chill when Michael walked up the High Street to *The Execution Dock*. Damp was turning to mist, which hung over the old mills on the Thames foreshore. The green cabin lights of the ferry lit up the commuters inside, as it glided up the river towards Woolwich. From afar came the rumble of a train on the Docklands' light railway.

As a child, his father had taken him for walks up that towpath where they would look at the ships sailing off to far destinations. Port Said, Aden, Mauritius, Singapore; even the names were magical. Dad had been a dreamy, under-nourished hippy with lank hair and denim jeans with patches on them, but he had known a lot about boats. He had pointed to the First Mate, high on the bridge in his blue jacket. Flags raised and horns sounded, then the ship would disappear beyond Rotherhithe reach. One day, his father had boarded one of those ships. Gone to India in search of something, his mother told him. After that, she never spoke about him.

At that age he associated ships with escape and adventure. He would think of ways in which he could get inside a crate which was being loaded from a dock, stowing away in the hold until the ship brought him to a Pacific island with waving palm trees, like the ones shown on the stamps he pasted into his album. To this day, he couldn't look at a boat or a train without wondering what might lie in wait for him in a new town, another country.

He turned into the pub. Inside it was filling up with evening trade: bankers, lawyers, journalists, estate agents. On the other side of the bar, he could smell roasting flesh: chicken, pork, and lamb on spits. The manager, a large woman with bleached blonde hair, gave him the eye, and went to fetch his order: Ricard on ice with a bottle of lager beer.

He found a booth with a bow window overlooking the river and sat down to look through the messages on his phone. The In box was empty. Fearing boredom, he went online and played backgammon. He found it a game which matched logic and chance asymmetrically, so you were constantly changing tactics in order to retake control of the board. The only thing wrong with it was that he sometimes had the feeling that, whether he won or lost, the outcome was always decided by the algorithm that had been placed there by an unknown programmer. That, too, disturbed him. But before long the alcohol and the mechanical game changing smoothed out the waves in his head, turning them into ripples as his agitation faded.

Someone had switched on a TV in the bar. A po-faced newscaster in a red twinset was reading from a prompt, while pretending to keep her eyes on the camera. Michael wondered what monkey training one had to undergo in order to perform the trick. The news was all about the incoming cabinet. A portrait photo of a sleek-looking blonde man appeared.

"Perry Winter is appointed Secretary of State at the Justice Department and he had this to say when emerging from Downing Street this afternoon…"

Michael went to the bar for a refill. On the wall was a print, dated 1743, of three men in a cart with their hands bound, trailing behind a marshal in a tricorn hat and ceremonial coat, holding out a silver oar. Around them, a heaving crowd gathered to view the execution. A lurking gallows stood over the dock.

Below the print was a description:

The condemned were served a quart of ale at a tavern on the way to the gallows. An execution at the dock meant sightseers would charter a boat to get a better view. For those convicted of piracy, a shorter rope was used. This meant a slow death from strangulation, as the drop was insufficient to break the prisoner's spine. 'Twas called the Marshal's Dance because the prisoner's limbs would jig from suffocation. Afterwards, the corpses hung in chains over the river until three tides washed over their heads.

Life in miniature, he thought. Now and then, a few are marked for death while the rest go on partying. In this type of murder, a sell-out crowd got drunk and taunted the victims while they dangled on a rope. Like most such rituals, it took the survivors' minds off their own approaching end for a few moments.

Someone tapped him on the shoulder: a tall, balding man in a blue raincoat.

"Dr Gereon? I'm Ralph Schoenman."

A pair of intelligent, deep-set, but not unkind eyes scrutinised his. Michael adjusted his dark glasses. They shook hands.

"Let me get you that drink you're waiting for."

"You don't have to do that."

"Per-lease. I insist."

Michael gestured over to the booth.

"I'm over there. I'll keep a place for you."

After what seemed a long time, Schoenman came over with a glass of wine in one hand and his pastis in the other. His briefcase was under his armpit. He put the case on the table between them and took off his raincoat. Underneath, he wore a grey polo-neck and designer jeans. His dark hair trimmed above the ears. He might have been anything between forty and fifty.

Schoenman raised his glass.

"Here's how!"

"How? How what?"

Schoenman gaped, snorted, and shook his head.

"I just love your English sense of humour."

He beamed and pointed to his briefcase.

"Shall I begin?"

"Please do."

"I'm a lawyer and I work for a bioscience corporation in Baltimore. Mostly, I work on the patents and licences that we file to protect our intellectual property. It's interesting, well-paid work. My hobby is collecting art, mostly European, but some from the US. Every couple years I travel to exhibitions and galleries with my wife, and we stay in some pleasant hotels and cities and I buy pictures. Some of these pictures I buy for investment and some because they appeal to me. Usually, the two go together. I have five Casiraghis."

He pulled out a wallet of photographs from his case and put some on the table.

"See, here are some early ones from the sixties."

He pointed to two pictures in dark brown with complex shading and an assortment of non-human figures. Michael knew these from similar works he had seen lying around in Casiraghi's studio.

"And these are from his transitional period when he

was moving to a bolder style. And this one you might know because it is similar in theme to your *Girl in a White Dress*."

It was a portrait of the same girl, who had been a friend of one of Casiraghi's students. Nude this time, except for her white panties. Casiraghi had tried to capture the same placid expression she had displayed in the other painting, this time contrasting it with pointed breasts figured in chiaroscuro. Titled *Sitting Semi-Nude I*. Michael stared at it in fascination.

Schoenman laid down a final photograph.

"But this one I don't know about."

It was a picture that looked like it might have come from Casiraghi's last phase: a bare style with emerging faces and torsos engaging with moving banks of secondary colours. This one titled *Moveable Wind:* it showed human figures issuing from clouds propelled along by the scirocco, which were trying to reach out to the viewer below. One figure, separating from the rest, looked vaguely familiar.

"There aren't too many of these around, are there? He must have been ill when he painted this."

"You knew Casiraghi well?"

"My brother-in-law is Wilf Rising. I used to stay with him in Lucca and we'd go round to see Casiraghi in his apartment above the studio. Sometimes he would invite us to have dinner with him in the *Osteria Pistoia*. He didn't speak much. Liked to watch other people having a good time and now and then he would get out his sketchbook. He drew me once and gave the sketch to my wife. He even signed it for her."

"What was he like?"

"Austere and hard to get to know. Dedicated to his art. That, and his boyfriends. He didn't even look like an artist. Most people mistook him for the janitor when they visited the studio. Partly because he spoke in dialect all his life."

"How did he die?"

"Cancer of the lungs."

"Was that why he changed his style?"

"He tired easily, so he used fewer brush strokes. People thought he was creating a new style, but he wasn't. It was just circumstance. Same way people thought Monet was an innovator before they found out he only painted that way because he was half-blind."

"Some people think the late stuff was his best work. You can pay a lot of money for one of those pictures."

"Art investment and artistic worth are clean different things. One depends on watching the market, the other depends on the artist's talent."

Schoenman laughed.

"Michael, you just crack me up."

"Did I say something funny?"

"No. Well, yes."

Schoenman looked puzzled, as if trying to decipher Michael's mood.

"Say, is there something wrong with you?" he said.

"What seems wrong to you?"

"The way you make conversation seem like hard work."

Michael had been told that before and his answer was always the same.

"If it's not hard work, then it's superficial. If you don't like the way I talk, then leave."

"Look, I don't mean to insult you…"

"Hey, this is beginning to sound like a real conversation. Insult me all you like. We might get to the point sooner."

Michael smiled for the first time that evening. While Schoenman looked like a dog just bit him.

"You were saying something about a painting you don't know about?" asked Michael.

Schoenman was thinking harder now, paying more attention to his phrases. That was the way it should be.

"I tried to speak to your brother-in-law about it, but he refused to see me."

"What did you want to speak to him about?"

"I think this painting is a forgery."

Schoenman tapped his finger on the image.

"You see this sepia that's been used to colour the edges around the clouds? So far as I know, Casiraghi didn't use it in any of his other paintings."

"Perhaps he experimented with that shade and decided he didn't like it?"

"That's expensive paint. I would expect him to experiment with it a few times."

Michael held up the photograph of *Moveable Wind*. There was something uncanny about it. He shivered and put it down.

"Perhaps you should take it up with the Bayes?"

"I intend to. Do you know Tristan Bayes?"

"I know him. When did you speak to Wilf?"

"A few days ago."

"What did he tell you?"

"The same as you: take it up with the Bayes. But he seemed angry about something."

"Well, I'm sorry, but I can't help you. I don't know the first thing about art forgery. Besides, I'm not really a collector like you. I bought my two pictures because twenty years ago Casiraghi wasn't that well known and you could get them for a song. I never thought they'd be worth what they are now."

"Which is maybe why some people are forging them."

"How do you know they *are* forging them?"

"Let me show you something else."

He produced a brochure from his case. Michael took it and read:

Bayes & Bayes are fortunate to have come into possession of six works produced by Fillipo Casiraghi before his death, released by the executors of his will. These are in his late, minimalist style...

There followed descriptions of the works, catalogue numbers and dates. Also a price guide, with figures between 400,000 and 600,000 euros.

Schoenman waited for him to finish.

"Interesting, huh? Casiraghi's been dead for over seven years and they're still 'releasing'. I'd sure like to look at the storeroom where all these paintings are lying around, waiting for export. The next best thing is to go over to that gallery. What do you say?"

Michael looked at the grid in his head. It was a hologram that came up whenever an unsolved puzzle appeared in the real world. Shaped like a Chinese Go board, it showed floating counters in various colours, some in an essential relationship to each other, some not. He saw instantly that the pieces for 'sepia', 'minimalist style', 'repetition', 'forgery', and 'cessation' bore such a relationship. But there were other pieces on the grid which were undecidable; some might lock onto those five pieces to form a new pattern, but some might not. The clicking noise slowed before fading away. Then the image switched off and he was back in the bar, conscious of the television, which was now showing a football match, at which people were shouting obscenities and shaking their beer glasses. Schoenman was staring at him to his left.

"You ok?"

"Yes," said Michael. "I was thinking about what you were saying. But let me ask you a question."

"Go ahead."

"What is your deeper interest in the matter? What do you want?"

"The truth," said Schoenman.

"Why do you want the truth? What good will it do you?"

Schoenman held out his hands in appeal, or perhaps in exasperation.

"The truth is the truth."

"A tautology?"

"No. I mean, the truth is the end product. It's worth having, for its own sake."

"I have to disagree. Beautiful lies work better for some people. Sometimes the truth is the last thing they need to hear about."

He was about to add that it was better, for example, that people didn't know they had no free will, but he foresaw where that might lead.

"Aren't you a philosophy don? Someone that teaches the difference between the true and the false?"

"What I do for a living has got nothing to do with the conversation we're having now."

"Ok. Don't get hot under your collar. But why are you advising me to give it up?"

"Because you might consider the personal cost of this pursuit to you."

"What about the money I paid for that picture?"

"If money is your prime consideration, then take it back to the gallery and ask for a refund. I'm sure Tristan Bayes would be happy to do that. He's a businessman, not an art lover."

It was Schoenman's turn to get lost in thought, tapping his fingers on the table, struggling to make sense of the conundrum Michael had posed. At length, he shook his head and sighed.

"No, I can't do that. I'm a lawyer."

"What's that got to do with it? That's just your job."

"It's more than a job. It's my life. I'm a poor boy from a little township in Kentucky. Went to high school there, got lucky, and went to law school on a scholarship to Yale. That life has given me everything. I can't just look the other way when people break the law."

"Well, be warned. I'm seeing some deep waters here. You might not like what you find."

He got up to go. Peggy would get angry all over again if he got back late.

"Wait with me a moment," said Schoenman, steepling his arched fingers to his mouth. He had a dazed look in his eyes. Michael sat down.

"I just want to say you've given me a lot to think about, even if it wasn't the conversation I was hoping for."

"You're welcome."

"Can I speak with you again when I have more information?"

"You can speak to me whenever you like. So long as you don't mind me telling you what you might not want to hear."

"No. I like that. You make a man think. Let me have your email address."

Michael wrote it down for him.

"I really have to go now," he said. "My wife is waiting for me. Good luck with your investigation."

"Nice meeting you," Schoenman called behind his back.

Outside, it was drizzling. He stepped back quickly for a motorcyclist who was heading out of the car park at high speed. A taxi trawled up the High Street. He hailed it and got in.

Ten minutes later, beyond Aldgate, the traffic slowed.

Seeing that there was some kind of jam up ahead and not wishing to waste time waiting for it to clear, he got out of the cab and walked up the street.

A few hundred yards short of the Market Square, he saw a Tesco Express and stopped to buy some wine. He didn't know what Peggy was preparing for dinner, but she ordinarily drank white wine before it, so he took a bottle of Pinot Grigio and paid for it at the automatic till. Coming out, he crossed the road and walked up to the square. Some workmen were erecting an artificial Christmas Tree; a trimmed, polyester cone with a star of David on top. Behind them, against an indigo sky and the swirling rain, skyscrapers loomed. Lit up in silver and blue lights, they were coming ever closer. Soon they would swallow up Spitalfields, turning it into a featureless wasteland, as most of the city was already.

He stared up at the night sky at a large star high to the north. Was it Mars? Then, keeping his eye on the celestial body, he repeated out loud a piece of verse, grim and hard, that he kept ready to banish melancholy:

Of what is it fools make such vain keeping?
Sin their conception, their birth weeping,
Their life a general mist of error,
Their death a hideous storm of terror.

He stretched out his arms high above his head and arched his back. Then, as an experiment, he leapt forward like a marionette. Two women passed by and giggled as he performed the ritual. Yet the mood had not altogether vanished, and Peggy awaited. He hurried up to Commercial Street and crossed over by Christ Church. A few minutes later, he was back at his front door.

11

The Man Who Came In
From The Rain

Peggy walked up the steps into the hall and found Michael wet through. She took the bottle from his hand and placed it on the sideboard. Then she helped him off with his mac. With both hands she held his face, in which there dwelt a mournful look.

"What's wrong, honey?"

He wrestled away from her, but she clamped her hands tighter and kept his face up close.

"Tell me."

"I saw what they did to the square, then I looked at the lights on the Gherkin and…"

"You think redevelopment is destroying the character of the place?"

He nodded, like a child confessing a bad dream had frightened him during the night.

"And you're upset because you think all you hold dear is ending?"

He rocked harder.

Peggy let go of his face and pulled him towards her.

She had on a white angora sweater that felt warm and soft. A faint smell of bergamot from the scent she wore came up from it.

"It's okay to feel that way," she murmured.

Slowly, the phantom dissipated. He took a deeper breath, and he was present once more.

"Go upstairs and get those clothes off. I'll get on with dinner."

He went up to the bathroom, dried himself, and brushed his hair. Put on a black sweatshirt and checked cotton pants that doubled as pyjamas. Found a pair of leather mules and put those on too. He looked into the mirror just as he had done that morning. This time his eyes were glistening, but with what he could not tell. Remembered despair that had been wept out, perhaps. But there was relief there, too. It occurred to him he was slowly getting used to releasing emotion. But it came out in such a strange way. Like an eruption from a geyser that shot steam into the air before subsiding again, as if some underground demon had switched off the tap below.

He came out and took *Girl in a White Dress and a Red Hat* off the wall and carried it down one flight to a drawing room, which he and Peggy used as a TV den. It was a large, bare room without carpets, as he had polished the floorboards instead, before Peggy put down a selection of Persian rugs. Beneath the windows were two industrial radiators he had found in a dump and restored in grey chalk paint. They gave the place the look of a warehouse.

He rested the painting on a table above which was another Casiraghi, called *Avian Scene*. It showed a multi-coloured bird erupting from a reddish-ochre cavern, over-looking an ultramarine bay.

He studied them both carefully in a way that he had not done for some time. They had stood on those walls for nearly twenty years, but he had stopped looking at them properly. Yet they were Casiraghi's all right. No one else could have drawn those graceful lines. Besides, he himself had picked out these two himself from the canvases the maestro kept in his private stock. His signatures were right there, in the bottom right corners. Each letter of his surname painted in the same squiggle.

While he was inspecting them, Peggy came up with two glasses of the wine and giving one to Michael, stood beside him.

"Is there anything wrong?" she said.

He told her about his meeting with Schoenman.

"He thinks these might be forgeries?"

"No, not these. Some more recent ones the Bayes sold."

"Why is he asking you about them?"

"He's been in touch with several owners. If there are forgeries on the market, then it affects the value of all the others bought and sold. That could keep an army of curators occupied for years."

"I see."

"It's time we had these valued and properly insured, anyway. Maybe we could put them into storage?"

He had been about to say: 'for when we get old' but stopped himself. As if divining his thought, Peggy avoided his stare and stepped forward to look closer at the macaw in the second picture.

"No. Don't do that," she said at last. "I like them on the walls."

"Why?"

"They remind me of those times in Lucca. When we were young."

He raised his glass.

"Cento di questi giorni," he said.

"Cent' anni."

She caught him staring at her face and her hand went up to the small scar on her cheek, which she habitually dusted with an olive blush. She went to the mirror over the fireplace and checked it.

"Does it show?"

"I keep telling you. No one can see it."

He kissed her eye.

At ten years old, Boyo had crashed the Audi while she was in the passenger seat. He had been drunk and the car skidded coming around a corner, going into a garden wall. Father and daughter both knocked unconscious. Peggy had broken her arms and a couple of ribs, and glass from the windscreen had cut her face. Surgery had left a scar under her eye, which grew smaller with time, but never erased. She had spent most of her life thinking she was Quasimodo.

"You think I look ok? You're not just saying that?"

He kissed her again. Then he told her more about the meeting at *The Execution Dock*.

"Schoenman told me he called Wilf. Sounds like Wilf gave him a flea in the ear."

"Wilf wouldn't have liked people saying things like that about Casiraghi. He practically worshipped him."

"It occurred to me to call him in the morning. We haven't spoken for a while."

Automatically, they turned to look at Wilf's painting on the wall at the end of the room. One he gave them as a gift: a painting he had finished before he became famous and his prices rocketed. A standing figure of a woman, recognisably Peggy, staring out of a window at a dock through which a sailing boat was passing. Wearing a green dress that contrasted with the mustard yellow canvas of the sail. Wilf had caught her characteristic look: half melancholy and half stern, gazing into the distance.

"Let's go downstairs and eat," said Peggy.

Over dinner, they stayed away from talk that might re-ignite the row that morning. Michael told her about his visit to Kennington, thinking, wrongly, that it might be a safe topic.

"What did Mom want to see you about?"

"She thinks Wilf is in trouble."

He told her about the drunk telephone call.

"But why is she asking you to go?"

"She thinks he will talk to me."

Peggy blew her lips as if she were spitting out a feather.

"What's wrong?" asked Michael.

"Mom never asks me how I am," she replied. "But if a man has a problem, everyone has to gather round with a handkerchief. Dad, when he got cirrhosis. James, when he gets stressed from making all that money, Wilf and his 'art', and you…"

"Yes?"

Peggy waved her fork in the air.

"You're the worst attention-seeker of the lot."

"I? A man who prefers to avoid people?"

"It's the most effective strategy I've ever seen. It fooled me for a long time."

"How so?"

"Poor little stranger. That's you. Gets everyone on your case."

"Sounds like a good reason for me to go to Doremouth and get on Wilf's case."

"You do that Mike. Might be just what you need."

"There is a problem. The book proofs came this morn-ing, and they want them back by the end of the week. Maybe I can go next week?"

Peggy chewed on her food and thought for a moment.

"No. You'd better go this week. Find out what's wrong with him."

"Do *you* know what's wrong with him?"

"I can give you a clue."

"Give it."

"Look inside Wilf's ego."

When Peggy was in this mood, things were likely to spiral. Unable to think of anything else that might be safe to talk about, he concentrated on eating, one small bite at a time.

When they finished, he got up to wash the plates.

"Don't do that," she said. "I'll put them away in the dishwasher. You make the coffee."

She didn't like the fact that his idea of cleaning was to scrub every plate, bowl, knife, fork, and spoon in boiling water. Saying that it took too long. Especially now she wanted to speak. He recognised the signal and went over to the coffeemaker, filled it with water, and spooned some coffee beans into the grinder. Then he put it all on a tray and carried it upstairs. Went back into the sitting room and put a vinyl record on the turntable; the second movement of Schubert's Second Piano Trio. It generally soothed him to hear the slow march on the piano interweaving with the lament on the cello, but not tonight. His mind circled over what it was Peggy wanted to tell him, for he feared the worst. Strangely, the cricket seemed not to agree. It was making an oboe-like sound that added a coda to the music. Hinting that whatever happened tonight would not be the end of something, but a stage on life's way. By degrees, his mind fell back on the funereal march of the music, building gradually to a crescendo, just as Peggy entered the room.

Coming over, she sat beside him on the sofa and put

her head on his chest, placing her hand over his heart. He put his arm around her, and they lay still as the trio went on its leisurely way to a conclusion. Then silence filled the room.

"I'm going up to the cottage for a while," said Peggy. "Don't be upset."

"Why do you want to go?"

She told him about the offer from Sarah.

"I have to create more stock so that I have enough to sell. That will take time. Easier if I stay up there on my own."

"Is that the real reason you want to go?"

"It's not the only reason," she said, still murmuring into his chest. "Having time on my own will give me some space to think about us."

Getting up, she poured some milk into her cup and filled it with coffee. Then looked back at him to gauge his reaction.

"I thought we were happy together?" he said.

"I'm not unhappy. But since we can't have children, what are we together for?"

"Like every other couple who haven't had children. Mutual companionship."

"You don't have to stay married to have that. We could live in separate places and still be friends."

"I see."

"Do you?"

"Well, I can see your logic. But I don't much like your conclusion."

Peggy laughed and shook her head.

"Doesn't it mean something that I love you?" he persisted.

"You don't really love me. You love what I do for you."

"That's not true."

"We've been married sixteen years…"

"I don't think I can live without you."

"You can, honey. Aren't you the loner? You always have been. At least since your mother died."

"It might look that way. But only because I had you to keep me sane."

"Maybe you should work on changing the things that drive you insane?"

"I am. That's why I gave up teaching."

"Mmm. But you have found nothing to replace it."

"It was you who told me to find something to do with my hands. So now I'm working on the house."

"It hasn't worked, has it? You spend most of your time upstairs in your office working on those gloomy stories. Besides, this house is part of the problem."

"How's that?"

"You're trapped inside it with your mother. At least when you were teaching, it connected you to other people. Sometimes."

"It seems I can't win. I try to give you what you ask for, then you tell me I'm doing the wrong thing."

"It's not my fault you don't know the right thing to do."

"Tell me again, then."

"I have tried. Maybe you should go back to that psychiatrist and ask him to tell you?"

"Adcocke? He's even more fucked up than I am."

Peggy threw up her hands in exasperation. A silence fell on the room.

"I don't think this is going anywhere," said Peggy at length.

"When do you want to go?"

"Soon. Before Christmas."

Michael thought now might be the moment to tell her about Sophie's condition. Was that the right thing to do?

What if her heart failed while Peggy was a hundred miles away in the middle of nowhere? On the other hand, Peggy might think it was a cheap trick to keep her in London.

He got up and walked out of the room, leaving her to finish her coffee.

Not knowing what else to do, he went down to the workroom. A thin bar of yellow light from the street showed through the cracks in the fastened shutters. Giving the place a peaceful, antiquarian feel. He flipped the switch, and the illusion vanished as the room filled with harsh, glaring light. Stacked against the wall were the moulded wainscots he had purchased for the conservatory downstairs. Perhaps they would not be needed now Peggy was leaving again.

Filling with anguish, he pulled out his mobile phone and looked up the trains to Doremouth. One from Waterloo left every morning at 8.55 am and would get him there by 11 am. Yet the thought of going to Doremouth depressed him. How could he fix on Wilf's problems when he had so many of his own?

He looked at his watch. It was 10.30, an hour past his usual bedtime, for he liked to read for half-an-hour before lights out. But he would not read tonight, he knew.

He stood there, irresolute. What to do? Then he remembered his insight the year before. That nothing anyone thought made any difference. That events would unfold in their own time, whether or not people wanted them to. Over and over again, until time ended. Endlessly, repetitively, automatically. Wasn't his body even now getting ready to ascend the stairs and look for the morphine he kept in the cabinet beside his bed? That, at least, would give him a necessary oblivion.

Half-way up, he heard a knock on the front door. He thought of ignoring it. If it was an emergency, the caller would surely have phoned? Only crazies knocked on people's doors at this time of night. The knocks repeated, louder this time. Giving up the impulse he had followed the moment before, he turned and walked back down.

When he opened the door, the rain was pelting down. A youth, or perhaps a man, with his face partly hidden in a grey hoodie was standing on the doorstep. A tall, dark guy with cropped hair. Underneath the jacket was a thin t-shirt and a crucifix hanging on a leather necklace. The garments were all soaked through.

"Yes?"

"This the Gereon place?"

"Yes. What do you want?"

The caller pulled his hood forward over his face but said nothing more. He seemed to wait for an invitation. Michael wondered whether he might be a mugger. A lot of them wore hoodies, he knew.

"Michael, bring him in."

He turned around and Peggy was standing at the bottom of the stairs in her dressing gown. Her hair in a towel.

"What?"

"Just let him in. I'll explain later."

Michael opened the door wider and summoned him forward. The man crouched his head deeper into the hoodie and stepped in. Stood in the hall mute, abject, and cold, with his hands in his pockets. As Michael closed the front door, Peggy took the man's arm and marched him down to the kitchen.

Michael was undecided about what to do. Should he go downstairs and risk getting in the way? Or go upstairs to bed and let Peggy deal with it? Whatever 'it' was. But that might look callous. He took the neutral option and stayed on the ground floor. Went back into the workroom, switched on the light and counted the tools on the racks. There were saws, chisels, hammers, scrapers, pliers, planers, and drill bits all lined up neatly in rows on the walls and on the long bench. Counting them would soothe him, as would the smell of linseed oil in the room. He numbered them up, slowly.

He had got about five-eighths of the way through when the door opened, as Peggy came through.

"I made him a sandwich and gave him some cocoa," she said. As if that was the usual thing to do at eleven at night for a stranger coming in off the streets.

He couldn't tell whether she was pleased or agitated. Perhaps both. She walked around the workroom, clasping and unclasping her hands.

"What's going on?"

"He's a refugee from the Shelter."

"But what's he doing here?"

"He's homeless."

"That doesn't answer my question. What is he doing *here*?"

In fits and starts, he got the story out of her.

The man's name was Isaias Adonai. An asylum-seeker who had entered the country on a boat nine months before. The border police took him to a detention centre in Kent, while the authorities examined his application for asylum. That was accepted, but the result was that he was told to leave the detention centre with nowhere else to go. So, he walked to London and was now living on the streets. Every day, except weekends when it was closed, he went to the Shelter for food and somewhere warm and dry. Meanwhile, looking for accommodation and paid work. Every Wednesday when Peggy volunteered there, she gave him English tutorials.

"Peggy, he can't stay here."

"Why not?"

"What do we know about him? He could be a thief."

It wasn't the real objection. A stranger would get in the way, just when he wanted more time with Peggy.

"Does he look like a criminal to you? He's a lonely, frightened teenager."

"But there must be other places he can stay. Isn't that what the Shelter is for?"

"We're searching. But we don't have enough guest houses. It might take days before we can find somewhere. Weeks, maybe."

"I see."

"Do you, Michael? If I weren't living here, I would take in Isaias and look after him until he's found a home to go to. As it is, I have to ask your permission."

"That's not true. When have you ever asked permission for anything?"

That came out the wrong way. Yet it was hard to keep the bitterness from his voice.

"Isn't this how it usually works?" he said. "Go along with what I want, or I'll leave you?"

"This has nothing to do with what I want. This has been a problem since before we separated and it's the reason we separated. That we have little in common anymore."

Just then, the youth re-appeared in the hall. He had walked up the stairs so quietly that neither had heard him. Looking as if he wanted to leave by the front door if uninterrupted. Possibly, he'd heard their raised voices. Peggy put out her hand to make him stay but turned first to Michael.

He took a deep breath. This was not the time to discuss their differences. Nor could they let the guy out to wander the streets in the rain at this time of night. In the morning, he would go back to the shelter, and they could go with him. Urge the people there to make his accommodation a priority.

"Let him stay the night," he said. "We'll talk about it in the morning."

12

The Marionette Theatre

By 7 am, Michael was up correcting the proofs for his new book in the kitchen. *Three Stories and One Essay*. By Heinrich von Kleist, translated from the German. Ordinarily, he would use the office for that purpose, but he hadn't liked to disturb Peggy, still asleep in the room next to it.

In his time he had written a few articles on the German poets and philosophers that interested him, as a lecturer of junior rank was expected to do. A short book on Nietzsche's genealogical method achieved a slight success, yet too specialist for most. Still, he kept up the habit of writing. Partly to find occupation, partly because it stepped up his war on words. Imprecise, sloppy, irritating words that people used to avoid thinking. Words that made him feel ill. Kleist's hard, terse style was the antidote for that.

He worked steadily for almost two hours, scanning each line and marking up corrections and alterations. Then he came to the essay Kleist had published the year before he shot himself: *On the Marionette Theatre*.

When he was a child, his mother had carved a few

wooden puppets for him, showing him how to play them. Manipulating the string bar so that their limbs danced to the music of a miniature hurdy-gurdy she bought for him in the market. On the barrel was a motto in italic script:

God turns the handle. Let us dance to his music.

He still had those puppets, which he kept locked away in a wardrobe along with the hurdy-gurdy, now broken. From time to time he would bring them out. But he was clumsier than mother, whose deft fingers could bring the puppets to life, their gleeful faces mocking the emptiness of existence. It seemed to him that the marionettes were happier than any children he had ever seen.

When he came across the essay years later, he saw Kleist had anticipated him. Marionettes, Kleist wrote, were blessed with charm and grace, where humans were not. Free from self-consciousness. Dancing elegantly on a stage with tinkling music. Unconscious of the past, the future and that which stood waiting beyond. Far better to be a marionette than a boy.

His concentration flagging, he closed the laptop and went up to the bedroom. Peggy's door was still shut. The youth was in the spare room downstairs, with his door locked, too. He wondered what mood Peggy would be in. Would she forget about her plan to leave? Or would Isaias' arrival speed that up?

He stopped and checked the cricket inside his head. Silence.

Before he got into the shower, he remembered he had promised Sophie that he would go down and see Wilf. Picking up his mobile, he texted him.

Are you free for lunch on Friday? Mike.

On coming out of the shower, he put on his jeans and the check shirt he habitually wore when working around the house. When he checked his appearance in the mirror it occurred to him that something new was forming inside him. He had forgotten to put on his chinos and polished shoes.

The phone buzzed: a text reply.

Have been thinking about you. Come to the university at 11.30.

The door opened and Peggy looked in. She crooked her finger and beckoned him into the next room.

The guest room where she often slept, was a work-in-progress. The walls painted deep blue with a brass bed by the window. But no carpets, for the floorboards wanted mending. He sat on the bed beside her.

"Thank you for letting Isa stay," said Peggy.

"I thought his name was Isaias?"

"He prefers Isa."

"Where is he from?"

"Eritrea."

"Why did he leave?"

"Everyone over fifteen has to join the army. He and his father refused to go, so they put them in prison camps. His dad died under torture. He escaped and went to Sudan."

"Doesn't he have other family?"

"His mother and sister are still in Eritrea, but they can't get out."

"What's your plan for him?"

"I don't have one yet. I'm going to the Shelter to find out more about him."

"Is Isa going with you?"

"No. I want him to rest. He's been sleeping in a cardboard box in that subway."

"Does he want to stay here?"

"He's not sure. He overheard us arguing about him last night."

She took his hand, resting her eyes on his.

"Will you do something for him?"

"What?"

"Stay here until he wakes up. Take him to the market and get him some clothes. I'll give you some money."

"I don't know, Peggy. Am I the man for that job? I'm barely fit for human consumption as it is."

"That's exactly why you should go. It'd be good for you to listen to his story."

"All right, I'll take him. But no promises."

Hopefully, the people at the Shelter would find him accommodation. If not today, then tomorrow. But complaining now wouldn't be a good look.

"When will you be back?"

"Late this afternoon. But don't worry about Isa. He'll find his own way back."

Two hours later, Isa came down while he was in the kitchen, still working on the proofs. Michael turned to look. Isa stood taller now that he was dry. He seemed more mature than he had thought the night before; maybe twenty years old. Standing in the middle of the floor, dazzled by the light, he had on the same ragged jeans; the dye washed out. Underneath the hoodie, Michael saw he was wearing a dry sweatshirt. He took a second look; it was one of his. Then he noticed Isa's smile. Not an ordinary smile, but a penetrating radiance that came through the eyes. It was a smile that made him feel ashamed.

"Do you want coffee?" he said.

"That would be most welcome."

Michael got up and poured some into a cup.

"Help yourself," he said, gesturing to the milk and sugar.

Isa leant over and put three spoonfuls of sugar in the cup. Michael winced as he drank it.

"Thank you for inviting me into your home," said Isa.

He had a sing-song voice, with both 'a' and 'e' similar. It was a pleasant sound.

"That's all right. Do you want to come with me to the market? We should get you some clothes."

"I don't want charity."

Michael realised he had said the wrong thing. It came from telling people things before they were ready to receive them. Peggy was always telling him not to.

"Call it a loan if you prefer. But you'll need better clothes than the ones you have on now it's winter."

"Can you give me work?"

"Sure. There's enough to do around this house."

"Then I accept."

"What kind of work are you used to doing?"

"If you show me what to do, I will do it."

Michael wondered at the way he said it. Like a man who knew there was nothing he couldn't fix.

"It's a deal."

They went out into the street. It had stopped raining and the skies had cleared. Bright sunshine, but cold. Mist came out of their mouths. Isa stood beside him while he locked up the front door, then they set off together. Three doors along their neighbour, an elegant woman in a dark business suit and a mackintosh, came out. She looked amused, being unused to seeing Michael in company.

"Good morning, Michael. Good morning to you," she added, turning to Isa.

She turned on her heel and headed off towards Bishopsgate, swinging her briefcase. It occurred to Michael that she treated him, too, like a displaced person.

They went into the corner store and bought cigarettes and a newspaper, and when they came out Isa offered to carry his bag. After some hesitation, he handed it over and

Isa put the strap around his neck. They walked up Commercial Street and turned off through the arch into the market. Already, there were Christmas lights hanging from the rafters below the roof. After some searching, they found a stall which sold clothes that teenagers might wear. The stallholder pulled out a tape and measured Isa's leg. As Isa raised his jeans, Michael noticed the burns and whip scars on his calves.

The man took them over to one rack of trousers and another of track suits, then left them to choose. Michael raised an eye at Isa, who hesitated, before walking over to look. Eventually, he selected a tracksuit, a pair of black cargo-pants, and a blue hoodie. He wanted to add two t-shirts, but Michael made him take two sweatshirts instead as those would be warmer. Michael added a three-pack of socks and the man folded them all up and put them in a shopping bag. Then they walked around to a shoe stall and Isa tried on a pair of Adidas trainers and seemed happy with them. So, they bought those, too. Michael handed over the bags to Isa, took back his shoulder bag, and they headed over to the cafe. But he noticed Isa avoided saying 'thank you'.

Inside, it was warm and steamy as before. They took a seat by the window. Fortunately, the menu carried small photos showing the things they could eat. Isa ordered pancakes and yoghurt and, guessing that this what he was used to eating for breakfast, Michael added a pot of jam to the order. Eggs and toast for himself, and latte for both of them. He took out the newspaper and began the crossword. Halfway through, he looked up and Isa was working through his breakfast with relish, spreading the yoghurt and jam on each pancake, folding them up and putting them into his mouth with both hands. From time to time, spooning some yoghurt in.

It didn't seem necessary to go into the usual yada-yada. Michael liked that, having no use for small talk himself.

In the end, it was Isa who broke the silence. Noticing that Michael watched him putting a carton of yoghurt in the shopping bag, he told him he had sometimes gone days without food in Malta and had learnt to eat well when he had the chance, always saving something for later.

"How bad was it?"

"Worse than people can imagine," said Isa. "In Libya, they made me work as a slave. The people who organise the boat traffic are evil men."

That was when he heard the whole story. About Isa's two years forced labour in a prison camp, with regular beatings by the guards; the long trek through Sudan in the heat; the year in Tripoli, trying to find enough money to pay the smugglers to get him across to Malta. Then months in a derelict refugee camp there before he stowed away on a cargo ship to London.

"Aren't you bitter?"

"No. What should I be bitter about?"

"I heard what happened to your father, and to you. Then the journey through hell you just told me about."

"It is not up to me to decide on what it all means. That is up to God."

"God? Why bring him into it?"

"Because I seek him. Through the lessons he shows me."

"He doesn't seem to be grateful."

Isa scowled for the first time.

"Please don't joke about it."

13

Train To Nowhere

On the Friday Michael got on the train to Doremouth at Waterloo station. The train was nearly empty, for there were no day-trippers heading for the beaches. He walked into a carriage with a single passenger in a seat by the far door and sat down at a table three rows down. Took out a bottle of mineral water and his book from a leather shoulder bag and placed them by his phone.

He texted Peggy:

Thinking of you. Love M.

The train moved off and gathered speed. To the right, the brown water of the Thames was flowing softly past the Chelsea Embankment. Moored pleasure boats floated in a line up to the Albert Bridge. It was a dull, overcast day but it didn't matter. One of the few times he ever experienced hope was on a train that was just leaving. A train that might go nowhere, or anywhere.

As the train moved out of London, it reminded him of the first time he met Wilf when they were fifteen years old.

One day the school organised a day trip to Oxford to visit an exhibition at the Ashmolean on the Odysseus legend. The party met outside the Great Western Hotel at the Paddington Station. It was a mufti day, so the boys competed by wearing expensive jeans and sportswear. Michael hadn't wanted to go and hadn't bothered to read the instructions; instead he came in uniform. This provoked a round of sniggers when he came on the train. Ignoring them all, he took a seat at the rear of the carriage. Mac, the Classics Master, took a roll call as the train moved off towards Oxford.

Perhaps that was the reason he felt sorrow for Isa. He reminded him of how he was as a teenager. Hadn't he, too, been friendless, alone and frequently depressed?

A few minutes later a blonde youth, also in uniform, asked if he could sit with him. He had a slight American accent.

"I made your mistake and forgot to put on the right things. No sense in sitting over there with the fashion parade; I'd like to sit with you."

That was how a random event led to his friendship with Wilf: the accident that both of them had been wearing the wrong clothes on the same day. For until then Michael had paid no attention to him.

Entering the school the term before, Wilf was fresh from a prep school in New York. There was something devilish, yet pure, about his handsome face with its high cheekbones, sharp chin, and frank blue eyes. Michael had heard that he was already in the first Fifteen and was a fast, aggressive flanker. From that, he assumed they would have nothing in common.

"Mind if I ask what you're reading?"

Michael showed him the cover. Nietzsche's *Beyond Good and Evil*.

"What's it about?"

"Do you really want to know?"

"Yes, I do really want to know."

"I can't tell you what it is 'about'. I read books like these because they give me new thoughts."

"What thoughts?"

Wilf's persistence might have irritated Michael if it had come from one of the other boys. But he recognised in him that curiosity that he possessed himself.

"That culture is founded on power, cruelty and repression."

"Could that be true? Or is it just a theory?"

"Look around you next time you walk back into that school."

"That's too deep for me."

"It's not that deep. Think of it as an empowering perspective."

"You mean like paintings do?"

"That's a thought I haven't had before," said Michael. "Thanks."

"You're welcome."

"Are you an artist?"

"I sometimes think I'd like to be one."

"Nietzsche thought art was the only possible justification for life."

"I don't know whether I'd go that far. I just draw a lot, that's all."

Wilf produced a sketchbook from his satchel and drew a caricature of a bossy prefect named Winter, sitting at a table at the far end of the carriage with Mac and the other prefects. Using rapid strokes, Wilf caught his pompous expression and showed it to Michael.

They both laughed. Whether at Wilf's sketch, or the fact they were discussing art and philosophy on a school trip, Michael didn't know. At any rate, they stayed together when the train got to Oxford and brought up the rear in their uniforms as the group headed up to the museum.

His father was Senior Vice-President at IBM, Wilf said, although the title didn't mean that much: Americans liked fancy job names. After living in New York state for five years they came back because Dad was now heading up the London office. They lived south of the river because it was convenient for the corporation's European headquarters in Waterloo.

Michael noticed that Wilf had outgrown school uniform; he was wearing it like party dress. He was tall and confident and had an athlete's grace. As they walked up George Street a couple of girls stared after them as they passed. They were not looking at him, he knew.

Wilf pointed to the gates of one college.

"Are you coming to this place, Michael?"

"Mac wants me to come here and read German. But I haven't decided."

"Too snooty for you?"

"Too depressing. Full of smug types like our classmates here, preparing to lead us all into the twenty-first century."

"Amen to that."

Just then, Perry Winter came back round the corner to reprimand them.

"You're to double up you two, and run up to the column ahead and don't dawdle behind. Or there'll be a detention tomorrow."

They looked at each other and laughed. He looked exactly like his sketch.

"Get lost, Winter," said Wilf.

After that, they were inseparable. Once it became known that Wilf was his friend, the other boys became more wary. On one occasion, Wilf punched one of his tormentors so hard the boy had to stay off school for a week. They kept away for good after that.

The first time he visited the house in Kennington, Peggy, who was then a shy 12-year-old with braces on her teeth, opened the door. She ran off into the interior shouting for her brother, leaving him on the doorstep. Wilf had been out on an errand, however and it was Sophie who came to fetch him.

The train was travelling south towards Winchester. From the windows he could see waterlogged meadows with bare trees hanging over them, with a wintry sun hidden behind grey clouds. Scenes from a vanishing world. He picked up his book, a collection of articles on the mind he had ordered from Amazon on impulse. For it was the one area left in philosophy that still interested him. But most of the articles were trivial and pedantic; the kind written by academics seeking to get their publication count up. What he really wanted to know was whether there was any such thing as an independent mind. Or whether, instead, humans were driven by genes, brain mechanisms, desires, instincts, cravings, social training, and random experiences. Leaving no room for choice at all. That what people thought were choices were really made-up stories about why they just did something; decisions programmed beforehand in the brain. But there was little radicalism of that sort amongst these papers.

The train inched its way out of a tunnel and into Doremouth station, with its white painted awnings and Victorian waiting rooms. He got out and headed for the exit.

He came out to a cab queue, and got in the first one, a blue Toyota Prius.

"The University, please."

The driver watched him in the rear mirror.

"Do you want the scenic route?"

"I want the direct route."

The car circled round and headed up the ring road. Michael hoped the driver wouldn't want to make small talk about the weather, how trade was doing now it was November, or the football results. Fortunately, the driver was a man in a reefer jacket who looked like he might be stoned by the way he was staring out of the window at the road ahead.

There was a lot to be said for sedative drugs, he thought. Life would be a whole lot easier if people just kept quiet and minded their own business.

14

A Serious Economic Crime

Dr Ben Adcocke was drawing to the end of his lecture to a group of police detectives.

"What marks out the psychopath-to-be from other children is his flight from the missing object. Which, to use a crude paraphrase, we can describe as a dismissal of the mother figure through which other children fulfil their capacity for attachment. There you have the psychopath's dilemma in a nutshell. And this dismissal is at the core of his most salient characteristic: Machiavellian Egocentricity. Which, as you will have noted, is measured in the Revised PPI test you have in your folders."

He paused for applause as he polished his gold-rimmed spectacles, but was met with a bemused silence. He turned to look at the Superintendent sitting beside him who, seeing the problem, got to his feet.

"I'm sure we are all very grateful to Dr Adcocke for his fascinating talk. Do please have a go at completing the PPI test. You might find some of your scores surprising. Not that all detective police officers are psychopaths, naturally."

The group dispersed towards the tea table laid out in

the room behind, DS Gary Gredic among them. As he made his way towards the door, DS Hammond fell into step beside him.

"What did the Super mean, Gary? What we doing these tests for?"

He sounded worried. Hammond wasn't the brightest button in the box.

"It was a joke, Phil. Just a joke."

"Not funny though, is it?"

"No Phil, not funny at all. And I can think of a better use of my time than sitting around all morning listening to mad doctors."

Gredic was in a hurry to get back to the station, for his workload had been giving him sleepless nights. Dumping his folder in the bin, he made his way to the exit.

"Be seeing you, Gary. Don't forget that drink you owe me."

"Any time, Phil."

Coming out to the car park, Gredic located his silver VW Golf and got into it. He put on his seat belt and switched on the ignition. The car phone rang.

"Yes?"

"Where are you, Skipper?"

It was Painter. One of the DCs from his unit.

"Bloomsbury. I'm on my way back."

"The DI's looking for you. He's in a flap about something."

"Know what it's about?"

"No idea. Could be anything."

"Usually is. Anything and nothing. Be seeing you."

Gredic drove off and headed up High Holborn towards St. Paul's. Took a left at the Museum of London, then a right to the Barbican. From there, it was a few minutes to the Art Déco police station in London Wall. He showed his pass at a side entrance and a security guard raised the barrier to the car park behind the building. He came in through the back entrance and bounded up the steps to the third floor.

The decor was standard civil service functional. Long corridors with grey walls, grey carpets, frosted glass, and strip lighting. Thick wooden doors with security locks. Partitioned open-plan offices with signs on the door. The one on his said SECU: The Serious Economic Crime Unit. Gredic shared this with two Detective Constables, two Financial Intelligence officers and an Administrator. When he came in, all except one were working at their computer screens. Half-eaten baguettes and coffee cups beside them. In Gredic's department few had time to go out to lunch.

Jack Painter looked up.

"Afternoon, Skip."

"Where's Halliday?"

"She's over at the Crown Court. Giving evidence on the KwikCash case."

KwikCash was a pawnbroking firm they had caught taking in jewellery and watches from thieves and selling them on over the counter. After evidence for money laundering came to light, the Unit was called in to examine the bank statements and account for the cash coming in and going out. Tracing the money all the way back through a maze of dummy bank accounts. Tedious work that had taken Gillie Halliday weeks to get through.

Gredic sat down at his own desk. On it was a note:

Debbie called. Says it's urgent.

He called his wife's mobile and she picked up instantly.

"Gary, we've got a problem."

"What problem's that?"

"Chloe's got a detention. Can you pick her up? I'm in the salon all day."

Chloe had not settled into her new school well and was forever cheeking her teachers. How was it his two sweet little girls had turned into stroppy teenagers?

"What time will she be out?"

"Should be about four forty-five."

"That could be tight," he said, trying to put it as diplomatically as he could.

"What's that supposed to mean, Gary? "

"It means I've got a lot on."

"And you don't think I have, is that it?"

He listened to Debbie giving him an earful for a few more minutes. About how he was never there, took no interest in the girls, and left everything to her. That she cooked, cleaned, laundered, took his children to school and back, all the while running a hairdressing salon in Buckhurst Hill. While he was away playing at cops and robbers. To mollify her, Gredic agreed to pay for a cab and put the phone down.

Gredic had never expected he would like it in the force. When he came out of school at sixteen with five GCSEs he went to work as a delivery boy with his uncle's fruit and veg wholesaler, working Saturdays in Spitalfields market. That had been all right when he was a teenager who only wanted money to go drinking with his mates, buy some smart gear, and travel away with the Firm when they took on their opponents at football grounds up and down the country. But the older he got, the better he understood he didn't want to be a market trader all his life. Besides, he had Debbie to think about. She wanted to get married, have children, and put down a deposit on a house in South Woodford. On her account, he had gone looking for something else to do and learnt the City of London Police were on a recruitment drive. He hadn't thought they would ever accept him, and he didn't know then he was amongst the last to be recruited without a degree. It was a sore point with him. Being a bobby on the beat had been so-so. Detective work was more to his taste. Especially SECU. The city was awash with smug, middle-class criminals, crying out for him to put them behind bars. But he had been a detective sergeant for fourteen years now and there was little sign he would ever go higher.

Time to visit the DI. He walked around the corner and knocked on the door.

"You wanted to see me?"

DI Gallop was seven years younger than Gredic. A graduate in Geography from a midlands university, fast-tracked on to a training course, and made Detective Sergeant in four years. DI in six. Then parachuted over Gredic's head into SECU, and lined up for Chief Inspector. Gredic had disliked him the moment he realised Gallop kept all the prestige cases for himself, while handing on the routine stuff to him.

"Sit down, Sergeant. Know anything about this?"

He held up an IPOC report.

"There's been another complaint about you. Accuses you of threatening behaviour with a suspect you interviewed last month. Perry Jacobs."

"Jacobs is a scrote who is up to his neck in crime. Now he's making a complaint he thinks will get him off. Anyone who actually has to deal with villains can see what he's up to."

"Sir," added Gallop.

"Sir."

"Tell me what happened. In your own words."

"In my own words? Sir?"

"Don't be insolent Sergeant."

"I brought Jacobs in for questioning in relation to the

passing of counterfeit fifty-pound notes. You may remember we have an enquiry going on about that?"

Gallop leaned back in his swivel chair and waved his hand for him to carry on.

"We wanted to ask Jacobs about a note which he used to pay for drinks in *The Blind Beggar* and another note we found in his pocket. I arrested him under caution and brought him back here."

"Did you threaten him?"

"Wouldn't it be a good idea to listen to the interview tape and make up your own mind? Sir?"

"I will. Don't worry. But what did you say to him before you switched on the recorder?"

"You do not have to say anything. But it may harm your defence if you do not mention, when questioned, something which you later rely on in court. Anything you do say may be given in evidence."

Gredic enjoyed goading Gallop. Although it was doing his career no good at all. Gallop's weakness was that he was a humourless twat. It was easy to get at him that way.

"Very funny. Was there anything else you might have done that provoked this complaint against you?"

"Other than calling him a scrote? Sir?"

Gredic gave him a look of wide-eyed innocence. The standard look of insubordinate NCOs to their superior officers in armies and police forces all over the world.

"It says here you called him a little cunt."

"Jacobs has grown used to people calling him that. Must have affected his listening skills."

"You're a bully, Gredic. I've a good mind to make you do the PEACE training again."

PEACE stood for Prepare, Engage, Account, Clarify, Evaluate. Something a psychologist who didn't live in the real world had come up with for carrying out interrogations. 'Engagement' was the best bit. Gredic couldn't imagine how that would work with the serial murderers, rapists, drug dealers and other low-lifes he had come across. But no use explaining that to people like Gallop.

"Always happy to improve. Sir."

"Two years ago, there were over two thousand complaints against this police force, and we have all been working very hard to bring that number down. Last year, we reduced it by twenty-nine percent. This year, so far, it is down by another eleven percent. Do you support that effort, Sergeant?"

"I do. Sir."

"Then why is your personal tally up by two hundred percent?"

"Meaning there was one complaint against me last year and two so far this year? I'd call that bad luck. Comes from having to mix with known liars, instead of sitting in an office worrying about statistics."

The thing about fake coppers like Gallop was that he treated his own like they were criminals under investigation. Never having done any real policing. Like the rest of his mates in the hierarchy, he was always looking for scapegoats when the numbers didn't come out right, before putting them on 'retraining' courses.

"You can tell that to the Chief Superintendent when he chairs the inquiry. I'm sure that last comment will go down well with him."

Gredic got up to go.

"Sit down, Sergeant. I haven't finished yet."

"Sir?"

Gallop picked up a blue plastic folder with three documents inside.

"I'm passing this case on to you. A fraud allegation from an American art buyer concerning a picture he purchased from a gallery here in London, which he says is a fake. His name is Ralph Schoenman."

Gredic raised one eyebrow with an unspoken question. There were tens of thousands of art fakes on the market. A few of them were in the National Gallery. Why should this one be of any concern to the City of London police?

"We also have here a print-out from InterPol relating to the activities of Ronald Pilcher. He's known to us, is he not?"

"Ronny Pilcher? I know him well."

Pilcher was an accountant caught cooking the books for a chain of travel agents ten years back. The firm was technically insolvent, but Pilcher had contrived to over-state their assets to make it look like a going concern. The firm had gone bust and the directors had absconded with two million quid in bank loans. Pilcher had drawn twelve months in Pentonville for that.

"Seems he might be money laundering for some very unsavoury people from Eastern Europe. Drugs and firearms trafficking across borders."

"What's the link between Pilcher and the allegation from Mr Schoenman?"

Gallop held up the third sheet of paper.

"This is the list of artworks under suspicion with their descriptions, plus information on their current owners. Courtesy of Mr Schoenman. Ronald Pilcher is on the list."

"What's the name of the gallery?"

"Bayes & Bayes. South Kensington."

Gredic had never heard of them. It was unlike Ronny Pilcher to mix in art circles. A pole dancing club in the Edgware Road would have been more his mark.

"I'll look into it, sir."

Gallop handed the file over the desk with an air of a teacher giving a pupil some necessary homework.

"You do that. And don't go treading on any more civilians. I've got enough to do without having the Chief on the phone, giving me grief about your misdemeanours."

"I'll bear that in mind. Sir."

By the time he returned, Halliday was back at her desk. He nodded towards the briefing room, and she followed him, closing the door behind her.

It was a bare room with a desk and three chairs. This was the DI's office, which Gredic had always thought would be his. But on arrival, Gallop had declared it was too small for him and insisted on taking over the office next door, which was the same size as the one Gredic and five other people shared between them. But Gredic did not like to commandeer the room. It was easier to lead the team when you sat with them. This room he reserved for briefings, plus the occasional bollocking.

"How'd it go, Gillie?" he said, putting the blue folder on the desk.

"Not guilty, sir."

"Straight up?"

"Straight up. Their brief smeared our key witnesses and made it look like their evidence was unreliable. The jury fell for it."

"Fuck. All that work for nothing. How do you feel?"

"You win some, you lose some."

Halliday was another graduate, but one of the okay ones. Hard-working, smart, and tough-minded. She was good-looking, too. She would go a long way if she didn't mind playing politics with the likes of Gallop.

He sighed.

"No point in mooning about it. Have a look at this."

Halliday pulled up the chair next to his and locked her hair behind both ears. Gredic could smell the scent she put there, but he tried not to think about that.

Taking out the sheets from the folder, he laid them on the desk.

"I want you to come in with me on this investigation. I'm going over to talk to this American buyer. While I'm doing that, I want you to see what you can find out about this art gallery. Get their company accounts and check the outstanding loans. See if you can find anything about them on the national database."

"Anything specific?"

"Check for criminal records. And get on to the NCA. Ask them what else they know about these money laundering allegations. Come back and see me at two-thirty. I want you to come with me when I go round Ronny Pilcher's for a little chat."

"Will do, Sergeant."

15

The Lucchese

The Dame Margaret Barry building was a grey concrete and glass construction encircled by yellow pavement on which the college had left some white PVC chairs and tables out in the rain. Four students were smoking outside the entrance. Michael went inside and reported to a bored receptionist with mauve hair. On her hoody she wore a security pass with a logo and the university motto: *Minds coming together*.

"I'm here to see Wilf Rising."

"Is he expecting you?"

Her green eyes bored into his, as if he were asking to meet the Wizard of Oz.

"He asked me to come and meet him here today, yes."

Ignoring his irritation, she leaned over the counter and pointed to a coffee bar in the corner, around which more plastic seats and tables were arranged.

"Wait there and I'll see if he's free."

He went over to the bar. Behind it was a big guy with a spreading beard over his red check shirt. Imbecilic grin.

"What can I get yah?"

After serving him a bitter coffee with powdered cream in a plastic cup, the guy told him all about himself and his opportunities at the university.

"I just love it here. Have a great day!"

He took a seat. At the far end was a conference hall with a sign outside:

Careers Fair Today. Come inside and tell us your dreams.

In front of him were some cleaners dressed in green overalls, carrying buckets and waiting for the lift. It had a glass door, giving the illusion that those inside were being propelled up to the lecture rooms in haste.

A figure came and stood over him. A middle-aged woman with a pleasant face. On her neck card, it read: *Karen Highet. Photographic Art.*

"Michael? I'm a colleague of Wilf's."

She held out her hand to him.

"Is Wilf not here?" he asked.

"We don't know where he is this morning. He had a class, but he hasn't turned up. We were wondering whether you knew anything about it."

"We're having lunch together."

"Has he texted you this morning?"

He checked his phone. No reply to his last message.

Karen shifted from one foot to the other and waited for him to say something, before giving up.

"We are concerned for his welfare," she said. "He hasn't been well…"

He realised that might be a euphemism for 'drunk and depressed'.

He would have to make a quick decision, which he disliked doing because it made his head spin. Thoughts cycled through his head. Which of them would turn into an action? He could stay here and wait some more. He could go back to the train station and go home. Or…

"Maybe I could see if he is on his boat?"

She brightened up when he said that.

"Oh, would you?"

Whatever was distributing intelligence in his brain had shuffled the options around like a pack of cards, revealing a random new spread. It was too late to pull back now. He took out his mobile.

"Let me have your number. I'll call you if I find him."

Karen's phone was in her hand, but she spoke each number slowly without looking at it while he stabbed at the keyboard.

He picked up his shoulder bag and turned towards the glass doors. It was raining again.

"I'd better go up," she said. "I have a class waiting for me. But THANK YOU!"

Before he could say anything more, she turned to catch the lift before the doors closed.

The marina was ten minutes' walk away, inside the harbour. Screened off from it by a suspension bridge that raised when one of the larger boats exited. Beyond the bridge was the peninsular and beyond that the North Cove, with a fishing pier which went far out into the Channel. Boats moored up for the winter jammed the place: for only the fishing boats on the harbour side went out at that season. There were yachts, motorboats and a variety of sail-boats and dinghies. Along the wharf, backing up the hill to the town centre, were houses, boatyards, a cafe, a general store, and an ornate Edwardian hotel.

Wilf detested campus accommodation, so when he came to the Art School, he brought his boat down from London and charged the berthing fees to the University. He stayed there during term time, going back to Kennington during the holidays. Some weekends he would take his cruiser for a trip over the Channel to Saint-Malo, or Cherbourg. Michael couldn't recall much about the boat except that it was white, had a cabin and a chrome rail around the hull. There were dozens of boats like that moored in the marina. He went over to the office and a weather-beaten man in dungarees came out. He pointed out Wilf's boat, which was fifty yards to the right: the *Lucchese*.

He climbed up the chrome ladder. There was no one on deck. He called out below and listened. To the left of the helm there was a hatchway and he went down some steps to the round cabin. In it was a circular cream sofa and a matching carpet, on which Wilf was lying. He had on a Barbour jacket, jeans, and boating shoes. His eyes fixed on the ceiling. From time to time, his arms and torso jerked and lifted his back off the floor. Next to his face was a lumpy puddle of yellow vomit.

He knelt down and put his hand on Wilf's left arm.

"Wilf. It's me."

He stared into his face. Every few seconds, the left eye and the right cheek twitched in a bizarre rhythm.

Wilf moaned:

"I lie here on purpose... not well."

His breathing was rapid, and his heart was beating fast. It looked like a high blood pressure problem. He had no first aid training, but he remembered it was best not to move them if you didn't know what was wrong.

Everything was unfolding as if in a dream in which scenes followed on one from the other, without necessity. He had to snap out of it. What did they always do in those TV dramas in medical emergencies? Call for an ambulance, naturally. But he didn't like to leave Wilf unattended. Nor did he want him to overhear while he made the call. So, he compromised and sat in the bedroom with the door open, dialling 999.

"Which service do you wish to speak to, caller?"

"Ambulance."

"Is it an emergency? One moment, sir…"

When he had finished, he went and knelt on the floor. Wilf appeared to be drifting in and out of consciousness.

"Mike? Is that you? It must be…"

Wilf's voice was husky. His flaxen hair was uncut and damp from sweat, sticking to the carpet. His eyes rolling as if trying to refocus. Michael took his hand and held it. He felt like weeping.

Over by the window stood the carving. Serene, yet implacable. It was too far away to see the inscription, but he knew it by heart.

You grieve for those for whom you should not grieve…

After what seemed an age, he heard a commotion on the wharf. Moments later, two paramedics came down the steps. They were both dressed in green jackets and cargo pants and carrying a stretcher. One of them patted him on the shoulder to move aside and guided him onto the sofa. The other set his bag down and put an ear to Wilf's chest.

"What is your friend's name?" asked the woman standing beside him.

"Wilfred Rising."

"Is he an epileptic, do you know?"

"I don't believe so."

He was still in a dream state. In which everything was taking place at one remove, regardless of his hopes and wishes.

"Sir? Are you alright?"

The woman was staring at him in perplexity, her hair tied back tightly over her skull.

"Is he on medication? Or any other drugs?"

Michael shook his head.

"I don't know. I haven't seen him for a while."

"Is this his home, sir? This boat?"

He understood; they wanted him to search the place. Getting up, he went into the shower room. No cabinets there; only a glass with some toothbrushes. Then he checked the larger bedroom, the one with the unmade sheets. He opened the bedside cabinet on the left, but it was full of briefs and socks. When he opened the one on the right, he found some sketchbooks. With a plastic bottle. On the label it said *Escitalopram 10mg*. Things must have reached a serious turn if Wilf was swallowing anti-depressants. He took it into the lounge.

"Is this what you had in mind?"

The man scrutinised it and showed it to the woman, who nodded, rummaged in her bag, and pulled out a syringe. She dabbed Wilf's arm and plunged it in.

"We'd best get Wilfred to hospital, now," said the man. "We'll try to get him comfortable. You can come with us if you like."

He watched them strapping Wilf on the stretcher. His chest was heaving every few minutes and he guessed they wanted to keep him still, but without tightening the belts so hard that he risked injuring himself. He was still half-conscious and insisting under his breath:

"I do so on purpose… on purpose."

They carried him out and put him in the back of the ambulance. By this time, a crowd had gathered: it watched them loading up: dinghy riders wearing Helly Hansen jackets, yacht owners wearing blazers and sailor's caps, and a lone motorbike rider in black leathers who had taken off his helmet to stand in watchful silence. Michael stepped up and sat in the seat opposite the stretcher. A few minutes later, the ambulance coasted up the wharf to a crossing point, before swinging back up the hill.

The Dwight D. Eisenhower Hospital was eight miles

away; a 1930s building which had treated US soldiers wounded in France after D-Day. After the war, some grateful American officers had set up a charitable fund for the support of the hospital, on condition that US citizens would receive free treatment if they were ever in the area and required it. Wilf didn't have a US passport, but it was fit that he should go there. Wilf had always been proud of the fact that he had spent five years going to school in the US, gaining an American outlook.

On arrival, the paramedics wheeled him into Accident and Emergency. After a long conversation with a nurse out of earshot, they both left for their next call. The woman glanced at Michael with a wondering look, as she went out through the revolving door.

Michael walked over to a drinks machine and put in two pound coins. He pushed the button for a sugar-free Coke. He sipped and it tasted of chemicals, but it gave him something to do with his hands.

He hated it when he didn't know what was going on, or what he should do. There was no one around who could explain what might happen next. Or when it might happen. But he had to make an attempt to find out. He went over to the reception desk, where a woman wearing rose-tinted glasses was staring at a screen positioned some way below the counter. She looked up at him.

He pointed at Wilf's trolley.

"Wilfred Rising? Do you know where they are taking him?"

"And you are?"

"His friend. I came with him in the ambulance."

She nodded in triumph and stared at the screen once more, as if decoding a message.

"He's waiting for a doctor to examine him. We're very

busy this morning. It will be some time before we can see him."

Wilf was sleeping when he returned. He had stopped sweating and his hair had reverted to its natural shape: a sort of blonde quiff which lifted off his forehead. It had always given him a youthful look. Michael sat on the chair beside him, took his hand, and felt him quiver slightly. But his breathing was steady, and he seemed at peace.

16

A Meeting In Belgrade

The two males were suspended upside down on meat hooks from the rafters. From the heads of both, blood dripped on the floor.

"The boy has passed out," said Zivko to the man standing beside him.

"Revive him," said Marko.

Zivko nodded to the accomplice behind him with the hosepipe, who, turning on the tap, let loose a jet of water over the son, then the father. Both spluttered, then awakening to their plight, sighed. The older man kicked briefly at the rope that bound his legs before resigning himself to what might happen next.

"Where is he?" repeated Marko.

"I know not," moaned the man. "Let us go. I know not. I swear. Neither does the boy."

"You do not know where your cousin lives now? You are surely lying."

The man with the hose came from behind Marko and slammed his first into the boy's face, breaking his nose again. Another muffled groan.

"We cannot tell you what we do not know," said the father.

Disgusted by his whimpers, Zivko stepped up with the ball hammer and broke the man's right knee. His calf sagged on the rope as the joint dislocated.

The man's howl echoed around the warehouse before evaporating into the silence outside on the industrial estate.

A door opened and Marko turned to inspect the man walking towards him with his hands inside the pockets of his leather coat. A burly figure with a shaved head.

"What is it Andrej?" asked Marko.

"It is the Colonel. He has been calling you. He wants you to go over to the Stari Grad."

"Now?"

Andrej held out his palms.

"It is necessary," he added. "We have a jeep outside."

Marko thought for a moment. His uncle was a man of whims who might have summoned him because he was bored and in need of a drinking partner. On the other hand, it might be something important. There was no way of knowing.

"You stay here, Andrej. Finish this off."

"Samuraj. You want us to continue with the questioning?" asked Zivko, waving the hammer.

"No. I think they are telling the truth."

"You want us to let them go?"

"No. Kill them. Take the bodies over to Borča and dump them on the street. It will be a warning to the others."

Coming out of the warehouse, Marko got into the dark grey Wrangler, which sped off past a row of derelict units, turning left onto the main road that led up to the centre. It was a Friday, and the traffic was heavy coming out of the city. The sun was setting, so far as people could tell, for smog and lowering cloud covered it. Beyond the waterfront development was the once-blue Danube, a smell of raw sewage emanating from it.

The driver deposited him outside the tunnel entrance to the hotel. Marko walked through it and headed for the bar. His uncle was at the back on the sunken floor, seated on a leather sofa next to an antique globe. A short man built like a bull, with one eye lower than the other. Two minders in ill-fitting suits that emphasised their chest muscles stood behind him as he approached.

"Marko, come sit beside me," said the Colonel, gesturing to his bodyguards to stand back out of earshot.

Amongst the Pumas, only his uncle ever used his first name. To the rest, he was always The Samurai.

"Have you found him?" asked the Colonel.

"No one is talking. I think he may be outside the city. Up in the mountains perhaps."

The old man's clasped, beringed fingers twitched under his chin.

"When we find him," he said, "I will cut his balls off."

It would be a high price to pay for raking off five bags from a cocaine shipment, thought Marko. But the man had no honour. Therefore, he had forfeited his claim to masculinity.

"What did you want to speak to me about?"

"Slow, slow," said the Colonel, pressing his hands down. "First, we speak of other things."

The Colonel stared around the room. A server sitting at the bar caught his look and fetched some more drinks. They sat wordlessly until they arrived. At the other end of the bar on the television, a rap singer in a tracksuit was being interviewed about her forthcoming appearance on a reality tv show.

When the server came back with the drinks, the Colonel gave him three thousand dinars.

"Go and switch that crap off."

"There will be complaints," said the server, gesturing to the watchers sitting around the television.

"If they complain, tell them to come and see me. Now go."

They watched as the youth explained to the viewers why he was switching off the tv. Some of them turned to stare and whisper. Slowly, they dispersed, leaving by the exit door to the street.

"Živeli," said the Colonel, raising his glass.

"Živeli," said Marko.

"You will be wondering why I sent for you?"

His uncle's voice had dropped, and Marko leant forward to place his ear closer.

"I have decided to make some changes. The future of our business demands it."

"It is time," agreed Marko.

"Our activities have been a necessary evil for a while. But now I think it is time to replace them with legitimate businesses."

Marko had seen that coming, for it was a logical extension of the Pumas' position. It had millions tied up in operations in the Balkans and also in Austria, Hungary, Germany, France, and Spain. Money from guns, drugs, and prostitution. With a sideline in snuff movies using kidnapped Romanian girls. But it was still a small clan, based in Beograd. To compete with the rest, it would have to expand. And what was more important, to divert money into safe outlets.

"I have been studying it," said Marko. "At the university there are some people we can recruit. People who know about finance."

The Colonel sighed. Not for the first time, Marko noticed how tired he looked. For twenty years, he had looked after the Pumas. There must be several hundred families in Beograd who depended on his generosity. Now he was worn out.

"I get old," said the Colonel.

"I will help you, Uncle. Rely on me."

"When I see you, Marko, I see your father. He was the brother I adored. I swore when he was martyred by the Bosniaks that I would care for his children. He was a great man."

Marko had barely known his father, for he had been away fighting the Croats, Bosnians, and Albanians while he was growing up. Commanding a para-military unit from the Delije, the Red Star football supporters' club. Marko had been just eleven years old when he was killed in a gun battle, a few months from the end of the war. Without his uncle, his mother and two sisters would have starved.

"We are grateful."

"You will not disappoint me?"

"Never," said Marko.

The Colonel stood up and they embraced.

"And now," said his uncle, sitting down, "I have some tasks for you. They will not be easy."

"Tell me."

"I want you to go to London and take care of some business there."

"What is it?"

"We have received a request from our friends in Naples. It seems one of their associates is a man named Carlo Casiraghi. This man builds hotels for them in Liguria. We, too, have money invested in these hotels."

"Are they profitable?"

"Very. In general, construction is a good activity for us."

"What investments do we have in London?"

"They are handled for us by a man named Pilcher. You will meet him and find out more about this."

"What is the favour the Camorra want from us?"

"They want us to take care of some people who have shown Casiraghi disrespect. It seems he sold some art pictures and there are men in London claiming they are forgeries. These pictures sold for over three million euros."

"But why have they come to us?"

"Because these slanders affect us too. We have money invested in the art gallery which sold the pictures."

"Through this man Pilcher?"

"Exactly so."

"Who are the men telling these stories?"

"You will find out from Mr Casiraghi. He is waiting for you in Genoa. From there you will go to London."

"What do you want done with these men?"

His uncle shrugged.

"You can talk to them. Help them see things our way. Otherwise…"

"It will be risky," said Marko. "We will not have protection from the police as we do here."

"I have thought of that. I had some false passports prepared."

"Passports? How many are coming with me?"

"Take Zivko and Andrej with you. You will need help, I think."

17

Despair

On the morning of Mike's visit, Wilf woke up feeling exhausted. He lay in bed hoping for more sleep, but none came. At length, he put on some overalls and went up on deck. Checked the instrument panel, filled the water tanks, and tightened the mooring ropes. Then back below to test the pump and ensure there was enough oil in the generator. After he had done that, he felt a little better. Over time, he had noticed that if he waited for the tiredness to go and the desire to do things to come back, nothing would ever get done. Getting on with things anyhow seemed to arouse his sluggish brain just enough for him to get through the day. He was hoping the new pills would work and give him more oomph. He had taken four, although it said on the bottle that he should take one in the morning and one at night. But pharmacists always erred on the side of caution; no wonder the pills never worked.

He took a shower and lay on the bed covered in towels, waiting to cool down. He felt the unfinished business in his head coming back up to the surface. Clamouring frustrations pushed forward, waiting for attention; worries circling around his head like a flock of crows; guilt clutching at his heart. Depression was weird that way. No energy, no sleep, and no desire to do anything at all except hibernate. All the while, his mind was on turbo charge. Going over and over the same problems, without ever reaching a conclusion.

He counted to ten and forced himself to get up before he gave into the urge to get back between the sheets. There was an art class to see that morning and it wouldn't do to have to cancel it again. He folded away the towels, put on some boxer shorts and chose some clothes that went with the role he was playing. Mr famous fucking painter offering a master class. One thing depression had shown him was how fake everything was.

When he finished dressing, he poured out some coffee and drank it at the table. His head still fuzzy with unexamined thoughts. The cabin lights flickered, and the carving caught his attention, standing on the shelf below the closed porthole. There was nothing serene about it this morning. Instead, it seemed to grimace at him with one eye open; its lips twisted in a smile of mockery.

He went over and picked it up, staring at it minutely. But it was no longer mocking him. He felt like smashing it on the hob. Did it not have a curse on it?

He went over to the shelf to put the thing away, but before he could get there, the fit came on. First, his jaw gurned like it did on MDMA. At first it wasn't unpleasant, but curious. He walked over to the mirror and checked. His pupils were dilated, but that wasn't the bad thing. A rictus distorted the left side of his face, so that it twisted his lip up towards his eye, while the right side was smooth. That worried him. By now his leg muscles were in spasm. He wondered whether he could dance it off, but his heart was beating so fast that would never be a good idea. Instead, he lay on the floor of the cabin and took some deep breaths. One slow, two slow, three slow, four, five. That helped a little. The sweat poured off him and he felt sick. His last thought before he passed out was that death might not be the worst outcome.

When he came round, Mike was standing over him. He refocused his eyes and saw that same saturnine face with the lined jaw and dark glasses.

"Mike?"

"Hello, you."

"Where are we?"

"I found you on the floor of your boat. The ambulance people brought you to the Eisenhower to run some tests. Find out what brought on the vapours."

"I'm feeling all right now…"

Getting up, Wilf sat on the edge of the trolley just as another paramedic came around the corner with an orderly, pushing along a red wheelchair with a high back.

"Mr Rising?"

"Yes?"

"Can you give me your full name and date of birth?"

"I can."

"We're going to take you round the corner. A doctor will examine you."

The medic gestured to the wheelchair.

Wilf thought for a moment before giving in.

"If you must."

He got down off the trolley and sat back in the chair. Looking fragile in his Barbour jacket, one size too large for him, his legs folded to one side.

"Mike, I'll be all right now. You go on back to London."

"No. I'll stay here."

Wilf spread out his hands in mild protest. With a smart turn, the orderly turned the wheelchair about and pushed him off into the interior.

Michael put on his bag and went outside. The rain had stopped, and a wan sun appeared amongst milky clouds. He was now in a vast car park. To the right was a long hall with blinds on the windows. That must be the canteen. An ancient man with a demented look was tottering up the walkway, supported by a woman who was twice his size, wearing a mackintosh and a bush hat. She looked like she might be his daughter. He made way for them. The man grinned at him as if he were on a schoolboy lark and they passed on through.

Over to the left were three ambulances parked up in front of the door to A & E; some elderly passengers were being helped down from the back door of the one in front. Beyond them was some parkland with a knoll on which a clump of trees stood. He walked towards it. A wind picked up and blew some litter back over the concourse towards the wheels of the last ambulance. When he got to the park, there was an empty bench with a memorial plaque in the backrest.

This seat donated by the family of Milly Davenant RIP. Who often stopped to admire the view.

He lit up a cigarette and tried to identify the view Milly admired. More ambulances were coming up over the hill towards the barriers; one had its blue lights flashing. Beyond the hill he could just see the grey waters of the Channel. On the horizon were a couple of boats which had somewhere to get to and were sailing gracefully on. Perhaps it was those Milly liked to look at while she was incarcerated in the hospital.

The shock was wearing off, helped along by Wilf's

revival on the trolley. He had a space now in which to survey the variables which had come into play around his friend. Wilf was lost, he could see that. Something he had never been before. There had always been a group around him: adoring and watchful, eager for the next adventure to which Wilf might take them, whether that was his next work of art, or to a bar or a restaurant in which he would regale them with his stories and artistic aperçus. Yet something had driven Wilf to despair. With himself, it was the reverse: despair was his natural milieu and a crowd was what he avoided. The cricket hummed and whined. Whatever it was, it was all deeply sad.

He called Peggy. She picked up on the first buzz, as if standing by.

"What's up?" she said.

He told her about his discovery on the boat and their journey to the hospital. He could hear her holding and releasing her breath as he spoke.

"Did they say what's wrong with him?"

"They're doing some tests now. I think the paramedics suspect something but aren't telling. Could be some kind of fit."

"You'd better stay with him. Find out what's wrong."

"Aren't you coming down?"

"I can't do that."

"Might help. Can't hurt."

It would be a lot easier for him if she were there. Or was that another evasion?

"Wilf won't want me there. Besides, I have Isa with me. I can't leave him in an empty house on his own."

Nothing more to be said. He put the mobile back into his coat and returned to the hospital. Inside, there was a queue waiting to speak to the receptionist, who was still deep in thought about whatever her computer screen was telling her. No sign of Wilf. He sat down in the waiting area and took out his book.

An hour later, Wilf re-emerged from the corridor, talking to a man in a white coat who might have been a Registrar. They stopped at the reception desk. The doctor was emphasising something with his finger tapping his hand. Wilf stood there pretending to listen, but at last broke off, saying he had to go. Signalling to Michael that he was heading to the door. Michael followed him out, hurrying to catch up with him, as Wilf headed for the taxi rank. None were about and the wind was blowing hard from the South, catching at their jackets. Wilf stopped and waited for him to come up before going into the bus shelter. Michael sat beside him on the bench and offered one of his cigarettes.

"No thanks. I'm trying to give up," said Wilf.

Michael lit up and they sat in silence together.

"What was the verdict?" asked Michael.

"There isn't one. Apparently I had a seizure, but they don't know exactly why. I'm to go back for a scan when they find me an appointment."

"Where do you want to go now?"

A cab, another Toyota, drew up at the rank.

"Let's go to the hotel," said Wilf. "Come on."

Two heavy-set men came hurrying over from the hospital to get the cab. Forestalling them, Wilf jumped up and walked round to hold the rear door open for Michael.

As they drove off, the men came up and one banged on the window, while the other threatened Michael with a fist, his face distorted by the rain on the glass. Wilf raised a finger at them both as the cab pulled away. They drove up to a junction with two green signs. One pointed to the right to Southampton, the other to Doremouth. They took the left up a long hill and by degrees came out to a heath with rolling hills, scrub, and gorse. From the top of the road in the twilight, you could see a long way off. Held in a vast sky, grey rainclouds were being pushed along by an invisible force.

18

A Farewell to Art

The *Admiral Jellicoe* was an Edwardian mansion on five floors newly repainted in white, with flags hanging out along the verandah below the roof: British, American, and European. Built when Doremouth was an exclusive spa, it catered now to wealthy holidaymakers, members of the Yacht Club, and business conventions.

They walked into a grand reception with blue carpets on which the Prince of Wales' feathers were embossed in gold. On the right was a brasserie, where they took a seat by a window with a view of the marina. Antique prints of sailing boats decorated the walls. A server in a black waistcoat came over with their drinks. Large gin and it for Wilf, and tonic water for him. Wilf took a deep draught without ceremony. Michael was about to warn him about his alcohol intake but thought better of it. It was talk, not arguments they wanted now.

By way of a diversion from the tangle, Michael told him about his recollection on the train coming down.

"I remember it," said Wilf. "I thought it was awfully

cool that you were reading philosophy amongst all those school-boys."

"I thought you were cool, too. The way those girls looked at you."

"You're being ironical?"

"Always."

They reminisced some more about their youth. Leaving school, going their separate ways. Wilf to Art School; Michael first to study German in Berlin, then on to University. Then deciding to spend the summer of 1997 together, first in Paris where Wilf wanted to look at the paintings, then on by train to Florence, where Casiraghi was teaching at the Institute there. The summers in Lucca that followed.

"Say, you remember that night we picked up those two girls in the *Deux Magots*?" said Wilf.

"I could hardly forget."

It had been the night he lost his virginity. He had done the translating during the chat-up, for the women were eighteen-year-olds from Koblenz, whom they persuaded to come back and share a bottle of Algerian wine at their hotel in Montparnasse. The following morning, over breakfast in the cafe next door, Michael told him he'd no idea that women enjoyed sex so much. Wilf had laughed so hard his chest hurt. After that, they looked at the Rodins in an old convent by the Invalides. Where Wilf was so taken by the portrait heads of Rose Beuret and the others that he got permission to sketch them, spending each morning at the museum while Michael wandered around the left bank, looking into the second-hand bookstalls.

"What happened to us, Mike? How did we get here?"

Wilf's eyes were blue-haunted in bewilderment.

"Life happened to us. You know, the thing that goes on while you're making other plans?"

"The hell it did."

On a table in the corner were some suits, who looked as if they all worked for the same company. They had that air of forced joviality which people who disliked each other adopted when out at a conference. A drunk woman in a grey suit was impressing the table with salacious gossip about the chief executive. Her voice so loud with a list of indiscretions that it echoed around the room.

He told Wilf about the call from Queen's.

"Why have you given up philosophy?" asked Wilf.

"I haven't given it up. It's the academic life I've given up."

"Ironic that. You give up teaching and can't find anything else to do, while I start teaching because I can't do the thing I want."

"Wessex isn't working out?"

"I hate the place."

"Why'd you come here?"

"Stop gap solution. Lucca didn't work out, so I accepted their invitation while I considered my future."

"Is that the only reason you're unhappy?"

A silence followed as Wilf gazed up at the ceiling.

"You remember those Masaccio panels in the Brancacci Chapel in Florence?"

Michael remembered them well. Early Renaissance frescoes on the walls of Santa Maria del Carmine. Of biblical scenes painted with weird emotional power. He and Wilf had not understood the expression of despair on the faces of Adam and Eve in the first panel. The garden of Paradise didn't look that inviting, and getting thrown out for eating an apple seemed bizarre.

"I went back and understood it better. It's the face people wear when they've made a mistake they didn't know was a mistake. One that ruined their lives."

"What mistake have you made?" asked Michael.

"I've made more than one," said Wilf, after a studied pause. "The first was marrying Cosima."

Michael recalled how Cosima and Tristan Bayes had come over to stay in Lucca, bidding for UK representation for Casiraghi's works. They had achieved that, though Filippo drove a hard bargain, giving them no more than 20% commission. Telling them to look at Wilf's paintings while they were there. Wilf had gone back to London with them, and his first exhibition came up that autumn. Cosima had seen to it that the society magazines covered it and the news spread that they were an item. Michael sometimes wondered who started that rumour.

"Was it so bad?"

"Like fucking a corpse. And a control freak, too. She and her brother make an evil pair. I always thought she was married to him, not me."

"What was the other mistake?"

Again Wilf paused, as if he were thinking of something else.

"I should never have signed a contract with that gallery. They make a brand out of you, take forty percent of everything you sell, and throw you on the scrap heap when they spot some other going concern."

Wilf seemed reluctant to say more, although Michael sensed there were other mistakes he did not want to talk about. He had the feeling that Wilf was ashamed of something; possibly to do with his failed trip to Lucca.

"Let's go back to the boat," said Wilf. "Get something to eat."

They finished up their drinks and walked out to the marina. It was night and the harbour lights lit up the buildings along the quay, their golden sheen reflected in the water. The wind was getting up from the southwest, blowing in their faces as they made their way back to the boat. Towards the end of the marina, it was pitch dark and they trod carefully on the quay for fear of falling in. Once they heard footsteps behind them. Wilf froze and looked back to see who it was, before moving on. Steadying himself, he heaved on the boat ladder and climbed up.

Michael set to work on cleaning up the mess below, while Wilf secured the deck. He scraped the mud from the paramedics' boots off the carpet and cleaned up the vomit. Leaving the portholes open to clear the smell. A gale looked to be coming on, for the wind caught at the cabin door and rocked it on its hinges.

While they made up the beds, there came the sound of a motorbike motoring up the quay. Its engine stopped, and moments later a voice came down the hatch.

"Mr Rising?"

"Who's there?" said Wilf, going up to the bottom of the steps to the deck. Once again, Michael noticed the alarm on his face.

"Delivery. For you."

"That will be the pizza boy," said Wilf. "Give him a tip, Mike. I'm out of cash."

After Mike finished eating, for Wilf had little appetite for the food, they cleared away the boxes and plates. Wilf went into the bedroom and came out with a battered brief-case. Picked up the carving and placed it on the table beside the case. The wind howled and the statue toppled slightly as the boat rocked.

"What's in the case?" asked Michael.

"Some paperwork and half-a-dozen sketchbooks. I keep them as provenance."

"Why are you giving them to me?"

Wilf shook his head in impatience.

"Because they will be safer at your house than here.

You saw just now that a delivery boy could walk on to this boat with nothing to stop him looking around."

Michael didn't know what to say to that, although he felt there was still something Wilf wasn't telling him. Not knowing how to coax it out of him, he tried a roundabout approach.

"I've been thinking about what you said about the art scam. Maybe it's time you gave it up."

"You've said that to me before."

"I've seen nothing since we spoke in May to convince me otherwise."

"Go over the point with me again."

"Because you're getting distracted by art that will sell. Art that will keep the Bayes happy. Twenty-five years ago, you painted because it was your calling."

"True. But what if I can't get the call back?"

"There you go again. You want the daimon to give you a guarantee? That's disrespectful. And cowardly."

Wilf winced.

"You don't sugar the medicine."

"Come and live with us in Spitalfields. Wait on the daimon there. In respect and humility."

"You forgot irony," said Wilf. "Never forget irony."

"I never do."

"Give me one of your cigarettes."

He followed Wilf up on deck. The rain was pelting down on the plexiglass roof, bouncing up in fat globules. A thunderclap lit up the rain clouds. The wind tore at the canvas at the back of the cockpit. Wilf sat down on the side bench and looked out into the darkness.

"I'm giving you back the carving."

"Thanks."

"Wish I'd never borrowed it though."

Michael thought it better to say nothing. He'd known

all along that no good would come of it. He blamed himself for letting Wilf take it away.

"What are you thinking about?" he said, after a while.

"What you said," replied Wilf.

"And?"

"My feeling is you're right. I'm going to accept your offer."

"That's a relief. You coming back on the train with me tomorrow?"

"No. I'll have to finish up at Wessex first. Make it the weekend after this."

"You could go sick? The doctors will give you a note."

Wilf shook his head.

"No, that wouldn't be playing straight," he said.

He stood up.

"We'd better turn in," he added. "It'll be another long day tomorrow."

Michael stood up himself and, for the first time in his life, he hugged his friend. The rain swept down on their backs.

He felt Wilf stiffen, but Michael clasped him harder. A few moments later, Wilf patted him on the back three times, before drawing back to look at him. Lightning flashed, and Michael saw in his lit-up face that Wilf was deeply moved.

"Thank you for what you have done for me," said Wilf, in a breaking voice, the rain running down his cheeks. "I won't forget it."

"Come back soon," whispered Michael, "for we have more to talk about. We have to find a way to get out of this nightmare we're both in."

19

A Cruise Upriver

Marko leaned back on the rail as the clipper sailed up the river towards the Tower of London. Gaily, it motored on, leaving behind a trail of foam, rolling back towards Canary Wharf.

"What does this Pilcher man look like?" he asked Andrej.

"Like an English gentleman. He wears a suit and tie. Always."

"How do you know that?" asked Zivko.

Andrej lit up a cigarette.

"I met him in Germany several times. Once in Antwerp. Whenever I bring cash over the border for him to load up in his car. He always dresses the same."

"Then he has no style," said Zivko, fingering his black Armani hoodie, purchased that morning in Canada Square.

Marko grunted, for Zivko was still a gopnik. Which was fine in Beograd, but conspicuous in London. He'd advised him to dress more discreetly, whereupon he had gone to the most expensive stores in the shopping mall and purchased designer gear with a platinum card. With the puma tattoo on his throat, the gold chain around his neck and a turquoise track suit underneath his hoodie, he looked exactly like a drug dealer from Zemun.

"Is this Pilcher trustworthy?" asked Marko.

Andrej shrugged.

"He is not Serbian."

"Put that cigarette out," said a steward, looking out from the cabin. "Can't you read?" he added, pointing to the *No Smoking* sign above Andrej's head.

Marko signed to Andrej to throw the cigarette over-board. Turned and waved to the steward, who retreated in disdain.

"You know, Andrej, you should show more awareness now that we are in a strange country. In not doing so, you draw attention to yourself. The same applies to you, Zivko."

"How long are we staying here?" asked Zivko.

"We can go back next week. Provided you focus on our mission rather than on your self-gratification."

Marko looked him up and down, slowly. The two of them stirred, nervously. That was as it should be.

"From now on, we will use the names written in our pass-ports when we are outside. You, Andrej, are now David. You, Zivko, are Miroslav. And I am Dragan. Remember this."

From inside came an announcement.

"The next stop is Tower. Alight here for the Tower of London and the City."

The boat slowed to manoeuvre towards the pier, on which a crowd of passengers were waiting to board.

"Do you see him?" he asked Andrej.

"He is there. The tall man with the briefcase. He has a moustache."

"Good. You will wait by the entrance and greet him. Then bring him to me at the table I have chosen. *Miro*, you will sit behind me while I talk to this man. Make sure no one is listening."

Marko sat down in a seat by the window and considered his position. He had a bad feeling about it. His uncle had been over-ambitious in extending their operation so far away. He didn't know for sure whose idea it had been, but it wasn't something his uncle would know about, so maybe it had been the Camorra or the Russians who had put him up to it. The problem was always what to do with the millions in cash. Restaurants, hotels, nightclubs, casinos, and grocery stores were all good. But there were only so many you could use and so few people to trust. Too often, the brotherhood had to be called in to make an example of the ones caught helping themselves. By degrees, they had shifted the money into the European Union. And now to England, where they were over-reliant on the man he was about to meet. Who was investing in things the Pumas had never touched before and knew nothing about. A recipe for disaster.

"Dragan?" asked Pilcher, standing over him, his hand outstretched, a frozen grin on his face.

Marko said nothing, as he did whenever he met someone new. Pilcher swallowed and sat down. Opening his briefcase he handed over some documents. On one of them was a list of their investments. Others displayed information about bank accounts and wire transfers. Marko read it slowly, but Pilcher interrupted his concentration.

"If you need help in understanding it…"

"My English is fine."

"Where d'you learn it?"

"From watching Mickey Mouse cartoons with subtitles," snapped Marko. "Now shut up."

The list was interesting. Two foreign exchange kiosks, a pawnbroker's shop, an antiques emporium, and an art gallery. Over the past two years, twenty million euros had passed through these outlets and out into wire transfers to offshore accounts. Maybe Pilcher wasn't as foolish as he looked.

"Why did you choose this art gallery?" asked Marko.

"It was Carlo who put me on to that. You see, it's a simple way to convert a lot of cash into high value articles we can put back on the market. That Cassy Raggy painting we own is worth half-a-million euros and we'll probably make extra when we sell it on."

Marko grunted and turned over a page.

"You have over a million pounds in interest-bearing deposits," he commented. "Why is that?"

Pilcher beamed.

"I put it there while I look for a home for it."

"But it earns almost nothing."

"True. But it's only been there a few weeks. I've got my eye on a car dealer we could purchase. Lots of premiums to be made on used cars."

"It's old-fashioned business," said Marko, throwing down the dossier. "Too conspicuous. We will do better investing in bitcoin."

"Always happy to come up with a new service. What sort of coins did you have in mind?"

Marko looked up at Andrej, still standing behind Pilcher. Who rolled his eyes.

"We are removing our money here in London," said Marko, after a weighted pause.

"Now what d'you want to go and do that for? Your investments are turning over nicely. You're getting twenty percent return on your money. Ten times the rate of inflation."

Marko raised his eyes and scrutinised the man a second time. What he saw disgusted him. A florid Englishman with small eyes and a weak smile. It brought shame on the family to employ such a man.

"You sure Mr Dmitrijevic approves of all this?" asked Pilcher.

"It is not for you to know what he thinks. I am in charge here."

Pilcher looked down at the table in mourning.

"As you wish," he said.

"How soon can you return the money to us?"

"At least three months, I would've thought. What is the hurry?"

"The 'hurry' comes because one of your investments is attracting too much attention. You know about these men who are threatening Casiraghi?"

"No. Who are they?"

"An American is making trouble with the police here over some paintings our Italian friend sold through that gallery."

"What of it?"

"Think, you fool. If the police investigate, they will find our money there."

"I promise you, Dragan, they won't be able to trace any of that money back to your people. I've kept it all nice and tight."

"That had better be true," said Marko, with a menacing look.

The loudspeaker clicked, and an automated voice came on.

"The next stop is Embankment. Alight here for the National Gallery."

"We will stop here," said Marko. "Before I go, I will give you another task. Go to the people at that gallery and warn them."

"Warn them about what?"

"That your arrangement with them is about to come to an end. But say nothing about the Pumas."

"I can do that. But why get off here? I can offer you and your boys a spot of lunch in Chelsea Harbour. Happy to show you around."

"We are not here for sight-seeing."

"You might as well enjoy yourselves while you're here."

"No. We have other business to transact."

"What business?"

Marko stared into Pilcher's face.

"You ask too many questions. Go about your business and report to me when you have carried out my orders."

"But how do I find you?"

Marko smiled and took him by the arm, whispering into his ear.

"We will never be far away. Watch and wait; we will come to you."

He pushed Pilcher hard so that he staggered backwards up the gangway, before Marko turned for the steps that led up to the pier.

20

More Delusions

Michael let himself in and stood in the hall. Silence. He went downstairs into the kitchen. No one there except Peggy's black cat, waiting to be fed. He turned on the light. It was supernaturally clean. Someone had polished the floor, the table, and the benches. Cleaned the sink and the wall-to-wall cabinet above it.

He went upstairs into each of the rooms. Same thing. All were dustless and immaculate. The scents of citrus cleaner, bleach, and floor wax everywhere, as if the house had been got ready for sale. He unlocked the workroom. At first, he thought it was undisturbed, but when we looked closely he saw that an unknown hand had removed each of his tools from the racks and cleaned those, too.

He took out his phone and called his wife.

"Hi. This is Peggy. Please leave your message and I will call you back. Ciao."

He went into his office. Papers and notes were in a neat pile beside the Mac. A jar full of pens on the other side. Underneath the desk was the printer, and a cabinet filled with the lumber of years: cheque books, sellotape, old iPods, batteries, cables, plugs and keys. Someone had removed the lot and placed them all in a plastic bag on the floor.

Behind him, covering the wall on either side of the window, was his library, which he kept in neat rows. Poetry at the top; philosophy in the middle; psychology at the bottom. The intruder had dusted them off, but in doing so had displaced an old paperback. It was a faded copy of the *Bhagavad Gita*, which his father had picked up on the hippy trail, somewhere in Kathmandu before he disappeared on it for good. A cheap paperback with Krishna on the front, wearing a bright yellow robe, driving a chariot. He had not looked at it since his mother died. He took it over to the sofa and looked for the passage she had used for the inscription on the carving. In it, Krishna was giving reasons why Arjuna should not flinch at the war that was about to start. On account of the fact that the soul never died, all was subject to the wheel of karma and death was an illusion. It was never an argument that Michael had found convincing, but he read on.

When the mind is cleared of its delusions, you will become indifferent to the results of action.

He let that sink in. Which delusions had Krishna in mind? He had spent most of his life with a malady that left him indifferent to the results of action. Thinking it over, he decided Krishna must be referring to the ego and its craving for control. Without that, people would be a lot more resigned, as he was. If that was true, he was already enjoying an egoless state of being. Yet he had found little peace.

He looked at his watch. It was now past one, and he had been up since six-thirty, travelling up from the marina. A drowsy slumber descended, and he drifted off.

Someone shook him and he opened his eyes to find Isaias standing over him.

"Doctor?"

"What is it, Isa?"

"You have to get up. There is a visitor arriving soon. Peggy asked me to wake you."

Michael grunted and sat up.

"Where is Peggy?"

"She is at the shop."

"Was it you who cleared the house?"

"Do you like it?"

"I'm not sure. But the point is: you don't have to do that. You're not a servant."

"I know that."

Isa sat down beside him. Tall and composed, his back straight and his knees apart. He had the same smile that was there on Thursday morning. The one that had disturbed him so much.

Isa picked up the book and riffed through it.

"What is this?"

"A sacred text of the Hindus. The teachings of Krishna."

"Is it good?"

"Some interesting stuff on the unreality of the self. The delusions of the mind and the senses."

Isa wrinkled his nose.

"Do you believe that?"

"I don't know whether I believe it. But it's an interesting way to look at the world."

"How can they be delusions? Aren't we here, talking together? In this room? Sitting on these chairs?"

"I think Krishna means that knowledge is impermanent."

"Impermanent?"

"Unstable. Something we now take to be true turns out to be not what we thought it was."

"I do not think I mistake it when I hold this book in my hands."

"You don't mistake that. But the stories you make up about it afterwards might be."

"Are we telling stories now?"

"Not now, but maybe later."

"Is this what you teach?"

For the first time in a while, Michael laughed; a deep, coughing laugh. Isaias watched him, then smiled along.

From down below there came three raps on the front door.

"She is here," said Isaias.

"You know who it is?"

"I think so. Someone from the Shelter."

They opened the door to a woman in a mackintosh holding a briefcase. Her treble chin wrapped in a scarf.

"Mr Gereon? I'm Jennifer. I've come about your host application."

"I have made no applications."

"You have a refugee staying with you without authorisation. Good afternoon, Isaias."

The woman brushed past Michael.

"Is your wife here?" she said, taking off her coat in the hall.

"No. Were you expecting her?"

"You have come too early," said Isa. "Two o'clock was the time."

"I know that, but I have a lot of homes to see today. Shall we make a start?"

The woman seemed irritated they weren't all lined up in the hall standing on a red carpet. Michael showed her

140

up to Isaias' room. Which was immaculate. The woman looked around in suspicion.

"This house seems ok. Does it belong to you?"

"It's been in my family for three generations."

"Is this room for his sole use?"

"He chose it himself," said Michael.

"You're aware you cannot accept money from him?"

Her flinty eyes, weary with the effort of charity, gazed at something behind his head.

"That's a shame." he said.

He was about to add something more when he caught sight of Isa standing behind her, gesturing at him to keep quiet.

"There is a bathroom next door," said Isa, leading the way.

A few minutes later, the front door closed and, seeing them on the floor above, Peggy came up the stairs without taking off her coat. She shook hands with the woman.

"I was just telling your partner here, about our terms and conditions."

"We have studied them," said Peggy.

"They are for Isaias' protection, you know. You need to keep in mind that he is a vulnerable adult."

"We're all vulnerable adults, sweety," said Peggy.

Turning to Michael, she ushered him away with her hands.

"Why don't you make us all some tea?"

He served it up in the TV room. By now, the woman seemed to have calmed down and was chatting to Isa and Peggy on the sofa opposite. He sat alongside his wife.

"Now that you're both in the room, I have to ask you formally: are each of you willing to host Isaias?"

Peggy turned to him, mouthing: "Yes?" He looked at

Isa, who observed him warily. He put his arm around Peggy.

"We'll do it," he said.

"And you, Isaias. Do you want to stay in this house? We have other places you can go, where you would have more independence than you have here."

"I want to stay here."

"We don't know how long you can stay in this place," she sighed. "Could be a few weeks or longer. We will call in and find out how you are coping from time to time."

She spoke as if Isa was in danger of having a breakdown if he stayed more than a week. Isa, for his part, attended to her as if she were speaking down a tin can.

"We can't pay you anything, you know," said the woman, turning to Michael.

"We don't need money from you," said Michael.

Seeing that the woman was irritating her husband, Peggy intervened.

"Will there be any money for Isa's education? Can you find him work?"

"We will carry out an assessment next week. Would you like that Isa?"

"I can do my own assessment," replied Isa. "I will have a look around before I find something to do."

"You don't have to do it alone, you know," said the woman. "That's what we're here for. My number's on that card."

Isa turned over the card in his hand and laughed. Flustered, the woman rose to her feet.

"I've seen all I need to see here. I will write my report and send you a copy," she said, addressing Peggy.

After the woman had gone, Peggy came up to see him in the office while he was working through Wilf's stuff. Photographs of works-in-progress, registers, notebooks, sketchbooks. He had not the time to look through them all, but he saw the newest one contained drawings Wilf had made of figures based on the carving, which stood on the desk.

"He gave it you back?" said Peggy, picking it up as if it were contaminated.

"Says he wished he'd never taken it."

"I can understand that. There's always been something creepy about it."

"In what way, creepy?"

"Like it's got a curse on it."

"That's what Wilf said. Don't you think that's a tad over dramatic?"

"No, I don't."

"My mother's not been dead that long."

Peggy put the carving back on the desk, lifting her fingers, gratefully.

"Her presence is still here. I can feel her in every room."

"I don't."

"That's because you're the transmitter."

"Explain."

"You carry her around with you. Maybe because you feel guilty that you weren't there to save her."

"You know I don't like talking about that."

It was an old wound that never closed. That he had known, on the morning of the murder, what was about to happen. That he had seen it, felt it. Even as his mother was packing up his lunch for school. He had looked at her and seen, also, that she did not know the fate looming over her. Something that confused him and made him think he might be mistaken. So, he had let her hug him and kiss his hair.

"You and me, we'll never be parted," she told him.

Then she waved goodbye to him on the doorstep, her skirt blowing in the wind and watched as he walked up the street.

Michael snapped out of his reverie and found Peggy leaning on the desk, staring down at him.

"You sound like that quack I saw on Wimpole Street," he said."

"You should take what I say more seriously. And lock that carving away."

"I'll do it if it pleases you."

"You do that. But first I want to know more about my brother."

She sat down on the sofa, and he told her about the last two days. When he had finished, she said:

"Do you think he took an overdose? Deliberately?"

"Can't be sure. It might be one of those situations where the person doesn't know what his intentions are any more. But I don't think he set out to kill himself. It was all too random for that."

"But you didn't ask him directly?"

"He pre-empted that by telling me he took the wrong dose after they changed his medication."

"What did the doctor say?"

"Seemed happy with the explanation it was all a mistake. Told Wilf it was most likely Serotonin Syndrome. That he should slow down on the tablets."

"But I still don't get it. What is he so depressed about?"

"He says he can't paint any more. That he's not happy at Wessex. He seems to have a grudge about Cosima. Says she turned his head while her brother was making a lot of money out of his paintings."

"I can believe that. When he married her, he stopped being an artist and became a celebrity. I remember when Wilf was a boy, he could draw anything and that was before he had lessons. We all knew that he had something special. But we never thought he would become famous. It was the worst thing that happened to him."

"He thinks that if he can get away from the art racket, then his muse might come back."

"Honey, his muse ain't going to come back if he's not around to listen to her."

"That job in Doremouth is getting him down. A clean break is what he needs. Anyway, whatever we think about it, he won't change his plans now. He's giving in his notice on Monday and he's coming here to stay."

"He's coming here?"

"Isn't that good?"

Peggy put on a puzzled look. As if he had done something unaccountable.

"You surprise me sometimes."

"How so?"

"The way you live in your interior castle for months on end. Then you snap out of it. Go round and comfort Mom. Save Wilf's life. Persuade him to give up his job. Give him a place to stay..."

"I only do those things to please you."

"Bullshit. You love Wilf too."

She embraced him and let him kiss her. That soft mouth he had always adored. Something choked him, but he didn't know what it was. He held her tighter, half afraid of what might happen if he broke the spell. Peggy stepped back and stroked his face, her dark eyes holding his.

"I'd better talk to Isa," she said. "Find out more about his plans."

Michael opened up a sketchbook and leafed through it. Most of the drawings were landscapes. Rather beautiful, he thought. They gave him the feel of the hill-top villages you could see in the Apennines all the way down to Rome.

But some of them were more abstract; semi-shapeless forms moving about in the atmosphere. Languid, haunting figures. Rather like the carving in shape.

Finding nothing else of interest, he put them all into another plastic bag and took the lot downstairs. Walking through the kitchen, up through the conservatory and out into the garden. There was the brick out-house with its rickety green door where he used to hide from his grandmother when she came to take him to school. Every day, for months on end, he would resist, kicking and wrestling with her while she dressed him and marched him up the road. For him, school was a place where they brain-washed children and the teachers scared him. Then, one day, he hid in the toilet, and no one had been able to find him. It became his secret hiding place until his grandfather discovered him there one morning.

It was disused now; the toilet basin removed. But it was still a place where he hid things. On the wall was the old cistern. He lifted the lid and put Wilf's secrets in it.

21

The Figure In The Picture

Michael's phone buzzed. When he picked it up, there was a text from Ralph Schoenman.

Please call me. I have news.

He didn't know whether to find Ralph impressive or boring. Twice he had emailed with details of his investigations over in Lucca. He had even been to see that peasant, Carlo Casiraghi, in the old studio. What he hoped to get out of him was a mystery. Carlo wouldn't be able to tell the difference between one of his uncle's paintings and a drawing by a five-year-old. To him art pictures were toys for stupid, rich people with more money than sense. Things to be off-loaded for as much money as they wanted to pay. When once he had seen Carlo looking at a Casiraghi on the wall one summer, it had reminded him of a chimpanzee staring at a Sèvres vase.

There was something touching about Ralph's dogged pursuit of the truth. It reminded him of the way he himself would spend months trying to resolve a problem in philosophy that gnawed at him, trying to see it from every angle until a flaw in reasoning appeared and he could put it to bed. Construct another position that was tighter and harder to break down than the original. But never letting go. Because giving up meant that there was a logical flaw in the world left unattended, leaving a trap for the unwary.

Ralph was undeniably different from most lawyers. For one thing, he wasn't an opportunist. Nor was he much interested in money. His idol was Justice. Maybe that was because he was a farm boy from Kentucky who had made it into Yale. At any rate, he would never give up on the Bayes.

He called him back, and they arranged to meet in the hotel where Ralph was staying with his wife, over in Canary Wharf.

Shortly before four o'clock, he alighted from the Docklands light railway at Heron Quays and walked across the footbridge over the dock. Then up the Westferry road, where there were hotels and restaurants catering for travellers who had business in the banking quarter. The Citadel was a thirty-five-floor building shaped like a broken bottle across the water from Rotherhithe. He went in, where Ralph awaited him in the lobby. Standing beside him was a woman in her forties with dyed blonde hair, wearing a green puffa coat with a high neck and holding a shopping bag. She looked like she was getting ready to go out. Ralph himself was wearing a grey hounds tooth jacket and a white shirt with a red woollen tie. He was clearly staying in. But it looked like they were having an argument.

"My wife, Mary-Beth."

The woman took his hand and appraised him with a look of candour.

"Dr Gereon, I'm hoping you can persuade Ralph to give this thing up."

"Oh?"

"He's spending far too much time chasing these pictures. He's neglecting his business and he's neglecting me."

Ralph stood beside her, stroking his new growth of beard and looking sheepish.

"Now honey, Dr Gereon doesn't want to hear about our private quarrel."

"Our quarrel won't stay private for much longer if you're going to spend the next six months acting like a private dick."

She put on her gloves.

"See what you can do with him, Dr Gereon. I hear you have as many doubts about this business as I do."

With a warning look at Ralph, she turned off towards the revolving door and went out to hail a cab.

Ralph was still stroking his beard, whether from embarrassment or irritation, he couldn't tell. Slowly, he turned around, put his hand on Michael's shoulder, and pointed to the lift.

"Come. Let's go upstairs. We'll have privacy there."

The lift took them up to the 30th floor where Ralph and Mary-Beth had taken a suite. Huge bedroom and shower room and, partitioned off from this by a storage shelf, was a sitting room furnished with grey-green fabric on the walls, leather easy chairs grouped around a glass coffee table and carpets that might have been designed by Mondrian. Out of the window was a panoramic view of the City. From there he could make out the Gherkin where, beyond that, lay Spitalfields. Ralph's desk faced the window and on it was a lap-top and a big sample book of the kind you could get from wallpaper shops. Beside it was a rolled-up canvas.

"Take a seat, Michael. Let me bring these things over to you."

The canvas was *Moveable Wind*. Somehow, it looked different from the photograph he had seen two weeks before. More beautiful. Or had he super-imposed what he knew about Casiraghi's style on the photograph when looking at it in *The Execution Dock*? The draughtsmanship in this painting was still unfamiliar. Instead of the hard lines and bold colours of the earlier pictures he knew about, this was dreamier, using light colours to distinguish human shapes from drifting clouds.

Schoenman came and sat beside him.

"What do you think?"

"I'm thinking that the man who painted this was not the same man who painted the two pictures that I own."

"You don't think it was by Casiraghi?"

"No, I don't mean that. I mean, he must have changed a lot by the time he executed this. Maybe it was his illness."

"That's a reasonable view. One that I went along with for a while. Until I realised that there are so many other things that don't add up. Using that sepia paint, for example. Which is why I commissioned a guy from the Italian Institute for Fine Art to take a closer look. I just got back from Florence with the findings."

Ralph opened up the sample catalogue.

"See these? Different types of canvas?"

Michael saw what it was now. Samples of linen and cotton canvases from an art store in London. There were many shades ranging from clean white to subtle creams and a variety of unprimed greys. The cheaper ones were light, the expensive ones heavier and more finely woven.

"The canvas used in this picture is made from rough English linen, which is unavailable in Italy. So far as we can tell it doesn't match any of Casiraghi's other canvases."

"That doesn't prove he didn't use it. He might have run out of canvas and ordered it online, with express delivery.

It's what a dying man would do if he didn't think he had much time left."

Schoenman slapped his thigh.

"You would have made a fine lawyer, Michael."

He got up and headed back to the desk. Rummaged about in the drawer and pulled out another wallet and brought it back to the coffee table. Opening it, he extracted some photographs and laid them out.

"I had these taken with the permission of the owners."

Michael picked up one of them, entitled *Shipwreck*. This one a series of brush strokes indicating ocean waves banking up on the shore, carrying one figure which appeared to be struggling to stay afloat, while another, hooded figure held out her arms on the shore. Michael studied it for a long time with growing recognition.

"A collector in Geneva purchased that for 450,000 euros from the Bayes Gallery. She let me take a sample from the canvas for testing."

The next one he picked up made Michael stop.

It showed an ascending series of violet and blue shades from which a figure was emerging with outstretched arms. The title was *Funerary Offering*. He got up and went to scrutinise it beside the window. Coming back, he laid the photographs side by side. Then he placed them next to the canvas. There could be no doubt about it: they all contained an image of the carving. Yet there was Casiraghi's signature at the bottom on each.

Schoenman came over and stood beside him before the window and gave him a quizzical look.

"Seen something?"

He told him about the figure his mother had made.

"I don't understand what it is doing there."

"Let me see that."

Schoenman took a magnifying glass off the desk and

peered through it. Turned the photograph on its side and looked at it that way. Then he did the same from the other.

"It doesn't look like those figures have been added at a later date. Seems to be part of the compositions. But we'd have to look at the originals to be sure."

Together, they re-examined Schoenman's purchase. This time Michael saw that the woman was in fact carrying an urn, which she was presenting to the other figures, as if in homage.

Michael felt sick. Was Wilf a forger? It was too dreadful to think about.

"Can I get you something to drink? You look a bit shook up," said Schoenman.

"Water."

Schoenman went over to the mini bar in the corner and took out a small plastic bottle. Poured it into a glass that was standing on the storage wall and gave it to him. He took a big swallow and tipped a little of the water over his face. Rubbed it over his forehead. That revived him a little. Schoenman walked off towards the bathroom and came back with a towel. Gave it to Michael and sat down beside him with his hands clasped together and his head down.

"Your brother-in-law, right?"

"Yes. My closest friend."

"What do you want to do?"

"I have to see him. Talk to him. Can I keep this?"

Michael held up the photograph.

"Sure, take it. I have others. Go see your brother-in-law. I have enough evidence for now."

"There must be an explanation. Wilf wouldn't do a thing like that."

Schoenman regarded him thoughtfully. Was there pity in that gaze?

"You know, I've had to look into a lot of forgery cases recently. Sometimes the perpetrators don't fully understand what they're getting into. What starts out as a bit of fun can turn into something nastier. The picture is only the start; the deception comes later."

"What are you going to do?"

"Me? I'm going back to the police. Find out whether they've found out anything more about Carlo Casiraghi and the Bayes. Get them to take this thing seriously."

"What about your wife? She seems to want you to drop the whole thing."

"Mary-Beth worries about deep waters. That it might be more than I can handle."

"Oh?"

"Something spooked her when we invited Carlo Casiraghi to meet us for a drink at our hotel in Florence. Nothing heavy, just a friendly enquiry. Then Carlo showed up with his lawyer, who translated for him. Seems Carlo doesn't speak English too well, but he knows the f-word. Called us a lot of awful names and said he was going to sue us for libel."

"Why is your wife worried about him? I've seen Carlo when he's drunk. Every Saturday night was fight night when we were staying there."

"He's not a nice man. Mary-Beth says he looks like a criminal. Thinks he might be mixed up with the Mafia."

"Is that what you think?"

"It's a possibility. But then something else happened this morning."

"What was that?"

"She picked up the room phone and someone asked for me. A man with a foreign accent. Said he wanted to come by and when were we leaving? Didn't leave a name or a call-back number. Said he'd call later. Now Mary-Beth is saying that we're being followed. But it's just imagination."

"Ralph. Maybe your wife is right. You should drop this."

"I can't do that."

"Why not?"

"Because I want to teach these people a lesson. Tristan Bayes ripped me off and he's not getting away with it."

"What are you? Some kind of vigilante?"

Schoenman winced.

"That's an ugly word. I prefer 'citizen'."

A few minutes later, Schoenman accompanied him to the door and shook his hand.

"I wanted to say, Michael, that I've really enjoyed meeting and talking with you. I hope, one day, when this business is over with, we can meet up and continue our conversations."

"I'd like that," said Michael, a little untruthfully.

Schoenman raised his right palm, his other hand making to close the door.

"Farewell, for now," he said.

Michael turned to the lift. He pressed the down button and saw that the lift was waiting on the twelfth floor. No doubt waiting to receive some guests before taking them to the ground floor. It would be a while before it elevated back up. To kill time, he went over to the wall behind him.

Along it was a series of pastiches based loosely on the paintings Monet had made of views along the Thames in his characteristic misty fashion. Six of them, all tripe. Smudged pictures of the Houses of Parliament, London Bridge, Westminster Abbey, and a few other landmarks.

The Go Board in his head switched on and the counters moved. He waited for them to stop, then the answer appeared. Satisfied, he walked back to the lift, which was just coming up. He got in and, on the way down, processed the answer some more. Clearly, he and Wilf had a lot to talk about. It was Saturday now, and they were expecting him on Foulard Street the next day. But he didn't want to wait that long. Pulling out his mobile, he texted him.

Please call me. There's something I want to ask you.

He waited until the lift got to the ground floor and the doors opened, before pressing the Send button on his phone.

Standing in front of him were three men. Balkan types, probably tourists. Except they did not look like people who would stay in a hotel like this. The middle one was a man in his mid-thirties, with eyebrows that knit in the middle, wearing a grey overcoat. A slight man with silk-black hair cut short over his forehead. To his right was a burly man with a shaven head, on the other a younger man in a lurid track suit. The man in the middle stood back slightly to let Michael out, leaving a tiny gap through which to pass. Michael could feel his breath on him as he moved around him. The cricket croaked as he stepped out.

He turned back to look. The man with the shaven head, he saw, was wearing motor-bike gloves and was whispering something in the ear of the man in the middle, who was staring straight at Michael. As if he knew who he was. A faint smile crossed the man's lips as the lift doors closed.

As he walked out of the revolving door to the street Michael recalled Wilf's fear when the courier with a pizza delivery drove up on the quay that night. He would have to ask Wilf about that, too, when he returned his call.

22

A High Class Gallery

Tristan Bayes leaned back in his swivel chair with his Timberland boots on the desk, spectacles perched on his spiky hair, skimming through the new Bayes & Bayes catalogue.

The night before had been one to remember. Starting out at Trumps, he had fallen in with Rory, Guy, and David. First a few bumpers and some coke to start with. Then on to Gaspers, where they had played baccarat, which had set him down a few hundred, before he won most of it back on the roulette table. Then on to a new club Guy had bought on the King's Road, where there were a lot of hot girls. One of them had almost broken his spine in bed afterwards.

He was still reasonably fit, he thought. Thanks to his annual skiing trips to Zermatt and his twice-weekly work-out on the squash court in Dolphin Square, where he played like a demon. Or so people said. He smiled at the thought. That was the thing about Harrow: it made a sportsman out of you. And that was great for the girls too; his physique was still that of an athlete's. Not all of them were bothered by his missing left eye. The result of a child-hood accident in which, getting on his father's racing bike without permission, he had spun down a hill and crashed into an upturned railing. One spike had gone clean through his eye socket. It had taken years of surgery to repair it all. Thankfully, his mental faculties were all still in place.

On the whole, he thought the marketing people had done a good job. They'd reproduced the art collections in high fidelity, with tasteful descriptions under each item in Baskerville italic. A nice photograph of Cosima and Abisola standing together in the upper gallery and one of himself standing proprietorially by the entrance outside, with Tabitha beside him. That would annoy Cosima, he thought. He wondered whether she had seen it yet. He could hear her whispering down the phone in the next room.

Lunchtime had gone and the gallery was empty. There were no riffraff coming in from the rain, staring at the pictures and pretending to be buyers. Time to do some work, for they had an exhibition to organise. A new artist at the Slade whom Cosima had met at an open day a few months back, with a striking set of found objects and installations to offer. Human figures in barbed wire, a series of collages featuring a deserted industrial estate, a derelict toilet decorated with graffiti in lipstick. That sort of thing. Mounting them in the upstairs gallery would require care and attention, for he could not always rely on Abisola to get the displays quite right; he would have to lean on Tabitha for that. Meanwhile, he had better get on with organising the opening night. There was a brochure to write, a mailshot to go, websites and social media to be updated and journalists rounded up.

He picked up the phone; it was engaged. Cosima was

still next door in a deep study with one of her chums. The call would have to wait, as he didn't like using his mobile for business transactions. Not tax-efficient, and you didn't know who might get hold of your private number. He got up and went into the gallery outside. There, he found Tabitha and Abisola packing up some pictures for the courier.

"Tabbie, can you stay on tonight?"

Tabitha turned to face him and adjusted her black belt, which complemented her red dress and black hair. She was a corker, Tristan thought. And gave the gallery exactly the right tone one sought from an intern. It was great, too, that while Abisola was from a princely Nigerian family, Tabitha's mother was the daughter of a viscount. One of mummy's chums. Ebony and Ivory; it just worked.

"We have a mail-shot to organise for Doris Teller and the brochure will have to be ready for the post first thing. When you've finished over there, come round and I'll go through it all with you."

Tristan knew it was a Friday and that she might have a prior arrangement, but he also thought it a good idea for an intern to gain a work ethic. He had spent four sodding years running errands for art dealers when he came out of Uni, and it hadn't done him any harm. Quite the reverse: it was what you had to do to get on in the art world.

He looked up at the plinth where the Aztec mask was still on display. Its yellow eyes, with their black pupils, stared down at him in disgust.

"And take that thing away, would you?"

Tabitha gave him a flirtatious look and turned back to the table to continue with her packing. Behind him, the street door opened and closed, and he turned to see who it was.

A slope in a grey, pin-striped suit and a furtive air,

Ronald Pilcher wouldn't have been Tristan's ideal choice for a business associate. He was a hangover from the dark days after the crash. Sales had dropped through the floor, and commissions with it. He and Cosima had tried to keep things afloat, but it had been hard. So bad it reduced them to opening four days a week and downsize on staff. There were some gambling debts to deal with, too. Fortunately, Pilcher had come along with an unmissable opportunity. A five-hundred-thousand-pound cash injection and fairly unlimited funds for new purchases. The only drawback had been Pilcher himself. Although he was an accountant, and lots of people did business with them these days, he was a bit of an oik and didn't understand the first thing about fine art. Not the sort of person Tristan would want in his club, although Pilcher had little chance of getting in there.

"What is it, Ronald? We're rather busy in here today."

"A brief word in your shell-like if I may."

Pilcher beamed and, pointing to his briefcase, couched his head towards the office.

"All right, come through. But it'll have to be quick."

Tristan stretched out his arm towards the door as if he were welcoming him there, watched him walk through and turned back to Abisola.

"Abi, give me ten minutes and then come on through. Say there's someone on the phone for me."

Abisola wrinkled her nose, as if a bad smell remained in the room.

"What does he want?"

"Search me. But ten minutes maximum."

He held up his hand and flashed five fingers twice, as he turned back to the office and closed the door. There was Pilcher, sitting upright on the chair opposite his, with the case perched on his knees.

"Now what's this all about, Ronald?"

Pilcher gave Tristan a conspiratorial smile.

"Has Carlo Casiraghi been in touch? I hear he's been having a spot of bother with one of your artists."

"Carlo has called me. What of it?"

"My consortium has spoken to me about it. They're not happy either. Apparently, your boy has been calling Mr Casiraghi at all hours of the night, making threats. Saying he's forged those artworks."

"It's all rot, you know. I doubt Carlo knows one end of a paintbrush from the other."

"My investors are most anxious to avoid unsavoury rumours. They want him gone."

"Well, I don't think there's too much to worry about there. Rising hasn't sold anything for a while now. They say he's all washed up. By all means, we'll drop him from the list if that keeps you happy."

"What about that painting we purchased? Is that kosher?"

"Nothing to worry about there. We have provenance."

"Providence?"

"Proof of origin. A letter from the lawyers confirming all six paintings were signed and produced by the artist himself. Abisola can print a copy off for you on your way out."

"That won't be necessary. It's the potential for adverse publicity that is the chief problem. As you know, members of the consortium are all wealthy businesspeople with European reputations."

"I don't know who they are. You've never told me anything about them."

"Naturally, they wish to remain anonymous," said Pilcher, tapping his nostril. "Which is why they appointed me to organise an investment pool on their behalf."

Pilcher was looking very pleased with himself, thought Tristan. All the same, there always been something a bit fishy about it. Ronald wouldn't have been his first choice to head up a multi-million-pound investment fund.

"There is another matter in the offing," said Pilcher.

"What's that?"

"We're making some policy changes to the administration of the fund. That will lead in time to a withdrawal of our investment in the gallery."

"Actually, Ronald, that's rather a good idea. How about if we repaid the investment to your consortium sooner rather than later? Your clients will be happy, and we can get on with taking the gallery to the next step without them having to worry about where the paper-work comes from."

Pilcher couldn't have looked happier if he had just won a holiday for two with Britney Spears.

"What would be the payback arrangement?"

"Your money back, plus an option to cash in on the Casiraghi you purchased. We can resell that on your behalf at the going market price. Less our commission, of course."

"A most interesting offer," opined Pilcher. "I would have to clear it with my investors, naturally."

"You do that."

The door opened.

"Time's up!"

Abisola's stony face appeared around the door.

"You have a phone call," she said.

Tristan got to his feet and held out his hand.

"It's been very nice talking to you, Ronald, but I must rush now. Please let your investors know about my proposal. See what they think."

He rushed out the door without waiting for an answer and, not wanting to hang about in the gallery before

Pilcher had gone, he went next door into Cosima's office. There he found his sister studying the new brochure.

She examined him with her grey eyes.

"Nice try, Tris," she said, putting her finger on the photograph of him outside the shop. "But I think we all know who's in charge here."

She always spoke in a whisper, so breathy you'd think she had asthma. Forcing you to pay attention to her every word. It was a trick she had.

"What did that awful man want?" said Cosima.

"Pilcher? Seems the people he represents have got a bee in their bonnet about your ex. They say he's fallen out with Carlo and that he's making trouble about those paintings we sold."

"Is there anything suspicious about them?" asked Cosima.

"Not so far as I'm aware," Tristan lied.

"Seems odd, nonetheless."

"How so?"

"That it's taken this long for Carlo to produce them."

"Ah. I can explain that. Apparently, they were hidden away in Filippo's farm-house. You know, the old family home up beyond Matraia. It's been locked up for years. Carlo found them when he went over to get it ready for sale."

Cosima cast him a sceptical eye.

"And what exactly has Wilf been saying?"

"Well, this is where it gets absolutely preposterous. Apparently, he said Carlo painted those pictures himself."

"Are you sure that's what he said?"

"That's what I was told."

"Very odd."

"At any rate, it's time Wilf found another gallery for his pics."

"He's rather fey now, don't you think?" said Cosima. "People want something more than narratives at this time. They're looking for something more pressing, more urgent. Less linear."

"Couldn't agree more, Sis. Shall I send him a letter?"

"Please do. It would free up more space for the talent we're trying to bring in. I've been hearing great things about Doris Teller. The Tate are absolutely crazy about her stuff and she's in line this year for the Bleacher Foundation Prize."

"That's been your doing, Cosy. She wouldn't have a foothold without all that press coverage you've been getting her."

Cosima closed up the brochure and considered for a moment. Then, leaning back, she shook out her hair, as if getting ready for close action.

"Sit down, Tris. I think it's time we had a serious talk about the running of this gallery."

Tristan knew better than to resist his sister when she was playing mother. Best to get your head down and wait for it to blow over. He sat down.

"What do you want to talk about, Cosy?"

Cosima's eyes had a faraway look, as they always did when she gave him one of her 'talks'. The same look Tristan had seen before in the eyes of headteachers, employers and police officers whenever there was trouble brewing.

"Tristan, is there something you're hiding from me?"

He thought of all the things he had hidden from her and from their parents recently, but could think of nothing that might end up in court.

"Nothing especially important," he replied. "What's on your mind?"

"Those loans. The ones you took out to pay your gambling debts."

"Now that's not fair, Cosy. That money was used to keep the gallery afloat. Something you agreed with at the time."

"I might not have agreed had I known more about this Pilcher."

She pronounced the name as if she were spitting out an olive pit.

"I've been making enquiries. No one we know has ever heard of him."

"Why should they? You don't ask for the name of the mechanic at the garage when you take the car in to get it fixed."

"One doesn't borrow nine hundred thousand pounds from a workman."

"I can put your mind at rest on that score. I've just offered to pay back the loan."

"All of it?"

"Yes, all of it."

"But we don't have that kind of money sitting in the account."

"Not to worry about that. I know a couple of chaps who are looking to invest. One of them being Ogilvie-Parkes."

He gave her a sly look.

"You've no objection to him, I take it?"

"None, if you're really serious. But Lou told me just the other day that she and Angus were having to rein in their expenses."

"I doubt Lou has the full picture. You'd have to get hold of Angus to find out the actualité."

"And Angus told you he has money he wants to put into the gallery?"

"He's straining at the leash for it."

"Well, if that's true…"

"Leave it to me. I'll get on the phone and get it all fixed up."

"You'd better do that sooner rather than later. I have another source who informs me that man…"

She jabbed her finger towards the door through which Pilcher had exited.

"… that man has a criminal record."

"Who's the source?"

She looked away.

"I'm not at liberty to tell you that."

"Well, I know lots of people with criminal records. Perfectly respectable people, too."

The door opened, and Abisola looked around.

"Your car's arrived," she said to Cosima.

"Car? What car?" asked Tristan.

"A ministerial car," said Cosima, getting up to put on her coat. "Perry sent it round to collect me."

"What? That chappy who came here for the open night?"

"Yes, that one. We're going to find some furniture for his new flat."

"I see. Deep waters, eh?"

Cosima paused at the door.

"And keep your hands off Tabitha," she said, as she went out. "Or you'll have me to answer to."

23

The Strangers On The Heath

Wilf's eyes opened. He stared up at the bronze glow from the dimmed ceiling lights. Checked for the heavy, wasting sensations that had dogged his head and his heart for months. All gone for the third day running. There was something miraculous about it, for depression had consumed him for so long, he no longer knew what to do with his time. He would have to learn how to live again.

Mike's visit had been the catalyst. The crisis of that day had pushed him over the edge and brought him face-to-face with that despair he could neither understand nor overcome. Yet the answer had been simple. Rather like the fly trapped in a bottle Mike had told him about. Which found that escape from prison came not from trying to break through the glass wall, but from flying up through the hole at the top.

He thought about the pictures he had executed in Lucca. The ones on which Carlo had forged Filippo's signature and put up for sale with the Bayes. Which had tormented so when he found out that his own work was to be sold as if by Casiraghi himself. Yet they had been amongst his best work. Although he had borrowed the master's style, he had infused new life into it with the power that came from the carving. They were works he might have signed with his own name; the beginning of a new style.

He was over his shame and would no longer make any trouble about them. To hell with Carlo and the Bayes. Let them satisfy their greed. It was enough that he was no longer in hell but starting out on a new and more exciting odyssey.

A fully formed image flashed to his mind. A new painting. He jumped off the sofa and climbed the stairs to the helm, where he kept his fresh drawing materials. Sat down on the passenger seat and readied the pad on his knee with a charcoal in his mouth. As a salt breeze nuzzled up the boat, then floated it back down again. Up and down, more slowly as the wind died away. On the next boat, the owners were mopping up rainwater on deck. The man was wearing tight white ducks which emphasised his thigh muscles like those of a sailor; the woman had on shorts which displayed her tanned, shapely legs. They looked like they were in their forties, about his own age. Two more subjects for sketches, but he must get this one down first.

He drew a long and menacing gallery with tiers of arches tapering away towards the vanishing point. It might have been a museum, a prison, or both. A pitiless sun beat down on the surrounding piazza. Marking out a hero holding a spear with his head bowed. His mouth twisted in anguish, his eyes blank with unseen suffering. The hero's shadow stretched out to the horizon, parallel to the gallery. Minute sightseers stared up in awe.

It was the start of a series celebrating his escape. Semi-abstracts fusing the bright colours he so adored, rather than the muted tones Filippo might have used. When he got back to London, he would hire a studio and start on the rest.

He turned over a new leaf and sketched the torsos of the couple next door. After a while the woman caught on to what he was doing and, without looking at him, she bent down and displayed different parts of her anatomy to him: her thighs, her bottom, and her hanging breasts, as if daring him to draw them in cruder outline. When he had finished and was about to go back through the hatchway, she turned to him with a smile which showed her whitened teeth. Her husband came up alongside her and placed his hands on the rail. Wilf had forgotten their names.

"Are you working on something new, Mr Rising?" said the woman. "Can we see?"

"They're just sketches," said Wilf.

"Still like to look at them," she said. "Are you doing anything tonight? We're meeting up with some friends for drinks. Would be great to have you there."

She stared at him in frank invitation. Her husband didn't seem to mind, standing there in friendly bemusement, as if he, too, was interested in the pickup.

"Where are you going?" asked Wilf.

"It's just the Jellicoe for a couple of hours. Tempt you?"

Wilf thought about it. He planned to get the train back to London in the morning and he still had some packing up to do. But whether he went tomorrow, or the day after, mattered little now that he was sane again.

"Sure. I'll come."

"Cool," said the wife. "I'll come and get you later. Five o'clock suit you?"

It was not yet midday and he wanted to keep up the momentum while he had the bug. Going back downstairs, he put on a water-proof anorak and walking boots, picked up his car keys and went back up. Locked the cabin behind him and descended the ladder to the quay. Above him, parked on the hill, was his red Audi TT. He walked around and got in.

As he turned on the ignition, a text appeared on the phone he had placed on the passenger seat. It was another message from Mike.

Did you get my last text? Haven't heard from you. Are you OK?

He remembered Mike wanted to ask him something. Most likely, it had to do with his accommodation in Spital-fields. Whatever it was, it could wait.

It was a fine day; the rain had dispersed, and it was mild, with bright sunshine. The car climbed a steeper hill which led out of town. Behind him, in the mirror, he could see the Channel stretching out beyond the port. Shortly after the last houses petered out, he drove past a campsite and turned left up towards open country. One reason the area attracted him was the existence of the heath a few miles outside the town. It was a place of rock, gorse, heather, and furze on which no crops grew, but on which wild-life teemed. Salt marshes and peat bogs proliferated; a danger to unwary hikers but a bird-watcher's paradise. Wilf had walked there many times in heavy boots and a stick, always with his sketchbook.

Fifteen minutes later, he turned onto the old Roman road. Straight and narrow, with a whitish surface, it bisected the heath like a neat parting on a dark head of hair. Shortly after that, he came to his favourite view, in which the road climbed a hill, at the top of which a valley fell away and he could see all the way to Wiltshire. In the far distance the vast sky met a horizon of blue, half-remembered hills.

He got out of the car and, fetching his things from the boot, he took the footpath which led down the slope. It was steep and overgrown with brambles that tore at his jeans. It was harder going than he remembered. By degrees, the path opened out onto scrubland, leading up to a knoll, on which was an ancient oak tree, like a bent octopus with its arms flailing. He sat down with his back to the trunk. He was quite breathless. After he had recovered, he took out his mobile phone and texted Mike back.

Still finishing up here. Coming up Monday. Talk then. Love to you and Peggy.

He switched it off and sat there for a while, contemplating the view once more. The sky was clear and azure-bright; it might have been spring rather than early winter. The heather, now dark pink, waved below him in the wind. He let the mood of the place sink into him. After a time, an invisible hand drew back a veil and he saw the place for what it was: a landscape that had been there for aeons and would be for ages more. Indifferent to human beings and their tawdry fate.

He picked out some crayons from the box and drew.

Two hours or more passed. Then he heard three motorcycles coming slowly up the road behind him. Their engines died away. Shortly after that, he saw a man in a grey overcoat striding down the hill, followed by two other men. Still euphoric after his release from depression, Wilf failed to register the tremor of fear that started at the sound of the approaching bikes. The same sounds he had heard from his boat late at night after his heated arguments on the phone to Carlo, who had threatened to have him killed if he ever dared go to the police. Along with the feeling of being followed in the morning when walking to the university through the marina. Now his mind was back on his art, he treated the strangers merely as a passing nuisance, unconnected to such incidents. Instead, he wanted to capture the shape of the heather as the wind caught at it, rather like sea waves hurrying to a shore. He sketched quickly in order to catch the moment before the wind died down.

A few minutes later, the leading man emerged from the trees. He was a lithe, dark man and seemed intent on approaching him. Wilf cursed under his breath and pretended to ignore him. But the man stood there, watching him. Perhaps he was lost and wanted directions. But what directions were there to give in this wilderness?

Irritated, Wilf looked over at him and cocked his head. "Yes?"

It was the last coherent word Wilf ever spoke.

The man said nothing and raised his arm.

Too late, Wilf felt the noose slip round his neck from behind the tree and pull tight. Taking him somewhere he did not want to go. The rope, thick and coarse, chafed his neck. He put up his hands and tried to pry it loose with his fingers, his back bucking against the trunk. But the rope bit harder into his Adam's apple and he choked. The man behind the tree was pulling him up onto his feet, up the trunk, with tremendous strength. Then a second man in a track suit came around and held his ankles. Wilf put out his arms and tried to push him away, but the rope kept him pinioned against the trunk. The man in the overcoat ran up and barked directions in a language he didn't understand. Expertly, the rope swung over a branch as they hoisted him into the air, his legs dangling. They tied the end of the rope around another branch and the three men gathered below to watch him die. Wilf looked down at their upturned, smirking faces. The one in the middle was wearing plastic gloves and holding up a gun. Wilf saw that he had only seconds left to live.

From nowhere a tremendous sorrow overcame him. Sadness that he was leaving behind the beauty of life, with his work unfinished. Sadness that he would never see Claudia grow up. Sorrow for all human beings, who would soon leave life behind.

"Pity," he tried to say, "pity."

But the only sound that came out of his throat was a croak.

He kicked into the wind hopelessly. Then he kicked again. The third time, he lost consciousness. His last thoughts were of his mother. How upset she would be when she learnt he was never coming home again.

Then the man shot him in the head.

24

Bonfire Street

Gredic and Halliday walked up Moorgate at three o'clock to Pilcher's office on Bonfire Street. It amused Gredic to think that Pilcher was only a stone's throw from the police station. That was convenient. For himself, of course, not Ronald. One thing Gredic enjoyed about his job was baiting villains. Toying with them, pressing them, winding them up. Until they broke down, as they always did. Either taking a run for it or coughing up the truth. Occasionally, some of them would have a go at him, but he was always ready for that. Few of them knew he had been a welter-weight boxing champion twenty years ago. When they found that out, it was usually too late.

They stopped at the lane that led into a warren of commercial office blocks.

"You ready, Gillie?"

"I think so, Sergeant."

"Why d'you always call me that?"

Halliday tucked her hair over her ear with a finger.

"It's more respectful, isn't it? Using someone's title."

"You don't have to be formal."

"I'll try to remember that."

Gredic looked up the lane in exasperation.

"We won't get anything out of him today," he said.

"I know. You want to squeeze him."

"That's right. It's what he tries to do after we've left that's going to be interesting."

"I leave the squeezing to you, right?"

"Yes, but what I want you to do is listen hard and see if you can catch him out. You got the bank statements?"

"In here," she said, patting her shoulder bag.

"Good girl."

"Watch out, sir. You'll be back on a course; you keep saying things like that."

Halliday's frank eyes met his. Gredic laughed and put his arms back into his coat pockets.

"Let's go."

Pilcher's office was on the third floor of a dull block of brown brick. Grey plastic panels with random holes like a binary print-out drilled into the outside wall, framing the smoked-glass windows. They went up some shallow steps into a reception area with beige walls, beige carpets and a counter made of pickled oak, behind which stood a man in a beige uniform with an identity tag.

The guard accosted them as they headed for the lift:

"Is Mr Pilcher expecting you?"

"He's always expecting us," said Gredic. "We're old friends."

They flashed their warrant cards and, without waiting for the man to phone upstairs, Halliday strode over to press the lift button.

The lift doors opened to a narrow corridor with three offices. The one on the left, at the far end, had a plaque next to its twin entrance doors:

Ronald I. Pilcher.

Chartered Accountant.
Investment Broker.

Inside, on the left, was a waiting area, with heavy armchairs in deep blue leather, old copies of the *Financial Times*, *Investment Observer*, and *Money Trove* on glass tables. A vending machine stood by the window. Opposite that were three rooms with glass walls screened by venetian blinds. In the first, a woman in a white shirt and triangular, retro spectacles was watching them. Ignoring her, Gredic sauntered up to the room at the end and went in.

Pilcher was sitting back in his swivel chair, tapping the desk with his fingers, his mind empty of thought. As Gredic came through the door, his eyes widened in alarm, then narrowed to a foxy look.

"Detective Sergeant Gredic. An unexpected pleasure, to be sure."

Pilcher paused for effect.

"It *is* still Detective Sergeant, I take it?"

"That's right, Ronny, still on the streets, doing what I do best. Locking up low-lifes."

"I wonder if you would care to close the door?" said Pilcher, looking at Halliday. Ignoring him, she sat down next to Gredic. With a sigh, Pilcher got up and shut it.

"What can I do for you two officers?" he said, resuming his seat.

"We're here to ask you some questions. Relating to your involvement with Bayes & Bayes," said Gredic.

Halliday took out a notebook and wrote.

"Is this a formal enquiry?" asked Pilcher. "You know, the kind that comes with an appointment to see me and some sort of forewarning?"

"You can come down the station if you like," said Gredic.

"I might do that if you get too cheeky. With my lawyer."

"Let's start with an obvious question. Why aren't you surprised that we're asking you about Bayes & Bayes?"

"I am surprised."

"No, you're not. You just asked us whether this is a formal enquiry. You didn't ask us why we want to ask you questions."

"Asking police officers why they want to ask people questions would be like asking a bear why he wants to have a shit in the woods."

Halliday placed some statements on the desk. Pointed to some entries she had highlighted with a pink marker pen.

"Do you recognise any of these transactions?"

Pilcher picked up the document as if it were a piece of toilet paper. Putting on his reading spectacles, he read it slowly, repeating the details under his breath, before handing it back.

"One is a loan to Bayes & Bayes, authorised by me. The other item relates to an art purchase. Nothing unusual about that."

"Three days before the forward transfers from your company account, equivalent amounts were wire transferred from an account in the Cayman Islands," she said. "Who controls that account?"

"I do."

"What is your reason for holding an account there?"

"Tax efficiency. Nothing more."

"Do you have bank statements for that account?"

"We operate a green environmental policy here. All our statements are paperless."

Pilcher smiled at them both as he leaned back. The swivel chair squeaked.

"Your investors. How well do you know them?" asked Gredic.

"Not all of them that well. Many of them come to me by word of mouth. They want a safe pair of hands. I'm noted for it."

"Do you have reason to believe that any of these... investors gained their funds through criminal activity? Be careful what you say now, Ronny."

"You'll have to ask them that."

"I would, if I knew who they were," said Gredic. "Now I'm asking you."

"Of course not, Sergeant. Who do you take me for?"

"A man who's done time for his part in a fraud, that's what I'm taking you for."

"We all make mistakes, Sergeant. That was over nine years ago."

Pilcher wriggled in his chair, as if trying to escape.

"Are the police going to come and see me every time someone commits a crime in this part of the world?" said Pilcher. "That would be a gross invasion of my rights."

"Spare us the theatricals, Ronny. A little bird told us you are associating with some very dodgy people who play with guns and drugs."

Gredic paused while Halliday sat back in her chair with her arms folded. Both waited for Pilcher to get over his agitation. Snorting through his nose and looking around the room, as if appealing to a fair-minded audience.

"I think this conversation is getting close to where I will need my lawyer sitting in here. That sounds like an accusation to me."

"Have it your way, Ronny. We've got something else we want to ask you about."

"Would you mind not calling me 'Ronny'? It's 'Mr Pilcher' to you."

"What's the nature of your relationship with Bayes & Bayes, Mr Pilcher?" asked Halliday.

"Purely investment. A consortium I represent comprises some gentlemen of high personal wealth, with an interest in acquiring art works, antiques. Top end stuff. You know the sort of thing."

Pilcher arched his fingers together as he got into his stride.

"They look to me to manage those acquisitions on their behalf. To that end, we have taken a stake in the art gallery you mention. Interest-bearing loans that we occasionally convert into art purchases."

"You are the registered owner of a painting called *Approaching Storm*, are you not?" asked Gredic.

"I am the registered owner, as you say. But the real owners are my investors."

"Where is that painting now?"

"Here, in this office, locked away in that safe room," replied Pilcher, pointing towards a steel door beside the vending machine.

"Can we see it?" asked Gredic.

"Why do you want to see it?"

"Because we received an allegation that it is one of six forgeries sold through the gallery."

"Who is making these allegations?"

"An American buyer, name of Ralph Schoenman."

Pilcher lifted his head up to the ceiling, as if hoping for inspiration.

"Doesn't ring a bell. No, I can definitely say I don't know anyone with that name."

"You sure about that, Ronny?" said Gredic, "I'd hate to think you were lying to me."

"I can categorically tell you I've never met him."

"What about that picture?" asked Gredic.

"We'd like to take a photograph," added Halliday, "for our enquiries."

Pilcher looked from Gredic to Halliday and back again, tapping his fingers on the desk.

"All right, to help you with your enquiries, I can do that. And I'd like that cooperation placed on record."

Pilcher got up and went next door. After a few minutes he came out again, followed by the woman with the retro glasses. Wearing webbed tights around her plump legs. She skipped along daintily, behind the loping stride of Pilcher. At the door of the safe, she placed a key in the lock. Pilcher pressed four buttons on the panel on the wall and the door opened inwards with a groan. The PA went in and, a few moments later, emerged with a picture frame which she placed on a chair. Holding out her arms, she invited Gredic and Halliday to contemplate it.

It was a canvas, three feet by two, that depicted looming blue-grey strips moving up from the right, against a restless backdrop of light grey sea and spray. To the left two shot ducks, sketched roughly in red and black, were falling out of the sky. Beneath those, a shadowy figure was holding out her arms to receive them.

Halliday turned off the ceiling lights. Then she took pictures on her mobile.

"Looks nice," said Gredic, "but what does it mean?"

"Search me," said Pilcher.

"It's an example of Expressionism, sir," said Halliday. "Where the artist tries to depict a mood on the canvas. I'd say this was quite a depressed mood, wouldn't you say?"

She looked at Pilcher for confirmation, who gave her a bewildered stare.

"Do you know the painter?" Gredic asked Halliday.

"Fillipo Casiraghi? I saw a retrospective at the Royal Academy, a few years back. Tickets sold out."

Gredic turned back to Pilcher.

"So why did you buy this picture, Ronny?"

"I bought it on the advice of people who know about these things. I may not know much about art, but I know a good deal when I see one."

"Which people would they be?" asked Gredic. "The Bayes?"

"No, Carlo Casiraghi, as it happens. I do business with him from time to time."

Gredic looked across at Halliday, who signed with her eyes she had registered it.

"Aren't you worried this picture might be a forgery?" asked Gredic.

"How can it be a forgery? I've seen the providence."

"That doesn't necessarily mean Casiraghi painted it."

"Well, who else would have wanted to paint a picture like that?"

"Mr Schoenman doesn't think he did. That's why he's asked us to look into it."

"There's no pleasing some people."

Later, when they got back to the station, Gredic called Halliday and Painter to the briefing room. Gredic took a black marker pen and stood beside the whiteboard.

"Let's look at what we've got so far."

He drew a circle on the board with RP inside it

"Ronnie Pilcher. Next to him we've got the Bayes Gallery."

Another circle for BG went up.

"The owners are a pair of toffs," said Gredic, "Tristan and Cosima Bayes. The woman is not known to us. The brother has a conviction for possession of a Class A drug. Nothing else on his record."

"Up here on the left we've got a man called Carlo Casiraghi, the nephew of a famous painter. Who sold some pictures through the gallery that may be forgeries."

Another circle for CC went up.

"What else do we know about him, Jack?"

"Seems he builds hotels. According to the Giudizaria in Genoa, he has links with the Camorra. Seems he's using their money to build them."

"Behind Pilcher, we've got a mob operating from Belgrade. Called the Pumas. We think Pilcher is laundering money for them."

"Pilcher let it slip that he does business with Carlo Casiraghi," said Halliday.

"Meaning we've got a potential link between one mob in Naples and another one in Belgrade."

Drawing two circles for both, Gredic drew arrows, pointing to Pilcher and Casiraghi.

"Here's where it gets complicated," said Gredic, drawing another circle for WR to the right. "This man, Wilf Rising, has been found dead. According to Ralph Schoenman, he is the maker of the six pictures reported to be forgeries. Dorset Police are treating it as a suicide. But let's assume for the moment that someone wanted him dead."

"Carlo Casiraghi?" asked Halliday.

"He's been in Genoa for the last few months," said Painter. "We can rule him out."

"Then who might have killed him?" asked Halliday.

"Could it have been Pilcher?" said Painter

"Ronny Pilcher might be a lot of things, but he's not a killer," replied Gredic.

"What would have been the motive?" asked Halliday.

"Good question. Any ideas?"

"To keep him quiet?" said Painter.

"Yes, that fits. But who would want to get at him?"

"It might be Carlo Casiraghi. Otherwise, it has to be the owner of one of the forgeries," said Halliday.

"Why?"

"Because if it got out that it was a forgery, the painting would be worthless."

"That ticks a lot of boxes."

"I've thought of something else," said Halliday. "If we prove the gallery is a money laundry, then all its assets would be seized. Including the loans that Pilcher put there."

"It must be these people," said Gredic, pointing to the Puma circle. "They're protecting their money."

"A contract killer?" asked Painter.

"Could be. That, or one of their own."

"If it's one of their own, then Pilcher would know who he is. Either that, or he knows the person who sent him here," said Halliday.

"I've got some names from the Pumas off Interpol," said Painter, "but none of them match the border records for arrivals into the country."

"How far back did you go?" asked Gredic.

"Six weeks."

"Try going back three months. They might have been scouting around for longer than we think."

"Can do."

"Any other suggestions?" asked Gredic.

"Maybe we should contact the CID in Belgrade and find out what they know," said Painter.

"No point in doing that," answered Gredic. "The Serbian Mafia are tolerated, so long as they export crime over the border. They won't tell us anything."

"I'll phone the National Crime Agency, then. See if they've got anything else they can tell us."

"Good going, Jack. Gillie, I want you to get a court order freezing Pilcher's bank accounts, as well as that Gallery's."

Gredic put his jacket on.

"Where're you going Skipper?" asked Painter.

"I'm interviewing another witness. A man named Michael Gereon."

25

At The Morgue

It was almost midnight as Michael followed the mortuary attendant down the long corridor. Alongside him was the police officer who had collected him from the station and brought him to the County Hospital.

It was the day after a woman on the heath had found Wilf's body by accident, having got lost while out walking her dog. The call had come through to Aunt Sophie, who had gone into shock. A neighbour called Peggy, who had gone with her mother to the hospital, leaving him to call back the Dorset Police. They wanted a family member to come down to identify the body. Said it couldn't wait and would he catch the last train to Bournemouth, where a police car would collect him? Travel fares reimbursed, courtesy of the Coroner's Office.

The attendant's plastic clogs slapped on the vinyl floor in an irregular rhythm. The man seemed to have something wrong with his gait, for it was the right foot that slapped, while the left shuffled along with a muted sound. They turned left into another corridor, longer than the first. Handrails along the lime-green walls, darkened consulting rooms behind locked doors, strip ceiling lights receding into infinity the further they walked.

At length, the man stopped outside two swing doors and pushed one open. Sheet plastic barred the entrance, and they sidled their way through into a small waiting room, with chairs and a low table with copies of *Mortician's Review*. A smell of wood preservative came from the further room.

"Have you done this before, sir?" asked the constable.

Thinking back to his mother's death, he had been first on the scene, but she was then still alive. As her only living relative, the police had been a long time questioning him about who she was and what she did. Asked him to find her passport and show them her bank statements and welfare claims. But he hadn't been there when she died later in the hospital ward. Aside from that, the only death he had ever witnessed had been Peggy's red setter when the vet put it to sleep. It was curious how the dog had flapped his tail before the needle went in, as if it expected a welcome release. Death had crept up slowly, like a quiet passage to nowhere in particular.

"No."

"You're going into the mortuary in a moment. The temperature may not be what you're used to, as we keep it at minus two. The body of the man we think is your brother-in-law is lying on a bed trolley with his face uncovered. His right arm is exposed in case you want to hold his hand. The attendant will stand at the back of the room so you can pay your respects. Take all the time you want."

The man waited for him to accept the information given.

"Do you know of any identifying marks on the body? Tattoos, scars, birthmarks?"

Michael thought of all the times he had seen Wilf

stripped in the school changing room and later on the beaches around Lucca. Naked in a hotel room they had once shared in Paris. Nothing came to mind. Then he remembered a thing Wilf had showed him after a fight he'd had with Cosima, who had stabbed him in a rage with a pair of scissors after she caught him screwing someone upstairs. They had stitched up the wound in A & E.

"He had a circular scar just here," he said, pointing to his upper arm.

The officer signalled to the attendant, who went inside to look.

"One more thing," said the man. "If it is your brother-in-law, he may not look as you remember him."

"How not?"

"We found him hanging from a tree."

It was the first he had been told about the scene of death. At once an image came of Wilf swinging from a branch, unnaturally still, his toes pointing to the ground. The cricket's voice clicked on with a loud whine. He looked away.

"Are you all right, sir?"

For the first time, he noticed how young the constable was. His skin was fresh and smooth like a boy's. He wondered how many corpses he had seen, how many people he had escorted to scenes such as this. Incongruous that a youth like this was a ferryman to the dead.

"I'm ready," said Michael.

They went inside. It looked like a cross between the lost-luggage department at a railway station and a funeral parlour, with wheel-in chambers lining the wall in front. The sickly, acid smell of fluid was stronger here. Behind him stood the officer. The attendant was standing before a barred window on the far side. Staring at the scene in front of him with his arms crossed, a grim smile on his face. A body covered by a newly pressed sheet awaited him under a harsh light. It occurred to him that the whole thing was like a dream in its combination of strangeness and startling detail.

It was Wilf all right. His face was puffy and yellowish, yet there was no mistaking that boyish quiff, or the large eye sockets that sometimes gave him the look of an angry owl in life. The sheet came up to just below the Adam's apple. Snaking red tentacles on his throat, partly cut open by the rope, but stitched up again. The right arm was resting on the sheet, exposed to the shoulder. Michael noted the stitch scar on the right arm and looked back at the officer. Turning back to the body, he noticed the round, blackish hole in Wilf's right temple, about the size of a 20p coin.

He had been told that the dead looked as if they were asleep, but it was not so. Rather, the body looked arrested in shock, the living man having abruptly departed. They hadn't been able to close Wilf's mouth, which might have been interrupted in mid-sentence. But at least his eyes were closed.

"Is that Wilfred John Rising?" said the voice behind him.

"It is."

He picked up Wilf's hand, as he had that morning he found him on the boat. It was cold and stiff, like a statue's; there would be no return to life this time. He recalled Wilf scolding him over drinks at *The White Devil*. That it was insane to think of life as a series of chaotic events, disguised by everyday routine and punctuated by random violence. Yet wasn't that what his death amounted to? And wasn't his corpse an ironic afterthought?

Somewhere out there, his killer was roaming free. Perhaps dreaming in a warm bed, safe from the cold outside. Or downing drinks in a bar, thinking with satisfaction about a life removed. Or on a jet plane, heading back to unknown, criminal shores. He realised, obscurely, that the man, whoever he was, had some connection with the phone calls Schoenman had complained about. But he felt too tired and overwhelmed to think about that now. What difference would it make if they caught Wilf's murderer? It wouldn't ever bring him back. The pictures Wilf might have painted would remain in the vast lumber room of potentially existent things, like emerging galaxies snuffed out by black holes.

The attendant to his right, and the officer behind, came up and stood beside him.

"You alright?"

The attendant took his elbow and shook it.

Abruptly, the thought chain vanished and he was back in the room once more. He looked down. Wilf's eyes were like the empty, white marble sockets on an antique bust. Michael let go of his frozen hand.

"I'd like to leave now," he said to no one in particular.

They walked him back to the car, which was waiting in the dark by the entrance with its lights on. The driver put away a garage sandwich when they opened the passenger doors. Leaving a smear of mayonnaise on his chin.

The car glided to the police station through half-deserted streets. His head reeled from the experience back there, something not helped by the droning engine and the dazzling headlamps of cars coming towards them. Had he been able to think of a suitable excuse, he might've stopped the car and walked. For he saw the world was closing in on him again.

A few minutes later, the car slid to a halt outside the station. Inside was the usual late-night crowd. Drunks, derelicts, and yobs waiting to be logged in by the burly sergeant behind the desk and led off to the cells. A woman with a black eye was weeping on a bench in the corner, while her friend consoled her.

"He's not worth it, Bev. You can do better than him. You'll see."

"Keep that noise down," said the sergeant. "I can't hear myself think."

The woman put a handkerchief over her mouth and sobbed into that, while her friend put an arm round her shoulder.

"There, there," she said, ignoring the sergeant. "Better times will come. You wait and see."

Michael followed his escort to a steel door beside the desk, which opened slowly from the inside. Off to the left was a warren of interview rooms and they showed him into one. Blue-grey walls and black PVC chairs stationed on either side of a bare wooden table. On the table a telephone. He sat on one chair. Up on the wall was a notice:

Warning. CCTV in operation. You are being watched.

He was grateful for the silence and in no hurry to be seen. The turmoil in his head subsided as shock descended. Giving him that familiar, spaced out feeling, like the world was very far away.

Fifteen minutes later, two more officers came in, a man and a woman. The man looked like someone had just woken him up. He had watery eyes and an air of carrying out a tedious chore. The woman was younger and more enthusiastic.

"Did your brother-in-law have another address, beside the boat?" asked the man.

"That would be his mother's address. Ninety-Eight, Kennington Park Road, London."

"Do you have access to that address?"

"His mother is in hospital with a stroke."

"We still have to look," said the man in irritation.

"As you wish."

The woman smiled and held up her palms, as if to say it couldn't be helped.

"When did you last see Mr Rising?"

"Twelve days ago."

"How did he seem to you?"

Michael didn't much want to share information about that day at the hospital. Somehow, it felt intrusive. But Wilf was dead and now the machinery of the state was taking charge of his relics. What choice did he have but to furnish information for its banal record? He told them about the events of that morning, keeping it neutral.

"Do you think he took an overdose, intending to kill himself?" asked the man.

"He told me he was confused about the correct dose."

"Did you believe him?"

"I didn't see any reason not to."

"What was his state of mind after you came back from the hospital?"

"Still confused, I would say."

"Was he depressed?"

"Yes, that as well."

"What did he tell you?"

"That he was handing in his notice and coming back to London to stay with my wife and I."

The man seemed disappointed with that answer but wrote it down.

"Did he say anything to you that indicated he might try to kill himself?"

He thought about Wilf's comment that he would have been better off left dead on the floor of the boat. But that was irrelevant now.

"Is that what you think happened? That he killed himself?"

The two of them looked at each other.

"The cause of death hasn't yet been determined ahead of the autopsy," said the man. "But we can't rule out suicide at this stage. There was a gun lying on the grass underneath his feet."

Michael pulled out his phone and showed them the text from Wilf.

"He sent this to me the afternoon he died. Why would he say he was still coming to see me if he was thinking of killing himself?"

They both peered at the screen.

"The Coroner will want to see that message," said the woman. "We'll take a copy for our records. Is that all right with you, sir?"

"Your brother-in-law might have sent that message for all sorts of reasons," said the man. "Doesn't prove he wasn't suicidal."

"Wilf didn't kill himself."

The two of them looked at him with suspicion.

"You seem very sure about that, Michael," said the man. "Care to elaborate?"

"The last morning I saw him, he wanted to come back to London with me. He only stayed on because he thought he should work out his notice."

"Maybe he changed his mind?"

"The text I showed you suggests otherwise."

"We have a copy of your brother-in-law's hospital discharge, here."

The man passed it over. In one box someone had written:

SSRI overdose. Suspected suicide attempt.

"That's speculation," said Michael.

"Isn't that what you're offering? Speculation?"

"No. It's…"

Michael halted, for this had gone far enough. It was no use arguing any more with these two. Let them take care of their own pre-programmed ideas.

"Anything *helpful* you can tell us?" insisted the man.

Michael wondered whether to tell them about his discovery over Wilf's pictures. He thought not. The superficial reason was that it was now one-thirty in the morning and he was too tired to talk any more. The real reason was deeper, but he could not identify it just now. He would have to talk to Peggy about it. It had something to do with Wilf's anguish the last day he had seen him alive.

"No, I don't think there is anything else that's relevant."

The man gestured to the woman to carry on. She held up a folded leaflet.

"This is an information pack produced by Public Health England. It's called *A Helping Hand*. It tells you all you need to know about coping with the bereavement process. On the back is a telephone number. Should you, or anyone in your family, wish to visit a counsellor."

He took the leaflet and placed it on the desk, out of sight.

"I have some questions to ask you," said Michael.

"We will try to answer them if we can, sir," said the woman.

"What happens next?"

"Your statement will go to the Coroner's office, ready for the inquest," said the man.

"When will that be?"

"We will notify the next of kin when we have an opening date."

"What about Wilf's body? When can we recover it?"

"There will have to be a post-mortem first."

"Is that necessary? You seem to have decided it was a suicide."

The man shrugged.

"We still have to follow procedure. Once the Coroner has established the cause of death, he can issue the interim death certificate. Then he will release the body to the family. It might take a while."

The man smiled for the first time. As if it amused him to think of the futility of waiting for the dead to return.

26

How The Dead Live

Michael watched the train roll slowly into the station from his bench on the platform. The information was all there: *Destination: London* posted at the front of the train. Up behind him on the departure board: *Waterloo: Calling at Southampton Central, Basingstoke, Clapham Junction.* After a beep, the doors opened and passengers alighted. It was time for him to stand up and get on. His hand reached out to his shoulder bag as if in preparation.

Yet nothing happened.

His mind ticked over the things to do next. Stand up. Walk to the door. Up the carriage steps. Find a seat on that train.

As it had for the five prior trains he might have caught that morning. Inside his head he yearned to get on one of them, but he stayed in his seat. Where before, he had suspected that there was something flimsy about human motivations, as if they did not really belong to the person, now he had proof. Sometime during the night, a neural circuit in his brain had quietly switched off, freeing him of the illusion that his actions were his own.

An elderly guard strolled by and stopped. Gave him a quizzical look, pointing to the open door of the train. Michael smiled sadly as the man shut the door and waved his arm up to the driver. Then he watched as the train worked up traction and moved off into the distance.

He looked up at the departure board. The next one was in forty minutes. Would he be able to get on it? But the feeling that came with the thought: that this was a purely hypothetical question, of passing interest to no one, told him all he wanted to know.

The same thing happened with the next train and the one after that. It was now past eleven and he had been awake on the platform for over four hours.

A vague, unconnected feeling of panic came up. Would it make any difference? Yet as soon as the self-question came up the panic fizzled out, and he returned to his torpor.

He couldn't have said for sure when this interesting malaise had settled on him. When he left the police station it had been three am. Wanting not to go to a hotel for four hours, he had insisted on being driven to the train station instead. There to wait for the early train back. Feeling drowsy, he nodded off in the waiting room. It was seven-thirty when he awoke to find a train waiting for him: solid, peaceful, inviting. He had watched it for some time with a feeling of wonder that a train was standing there waiting just for him. It seemed like a travesty to get on it. Motionless, he watched it slide away. Along with the thought that there was a place he had to get to. A place with the abstract label of 'home'.

His phone buzzed. A text appeared.

Where are you?

It was from Peggy, who might have expected him to have come through the front door by now. The picture in his head, of her staring at the kitchen clock in surprise, amused him.

The display on the departure board flipped. The next train to Waterloo would be in fifteen minutes. He wondered what would happen when it came in.

The phone buzzed again. This time, it was a call. He stared at the screen and noticed, as if it had occurred to him for the first time, that all that was required to answer a call was to press the green logo. He pressed it and waited to see what would happen next. A voice emanated from the speaker. He held the phone to his ear.

"Hello?" he said.

"Where are you?" said Peggy.

"At the station."

"Which one?"

"Bournemouth."

"Is there something wrong? You've been there since how long?"

"Three am."

"Are the trains running?"

"Yes. There have been a few."

"Why aren't you on one?"

"It's the strangest thing…"

He did his best to explain the absence of desire to do anything about his thoughts. But it ended up sounding like a philosophy lecture. He tried a metaphor.

"… like an electric car with a flat battery. Nothing happens when I press the starter button."

He heard her gasp. Then the line went quiet.

"Hello?" he asked, with the same remote curiosity with which he watched the trains go by.

"Michael. Is there a guard standing near you?"

He looked up. A few yards away was a younger man, who was watching the railway track back yonder.

He gestured to the man to come over, for something in Peggy's voice imparted urgency. He flapped his fingers harder. The guard caught sight of him and came up. Without a word, Michael handed him the phone.

The man listened hard. Now and then directing looks at Michael, as if verifying something he was being told. At length, he closed the call and came over. Beckoned to Michael to stand up, then picking up his bag, he walked him up the platform. They stood side by side behind a yellow line. The man smiled at him.

"Here. The train is a coming now," he said, pointing up the track to the next train rolling in. "When it gets to Waterloo, your wife will be waiting to collect you. She says you are not well, sir."

Michael wondered if he should thank him. But the man looked pleased now he had taken charge. What was the sense in thanking people for doing something that made them happy?

The train rolled to a stop and a few passengers got off while the guard held his arm. Then he helped him up the steps through the door and stood back.

Michael turned around and stared back out of the open window. The guard looked up.

"Go inside," he said, shooing him on. "Your seat awaits you."

Michael smiled back and looked along the platform. It was curious how many travellers were waiting to get on. What were they waiting for and where were they going? Then the guard hopped up and, taking him by the arm, propelled him through the carriage. Not resting until he found him an empty seat. He took the shoulder bag from him and placed it on a rack. Sat him down in the seat below. Michael had the feeling that if the train had been equipped with seat belts, he would have pinned him down.

At any rate, the guard seemed cross that Michael wasn't able to do anything for himself. He thought of trying to describe his loss of volition but thought better of it. He had the feeling the guard would not welcome explanations that unknown puppet-masters pressed 'stop', 'pause', and 'go' on people's actions.

A whistle blew and the guard made haste to get off the train. Stood on the platform watching Michael as the train pulled out. A look of intense disgust on his face as he raised his arm in farewell. Michael watched out of the window as the guard, and the station, disappeared back into the past.

By now his mind was spooling through the experience, like a computer processing thousands of bits per second, whether or not the program was still of any use. What did it amount to? On cue, the answer appeared: that where, before, he had thought that human beings were mari-onettes, he had no direct experience of it. Now he was having it. And although it was inconvenient, it was also pleasant. He was a ghost come back from the dead, watching the living go through the motions, without the power, or even the wish, to interfere. Entirely free from care.

Two hours later, although it felt like two minutes, the train entered Waterloo and rolled to a halt on the platform. He stared out of the window at the passengers hurrying up the concourse to catch taxis, buses, and trains. It was wonderful how tenacious people looked when they had somewhere to go and something to do. On the whole, he decided, it suited human beings to have a purpose. It gave them the illusion of control.

A tall, dark youth came up and placed his forehead between his palms and stared through the window, scan-ning the carriage. He looked like he might be worried about something. Michael turned his head to meet his gaze. It was Isa.

After what seemed an age, Isa came up the gangway towards him, followed closely by his wife.

Peggy had on a peculiar red beret which contrasted with her luscious black hair. How beautiful she looked; he had always thought so.

Isa bent down before him and looked into his eyes, concern on his face. Behind him, Peggy stared at him with her hand on her mouth. Then Isa lifted him up by his arms and led him away.

27

The Seated God

The first thing Michael saw when he awoke was the familiar wallpaper with its climbing cherry trees reminiscent of a Taoist garden. Early December light filtered through the shutters on the windows. A smell of fresh, white bed sheets. The warmth of soft pillows. The house filled with heavenly peace.

From below, he could hear the faint sounds of people going about their business. Peggy, or perhaps Isa.

He had a partial memory of their bringing him home from Waterloo station in the old Volvo and putting him to bed. He'd overheard Peggy telling Isa they ought to call a doctor. Isa saying it was too soon to involve people like that and they should let him sleep it off. After that, Isa went to fetch something. Coming back into the room, he sat on the bed and took Michael's hand. Opening it, he put there an old coin. It felt curiously warm.

Isa closed Michael's hand over the coin.

"Hold it and feel the heat that comes from the coin. Count to ten slowly. Before you finish, the coin will drop from your hand…"

He remembered counting, wondering idly how it would happen as Isa said. On the count of eight, he felt the coin quiver. Automatically, his hand opened, and it dropped on the bed. Isa put his hand on his forehead and chanted something in an unknown language. It sounded like an ancient prayer, delivered in a sing-song lilt. Before long, he was asleep.

He looked down and there it was on the bed. He picked it up; it was still warm. An ancient silver coin with a flowering shrub and coiled serpent on one side; a seated god holding a staff on the other. Aesculapius, perhaps. It might have been two and a half thousand years old.

While he was examining it, Isa came into the room and opened the shutters.

"You ok?" he said.

"Where did you get this coin?"

"My father gave it to me."

"How did he come by it?"

"I will tell you the story, but first tell me how you are."

He felt more alive than he had for years. A current flowed through his body with raw power. Natural light lit up the room; far more than the weak sun lying low in the mist outside might justify. Every object in the room rested there as if unveiled by an unknown maker, shining forth in splendour.

"You've been asleep a long time," said Isa, still looking at him.

"I've never felt better."

"That is as it should be."

Michael sat up, gesturing for Isa to sit beside him.

"Tell me the story."

"When I was fifteen my father took me on a walk through the mountains that overlook the Red Sea. Up there are Coptic monasteries. We went to one of those."

"Describe it."

"It took two days to climb to it. When we got there, we found a chapel and a lot of cells where the monks live. Many of these buildings are crumbling away. My father offered to repair two of them if they let us stay. We were there for two months. It is called Gebre Selam."

"What was it like?"

"Peaceful. People go there to meditate. Also to visit Abune Filippas. It was he who gave my father this coin when we departed. He had the gift of healing."

"Had?"

"The soldiers took him away when they closed the monastery, and he died in the prison. He was eighty years old, and the ordeal was too much for him."

"Is that the place where you found your faith?"

"No. That came from my father. But when you go to places like that, you see the power of the spirit. I once saw the Abune restore a man's sight."

Michael wanted to ask him more but, just then, Peggy appeared at the door. Isa got up to make way for her and she sat on the bed. Took his hand in hers and held it tight. Turned back to Isa to signal that she wanted to talk.

"You two want breakfast?" Isa asked.

"I'm starving," said Michael.

"Make me a little, Isa," said Peggy.

Isa made to go out of the door, then turned back.

"I had a letter this morning. From that charity. They've found me a job in Warrington."

"Doing what?" asked Peggy.

"Building trade."

"Are you taking it?" asked Michael.

Isa's eyes widened.

"I don't think so. Who's going to look after you two when I'm gone?"

After he disappeared, Peggy turned to Michael.

"Isa's right, you know. He's becoming indispensable. He dug up the garden the day before yesterday."

"If he's doing all that work, we should pay him some more money."

"He says he doesn't want anything more. He likes it here."

"Still, he should get a trade. He has to think about his future."

"I agree. But let's not talk about that now."

He sat up and swung his legs over to sit beside her.

"What happened to you?" she asked.

He wondered how much he could tell her. He didn't want her to think he was having another 'moment'. For this was something else; something that he hadn't experienced since he was sixteen years old: the feeling of being fully alive and connected to the world around.

"I went into this weird trance state after I saw Wilf in the mortuary. Maybe it was the shock, followed by state of suspended animation. But Isa did something to me with that coin and that state has gone."

"You seem different," she said.

"I feel like my brain's been reset. The state I am in now feels a little overwhelming."

He caught sight of the porcelain vase on the bed-side table. A white vase, with dragon tracery in blue. It stood forth as if made especially for him by a spectral artisan a thousand years before, toiling over it on a Chinese kiln. He couldn't take his eyes away from it.

Peggy touched his hand to get his attention.

"Sorry. Everything in this room seems so beautiful just now," said Michael.

"What did Wilf look like?"

"He looked at peace," he lied. "As he never did in life."

"You know, I've been going through the wringer the last few days," she said. "When I first heard about it, I resented it. Why does it always have to be about Wilf, I thought."

He took her hand again.

"I can understand that. While Wilf and James were jetting all over the place, you were the one who looked after your father, now your mother."

He might have added himself to the list, he thought. Hadn't he, too, added to her burdens?

"I didn't mind that so much. It was the unfairness I minded. Then I got angry with myself for having bad thoughts about him…"

She dabbed at her face with a tissue she picked up from the bedspread.

"Now I discover he's left half his money to me."

"How did you find that out?"

"It's in the will he left in that old bureau in the front room. I expect he only did that because he wanted to be sure James or Cosima wouldn't get any of it," she said. "He put the rest in trust for Claudia."

"He loved you, Peggy. That wasn't the only reason."

"You really think that?"

"Wilf wasn't a man who could talk about his emotions. He put them all into his art. But he cared about you deeply."

"Why couldn't he tell me that?"

"Maybe he thought there'd be plenty of time left to tell you before death came around. But he told me often enough."

"How do you feel about it?"

"About what?"

"His death."

"Sorrow. But anger too, I think."

"You? Angry?"

"Don't look surprised. He was my best friend."

"I know that. But I've never known you to be outright angry about anything."

It wasn't exactly anger that he felt. Rather, it was a disturbance. A feeling that something unnatural had happened, which left a stain behind. Something it was his duty to make clean. Something to do with Wilf's shame over the paintings he had executed, and the way he had been compromised in a forgery.

"Why did he kill himself? Do you know?"

"It was murder, darling. It wasn't suicide."

"How do you know that?"

"It was a feeling I had when I saw him on the boat the last night I saw him. Like he was afraid something might happen to him. It's got something to do with those pictures Wilf created in Lucca."

"Who would want to kill him?"

"I don't know. But I'm going to find out."

28

The Entrepreneurs

Close by Spital Square was a garden; all that was left of the fields that once surrounded the Spital, the leper hospital founded outside the old London wall in the 12th century. Enclosed by the backs of houses on one side, the market on the other, it is a quiet place. It was cold and deserted as Michael read the morning newspapers on a bench. Two days had passed and the shining wonder that gripped him had faded to a peaceful glow. Yet still enough for him to feel a deep connection with the enclave: the sycamore, beech and willow trees hanging over the winding path around the little park; the lowering mist; the silence which resisted the ceaseless roar of the traffic in the background.

Earlier, he had gone out for breakfast in the market but, instead of going back home, he stayed out and bought the papers. Not wanting to take them to the house, for seeing them would upset Peggy. Ordering a take-away coffee from the restaurant next to the garden, he retreated into it and read what they had to say about Wilf.

One thing that angered Peggy was the way the police

leaked information to the press, despite her request for privacy. Now the tabloids carried headlines like '*Massive Police Hunt Ends in Gruesome Discovery*' and '*Artist Found Dead In The Woods*'. Most reported Wilf's admission to hospital the week before, his 'struggle with depression' and, what was more insulting, the 'failure' of his career. Somehow, also, rumours about the forgery had circulated and the house phone had rung for hours with reporters demanding information. Two of them had got hold of Peggy's mobile number and pestered her on that. To all of them, she replied 'No comment' and switched off.

Most of the articles contained little he did not already know. Two of them referred to an interview with the couple on the boat next to Wilf's. Relating that on the day he disappeared they had seen him on his boat drawing and he seemed in good spirits. Had smiled and waved at them, before driving off to his death. They hadn't known him well, they said, for he kept himself to himself, but that night they had been looking forward to getting to know him better at an informal drinks party.

He turned to the obituaries.

The one in *The Guardian* was sniffy. An artist who worked in a modernist style which became 'somewhat dated', owing much of his inspiration to Filippo Casiraghi. But 'struggled' to create an original style of his own. *The Daily Telegraph's* was the longest but went into gossipy detail about his private life. That he spent his early years going to a school in New York, about his alcoholic father, that he had been expelled from Lauds (which was not exactly true, for Wilf had left before they could do so), and his acrimonious divorce from Cosima, described as 'the beautiful, high society photographer to whom Rising owed his celebrity'. The column in *The Times* was more appreciative, trying to explain what Wilf wanted to achieve through his art. Taking his cue from Nietzsche, he had depicted 'a mythical world of savage force, divine ecstasy, and human insignificance, placed in a beautiful, but alien landscape, reminiscent of Claude Lorraine'. Reflecting Wilf's 'spiritual yearning for a better world'.

He thought about his own obituary, were one ever written. It was a downbeat prospect. For what had he achieved in his own life, when compared to Wilf's? Hadn't he always lived through repetition? Driven by the fear that he was one step from the mad house? To escape that he had observed the others: at school, at the university, in the very streets where he lived now. Carefully noting what people did to look ordinary. Speaking like them, gesturing like them, dressing like them. Taking morphine when the effort became too much. All the while living like a marionette gyrating on a stage. And what was he doing now but living in a cocoon, writing books that nobody read, turning the house in which he dwelt into a museum? What good was that to anyone?

It was time to act. Fetching out his phone from his jacket, he dialled the gallery.

"Is Tristan Bayes there?"

"Who is this speaking?" asked a gruff voice in an African accent.

"Michael Gereon."

"What is it about?"

"It's a private matter," said Michael.

"Hold on."

There was a lot of confused muttering and the sound of the receiver being picked up, put down, and picked up again.

"Bayes here."

"Tristan? You may remember me as Wilf Rising's brother-in-law."

"I know who you are."

"It's about the Casiraghi series sold by the gallery recently. The ones painted by Wilf."

Michael paused for effect.

"Steady on. That's a wild thing to say," said Tristan.

"I wouldn't be the first to say it. Ralph Schoenman told you the same thing."

"I told him the same thing I'm going to tell you. There is no substance to these allegations."

"I have proof."

"I seriously doubt that."

"I could come and show you? Wilf made sketches for each painting in the series. He also put a sculptural figure in each of the paintings. I have the original of that figure in my possession."

The line went silent.

"Hello?" asked Michael.

"I'm here."

"This needn't end in a claim against the gallery. What I really want to confirm is that Carlo Casiraghi placed the pictures with you. Is that correct?"

"Now I'm not getting dragged into this. You'll have to speak to Carlo."

"I intend to. Do you have an email address or a phone number for him?"

"No can do. Private client information."

"It's in your interest to have this matter cleared up. Full disclosure and I can tell the police about Carlo's activities. No accusations need come your way."

Another silence. Then he heard more mutterings as Tristan spoke to someone in the background while holding his hand over the receiver. The other voice sounded as if it might be Cosima's.

"Tristan?"

"Yes?"

"I can meet you in an hour?"

"Go to hell," said Tristan, before the line went dead.

Forty-five minutes later, the phone buzzed again. He looked at the screen. It wasn't a number he recognised.

"Hello?"

"Is that Mr Gereon?"

"Who is this?"

"My name is Ronald Pilcher. I'm a business associate of Tristan Bayes."

"Did Tristan give you my number?"

"Tristan's most upset about your call this morning. I've been delegated to discuss the matter with you."

"You have information on those art works?"

There was a pause.

"I have information. And a proposal to make to you."

"What sort of proposal?"

"That's something I'd prefer to tell you when we meet. Will you come and see me at my club? In Chiseller Street?"

Michael looked at the map in his head. It was fifteen minutes' walk away, on the other side of Finsbury Square. He had nothing else to do that morning.

"I'll be there about twelve."

The Entrepreneurs Club was in a mid-Victorian building that had once been a town house on three floors. The club was on the ground floor, with a few bedrooms and meeting rooms upstairs. A doorman in a blue coat and a top hat stood outside and bowed to people who looked as if they could be members. A motorcyclist in a leather jacket, who might have been a courier, drove up by the entrance. Michael stepped past him and walked into a lobby with a mezzanine floor and an old desk by the wall. Behind that sat a youth in a blue waistcoat who took his name and went off to enquire within for Pilcher. Ten minutes later, a man in a blue club tie with a florid *E* woven inside a parallelogram came out, switching off a mobile phone as he emerged through the door.

"Mr Gereon?"

Pilcher held out his hand. A man in his fifties who might have looked like a prosperous undertaker were it not for the furtive, anxious look on his face.

Michael followed him into a sitting room decorated in imitation of a St. James's club. Deep crimson carpets, green leather chairs and mahogany furniture. A portrait of William IV over the fireplace. Over at the bar stood a bunch of venture capitalists telling funny stories to each other in loud voices. One, an obese man in a three-piece suit, turned to stare at Pilcher, decided he was of no account and turned his back. They walked through to a dining area with people seated around the room consulting oversized menus and wine lists.

"Let's sit in the corner," said Pilcher. "It's cosy there."

A server came over and took their drinks order. Whiskey and soda for Pilcher and a spritzer for himself. Pilcher took a deep draught and looked around the room in satisfaction.

"They do you quite well in here, and they don't just let anyone in you know. You've got to be a citizen in high standing within the business community. I could tell you some very well-known names who were never allowed in."

He caught Michael looking at the signet ring on his pinkie finger. He held it up.

"I come from a very old family," he said.

"Everyone comes from a very old family," said Michael.

Michael wondered why Pilcher was trying so hard to impress. From his accent, he guessed he was from south of the river. Croydon, or somewhere like that. It occurred to him he had been so long away from ordinary life that he was all at sea when it came to people like Pilcher. What they wanted from life was a mystery to him.

"Would you like a spot of lunch?" asked Pilcher.

"No, thank you."

"You sure? I'm happy to pay."

"Let's get this over with."

A look that might have been hurt crossed Pilcher's face as he considered the rebuff. After a struggle, he gave up and leaned over the table.

"May I call you Michael?"

"If you like."

"That's me."

He handed over a business card.

"Well Ronald. What did you want to see me about?"

"Business. Always business!"

Pilcher beamed as if he had just said something witty, showing his yellow teeth.

"Let me explain something about the Bayes Gallery to you…"

"I'd rather you didn't. I want to know who you are first."

Pilcher froze, as if the question was unanswerable.

"What it says on the card. I'm a businessman."

"Why has Tristan Bayes sent you along instead of coming himself?"

"It wasn't Tristan's idea for me to call you. It was Mr Casiraghi's."

"What does Carlo want?"

"He wants to make peace with you. Told me to say that he remembers you well from the old days in Lucca. That he has no quarrel with you."

"Tell Carlo that this quarrel will end when he admits to putting six forgeries on the market."

Pilcher winced and looked around to see if anyone was listening.

"You know, saying that could get you into trouble in some quarters. A court of law, for example."

"That right?"

"Michael, be reasonable. We have signatures on all those paintings. And we have providence, confirming that all the works in question were produced in the artist's studio prior to death."

"But not by him?"

"By him, with him, through him. What is the difference?"

"So, if I mix an omelette in your kitchen, that means you made it?"

"You can't compare an omelette to a painting by Casiraghi. No, it won't do Michael. Won't do at all. We have his signatures, and we have the signed certificates. That's enough for most punters."

"But you don't have the sketchbooks."

"Casiraghi's sketchbooks?"

"My friend's sketchbooks. Wilf Rising's sketchbooks."

"Ah, about those. We'd like to have them back."

"That might be a tad difficult given they belong to his family."

"We believe those were the artist's sketchbooks and your friend - his student - borrowed them. They rightfully belong to his estate. Carlo was most insistent on that point. In fact, I know he's consulting his lawyers about it as we speak."

"Tell Carlo from me he's welcome to try."

"We were hoping to come to an amicable arrangement rather than involving the lawyers."

"What arrangement did you have in mind?"

Pilcher fetched out a pen from his jacket and with a

conspiratorial wink wrote something on the paper napkin that came with his drink and handed it over. It said £50,000.

"You want to give me all this money for sketchbooks that you say belong to you?"

"And the carving. That is included in the price."

"All for fifty thousand pounds?"

"It would cost a lot more than that to pay the lawyers to get them back for us. So, consider it an out-of-court settlement."

Pilcher beamed again.

"Everybody's happy."

"No."

"No?"

"I'm not going to sell them to you."

"I could go a hundred thousand, if it's more money you're after?"

Michael ignored him. The lamp that illuminated William IV flickered and died. A bust of a lawyer in a toga sneered at him across the room. Raucous laughter from the crowd next door rose and died away. Once more, he felt the weight of a falling world pressing down on him. With it came the familiar lassitude. For too long, he had confused it with indifference. But he understood it better now. He shook his head.

"Mr Pilcher. There is one thing you haven't told me."

"What is that?"

"Who killed my brother-in-law?"

"I've no idea."

"You're lying. If you really didn't know, you would have given me your condolences when you came out to meet me in the lobby. The fact you didn't tells me you're hiding something."

"I am sorry about your friend," he whispered. "But what happened to him had nothing to do with me."

"No? Then why are you here offering money for his possessions?"

Pilcher took a long swig from his drink.

"Listen to me, Michael. It's better that you don't know who killed your friend. Best let sleeping dogs lie."

"Better for whom? You? Tristan Bayes?"

"You, Michael. It's better for you. You've no idea about the people you're dealing with."

"I know you're shielding them. Whoever they are."

Pilcher winced, as if someone had just stuck a pin in him.

"Listen, Michael. Take my advice and take the money. That's my last word."

Michael stood up. There was nothing more to see here.

"Damn you, Pilcher," he said.

29

The Blade On The Bone

On leaving the club, Michael walked back to Spitalfields through a complex of steel and glass brutalism: banks, lawyers' offices, and insurance firms. All in black and grey against grey skies on granite pavements. Walked up Sun Street, then up a stepped causeway punctuated by surveillance cameras and out into Bishopsgate. Here, amongst the crowd, there were glimpses of human life beyond the machine. He crossed over into Spitalfields and back through the market.

It was past three o'clock, and the place was filling up with festive shoppers. An undressed pine tree stood beside the main door and two loudspeakers on either side relayed *I Wish It Could Be Christmas Every Day*. Then he caught sight of Isa wandering around the stalls, looking for something. At the same moment, he looked up, saw Michael, and strode over.

"What's up?" said Michael.

"I looked for you."

"Why?"

"There is a man to see you. He waits at the house."

"Who is he?"

"He says he is a police officer."

"What does he want?"

"He won't tell me."

"Let's walk back slowly, Isa. I have another favour to ask."

"What is it?"

"There's something I want you to make for me."

In precise detail, Michael explained the idea that had come to him on his way back through the City. Right down to the dimensions required and the instructions on what to do with it.

When they arrived back, the man was waiting for him in the sitting room. Staring at the Casiraghi on the wall. A shaven-headed, stocky man in a green mac, with hard, cynical eyes.

"Dr Gereon? I'm DS Gredic."

The man showed a warrant card, which Michael scrutinised. For this man did not look much like a police officer. Rather, he looked like a night-club bouncer. His face was vaguely familiar.

He went over to the window and stood with his back to the light. He did not take his dark glasses off or ask the man to sit down. Better to get it over with quickly. He had talked enough to dim police officers.

"What is this about?"

Gredic pointed to the painting on the wall.

"A Casiraghi?"

"You haven't answered my question."

Gredic caught his hostility and regathered himself.

"Might be best if I gave you some background... so. I'm from the Serious Economic Crime Unit. We investigate things like fraud, forgery, and money-laundering. You may know that's big business nowadays, which is why we have a department to ourselves."

"You're investigating Bayes and Bayes?"

"Ah. You know them?"

"Not well. But I've been hearing a lot about them from Ralph Schoenman."

"Ralph Schoenman is dead. We found his body washed up at Rotherhithe two days ago."

"I see."

"You don't seem surprised."

"If you'd told me something like that six weeks ago, I might have been. Now I've come to expect it. As people do when the plague comes to visit, and bodies start dropping on the streets."

"That's an interesting way to look at it," said Gredic.

The room went silent. Gredic was leaning back on the radiator, his polished shoes gleaming on the varnished floor. He had a strange sort of smile, Michael decided. Grim, but also impish, as if all the evil that went on in the world was a source of satisfaction to him, confirming a long-held prejudice. At that moment, he realised who Gredic was.

"Hey, you're a police officer now, Gary?"

Gredic put his hand over his eyes and scrutinised him. Then he laughed.

"It is Little Mickey. I knew it."

Years before, on the council estate by Quaker Street, Michael had hung out with a group of tough, older boys, known as the Wall Street Gang. Dave Tavey, Two-Ton Tony, Jonny Beck, Devon Henry, and Gary himself. They all had in common that they disliked being children. They dressed up in expensive sports gear, smoked, drank, and swore, and on Saturday afternoons fought with other football firms. One day, he had been walking home from school with Jonny's little brother, Franky, and they had let him play football with them. After that, two or three evenings a week, Michael would skip homework and join them. His mother had tried to keep him away from them, but he would meet them behind her back. He liked the fact that they ignored he went to a private school, including him in the gang because he was still a working-class boy from Spitalfields. Gary had taught him how to box a little and he had even gone to football matches with them. The gang went to the Comprehensive school and left as soon as they could. They had all gone their separate ways and he had lost touch with them after he went up to University. He was about to tell himself that he had 'escaped' where they had not. But that was not really true. The trap had closed on him later.

"You used to fancy my sister, Paula," said Gredic.

Michael laughed. Paula had been a very attractive girl, but way out of his league. Like the rest, she had listened to his problems and given him cigarettes. She had even let him kiss her once.

"She's a big wheel now. Got her own business. Doing well. Married with a daughter."

"It's good to see you again, Gary."

"Likewise, you. I think this calls for a little celebration."

"What did you have in mind?"

"I'm going off duty at five. Why don't we go down to the Blade and have a couple of drinks?"

"Suits me."

"What are you called nowadays? Can't go on calling you Mickey, can I?"

"Mike will do. Let me go downstairs and get you some coffee."

"Let me come with you. I'd like to look at the house now all these years have gone by."

After Michael had shown him around, they took their coffees back to the drawing room, where Gredic updated him on the others. Dave Tavey had done time for actual bodily harm in a brawl outside a nightclub but was going straight now. Two-Ton Tony had slowed down after a triple bypass op and was selling fridges from his back room. Jonny Beck, a very handsome boy who wore sharp mohair suits, was still chasing women around the manor and sold insurance. Devon Henry had gone back to Jamaica to be with his extended family.

"And what about you? Never had you down as a police officer, Gary."

Gredic grimaced.

"Me neither. But I'm thinking of packing it in."

"To do what?"

"A mate of mine's offered me another job. Running security for banks in the City."

Gredic looked down at the floor glumly

"Pays well," he added.

"You don't sound enthusiastic."

"I'd miss working on crime. It's something I'm good at. Security work is more hum-drum."

"Why leave, then?"

"The force is not what it was. It's all about politics now, not what you can do. Like repeating the right slogans loud enough."

"I know the feeling," said Michael, thinking about his own war on banality.

Gredic looked at him shrewdly.

"You always were a loner, even as a boy. Wicked clever, too. What are you doing now?"

Michael told him about academic life at Queen's, leaving out the reason for his sabbatical. Then his marriage to Peggy and his turn to translations and house restoration.

"You doing up this place?" asked Gredic.

"It's a temporary project. Like you, I'm in between vocations."

There followed another silence as the two of them adjusted to their new footing. Gredic sighed.

"Let's talk about the personal stuff in the Blade. There are other things I want to ask you about."

"Your coming here is providential. It's about time I had a talk with a proper detective."

"What did you want to talk about?"

"My brother-in-law's death, for one thing."

"That's one of the reasons I'm here. To tell you that your brother-in-law's case is now a murder enquiry."

"Why so?"

"Autopsy report. The angle of the bullet in his head was all wrong. He couldn't have shot himself."

"What else did you come to see me about?"

"Wait. Why aren't you surprised?"

"About Wilf? I've known all along he didn't kill himself. I tried to tell the police in Bournemouth that, but they had other fish to fry."

Gredic looked at the floor, as if police failures were a badly kept secret.

"These forgeries," said Gredic, "Ralph Schoenman told me to ask you about them before he disappeared."

"I discovered Wilf created those pictures. I was going to speak to him about it before his murder."

"How did you come to know it?"

Michael told him about the images of the carving.

"He gave me some sketchbooks to keep for him. They show the pictures in the making."

"Can I see them?"

Michael went down to the out-house to fetch them from the cistern. The sketches, the other documents, and the carving. Brought them back upstairs and laid them out on a coffee table.

Picking up one book, Michael showed Gredic the sketches Wilf had made for *Funerary Offering*. Pointed to the carving and back to the sketch. Took out the photographs Schoenman had given him and lined them up on the table. Then he got up and left Gary to it.

He went downstairs to look for Isa, and found him in the workroom, finishing the box. A discarded crate for which Isa had fashioned a lid.

"That will do nicely," said Michael.

Isa ignored him, edging the panel in his hands to a precise fit over the opening. Then he got to his feet. Stood back and inspected it. Satisfied, he turned to Michael and awaited his question.

"Where's Peggy? She not back yet?"

"She is with her mother."

"Fine. Tell her when she gets back that I went out for a drink with the police officer upstairs. He is a friend I haven't seen for a while."

"I will tell her."

"You know what to do?"

Isa turned to look at the box on the floor. On one side, he had stencilled *The Carving*.

"You want me to put it in a hiding place where it will be easy to find."

"That's right. But don't wait around inside the house. Just lock all the doors and windows and keep away. We'll be back from the funeral around four o'clock. Remind Peggy."

Going back up, he found Gary finishing his notes. Precise notes in which each letter was printed rather than in cursive script. The Go Board came on in his head, and he went over to examine the Casiraghi on the wall. A few minutes later, he looked back to find Gary staring at him. He motioned him over and pointed at the signature in the bottom right corner.

"See this? You will find when you examine the pictures sold by the Bayes that the signatures on those do not match this one. But you'll have to get an expert to verify that."

"How do you know that?"

It was too complicated to explain how the grid in his head worked, so he left that out.

"The way you print your letters when writing gave me the clue."

"Any idea who forged the signatures?"

"My guess would be someone hired to do it by Carlo Casiraghi. Wilf created those pictures in homage to the artist he loved more than any other. He never intended them to be sold. But he made the mistake of trusting Carlo Casiraghi with them. Bayes & Bayes hold the UK rights for the sale of Casiraghi's works, so Carlo commissioned them. Most likely, he thought it would be easier to pass them off in London rather than Italy. But Wilf found out about it and made trouble for them."

"There's something else I've been waiting to tell you," said Gredic. "I've been saving it 'til last."

"Oh?"

"Come on. Let's go down the Blade. I'll tell you there."

The Blade on the Bone was filling up with evening trade when they went in. Mostly yuppies moving into the area now that it had become fashionable. A few market-stall traders were drinking Guinness at the bar, along with some tourists, who were staring at the poster on the wall, advertising a *Jack the Ripper Experience* around the corner in Hanbury Street. A couple of stallholders recognised Michael and made room for them. Steph, the landlady, pulled a pint of lager for Gredic and went out the back to pour him his Ricard. Winked at him mischievously when she placed it on the bar in front of him. Like he was a suspect in a case Gredic was investigating.

"Let's go upstairs, it's quieter," said Gredic.

They went up to a lounge with old furniture and newspaper prints from 1888 on the walls, containing lurid illustrations of the Whitechapel murders.

Taking a worn leather sofa in the corner, they sat down with their drinks.

"This is all off the record, mind," said Gredic. "You'll have to come down to the station and make a statement tomorrow."

"Can it be the day after that? Wilf's funeral is tomorrow."

"Funeral?"

"We're not burying him. It's a memorial service. At Westminster Cathedral."

"What? Like a state funeral?"

"You're thinking of Westminster Abbey. The cathedral is the Catholic place in Victoria."

"He was a Catholic?"

"Wilf wasn't. But his mother is."

Michael changed the subject.

"Is there going to be an announcement about the murder enquiry? Before the service, I mean?"

"It'll probably be on the news tomorrow."

Michael wondered how Peggy and Sophie would take it. Sophie was in a fragile state. Might be best to keep her away from the television until the service was over. He would have to speak to Peggy about that before they set off in the morning.

"What else did you want to tell me, Gary?"

"It's about these murders."

"Yes?"

"We think the people behind them might be a mob from Belgrade. A man called Ronald Pilcher has been laundering their money for them through that gallery."

"Do the Bayes know about this gang?"

"Unless they're short of a few brain cells, they must have some suspicions. Maybe they just turn a blind eye to it."

"It seems like a risky thing to do. They're a well-known family."

"Throw a stick in the Brompton Road and you'll hit another upper-class degenerate just like Tristan Bayes. There's not a lot of difference between middle-class crime and the lower-class variety. It's mostly about thieving and drugs when you get to the bottom of it. But toffs are better at covering their tracks."

"But if what you tell me is true, then surely he's in danger too?"

"I doubt this mob will go after him directly. It's Ronny Pilcher who has control of the money."

"I saw Pilcher two hours ago."

It was Gredic's turn to be shocked, nearly spilling his beer.

"The bloody hell you did."

Michael told him about the call to Tristan Bayes and Pilcher's subsequent offer in the Entrepreneurs.

"Sounds like Ronny's digging a deeper hole for himself," said Gredic. "I wouldn't be surprised if the mob put him up to that."

"But what's a gang from Serbia doing here? Killing people, I mean."

"The joys of globalisation," said Gredic. "Open markets and open borders. Crime is just another export now, along with Belgian chocolate and Chinese watches.

It's a lot easier to transfer money you don't want other people to know about now we have the internet."

"Wilf and Ralph were killed because gangsters didn't want the police investigating the gallery?"

"That's about it."

"Do you know who they are?"

"We don't know their names. We don't even know what they look like. They're probably here on false passports."

"There are three of them. One has a puma tattooed on his throat and wears a turquoise tracksuit. Another has eyebrows that meet in the middle. The other one has a shaven head like yours and wears leather gloves. The one with the eye-brows wears a grey overcoat."

"How do you know that?"

Michael told Gredic about the men he had passed on his way out of the lift in The Citadel.

"You can't be sure they're the people who killed Schoenman."

"I had a feeling they were up to no good."

"Have you told Dorset CID about the men you saw?"

"No. They seem like a stupid lot down there. And, like you say, I can't be sure."

"I'll pass it on, anyway."

"Maybe they've left the country?"

"I doubt it. They haven't closed down their witnesses yet."

Gredic gave him a meaningful look.

"You mean, me?"

"You're the last man left. Apart from Pilcher."

"What about Tristan Bayes?"

"He's done a runner. Last seen getting on a plane to Zurich four hours ago."

"What do you advise me to do?"

"I can take one problem off your hands. I'm going to have to impound those sketchbooks."

"Do you have to do that?"

"Afraid so. They're criminal evidence."

"But Wilf didn't commit a crime."

"I know that. But his paintings were sold with false signatures. The sketches form part of the case against Carlo Casiraghi and Tristan Bayes."

"I'm not giving you the carving."

"Why not?"

"It's my mother's. The only thing I have left of her. You remember?"

Gredic thought for a moment. Michael wondered how much he recalled about the weeks that followed her death. How he and the gang had come round to see him at the house and had made him come out with them to the same pub they were sitting in now. Had sat with him in the house and listened to reggae music. Helped him refurbish the rooms for let. They had been there for him as few other people had ever been. Wilf being one exception.

"Keep it, then," said Gredic. "The sketchbooks are all dated in your brother-in-law's handwriting anyway. That should be enough. But mind, if the lawyers ask to see it, you'll have to give it up to the court."

"Thanks, Gary."

Gredic raised his glass.

"The Wall Street Gang."

"The Wall Street Gang," said Michael.

After they had supped, Gredic resumed.

"The problem is that these killers, whoever they are, won't know that the sketchbooks are no longer in your possession. They might come after you if they think they can get them back."

"I know it."

"Maybe you and your wife should go away for a bit?"

"We can't do that. Peggy's mother is seriously ill, and she won't leave her. And I can't leave her on her own."

"You could take your mother-in-law with you. You should go if you can."

Gredic looked worried.

"These people are maniacs," he said. "They won't think twice about wiping you out."

"Like the man who killed my mother?"

"Why are you bringing her up?"

"Because that's another reason I'm staying. I don't want to run away anymore."

He told Gredic about his premonition that she was in danger. How he might have saved her had he acted in time.

"That's a long time ago, Mike. You weren't to blame."

"It's still on my conscience. If I'd listened to that voice, she might still be alive."

Gredic rubbed his face all over with his hand to wipe away his exasperation.

"I'll see if we can get you some protection," he said at last. "After all, you're a key witness now."

30

The Samurai

Marko took off his delicate kimono and placed it on the chair. Adjusted his white headband and flexed himself, feet apart in the prescribed manner. Looked at himself in the vast mirror of the apartment and practiced. Hard chopping movements with his palms, fists, and elbows. Pirouettes to deliver neat kicks with heels and knees. Now and then coming to a rest before the next series of movements. Swinging round to face himself in the mirror once more. His face taught with struggle.

Whenever he watched samurai movies, it was never the fight scenes he lingered on. Rather, it was the scenes in which the warriors meditated, watched, and prepared for battle. How they floated as they walked, without expression, letting nothing disturb their concentration. It was that composure he sought. He knew from *The Book of the Samurai* that it rested on two things: the realisation that life was a dream and that death awaited like a running fountain ready to wash it away. On those foundations a Samurai was attached to nothing except his appearance before others and his honour.

He had read in a travel guide that there were schools in Japan in which those who trained in the samurai arts lived and worked like monks. Some day he would go there and see for himself. Perhaps it would be possible to combine such a life with the business interests he ran for his uncle.

He came to a halt, for he had made a false move and would have to go back and start again. Something was breaking in on his composure: the encrypted call he had received from his uncle after midnight. He sat cross-legged and meditated upon it.

His uncle sounded like he had been drinking with his friends from the Delije at the Excelsior hotel. When he was drunk, he had a way of spitting his words as if catching his breath. That was the rage talking. All over a message from inside the Ministry of the Interior in Beograd. Stating the police in London were investigating Pilcher and the gallery, and were about to make an arrest. That Interpol had put out an alert for information on the syndicate. Their friends in Naples were growing restless and his uncle was afraid that losing the money would start a war. The Colonel had finished by berating him for his failure to contain the situation, ordering him to finish it now. Or else.

That had hurt. He, whose devotion had been total. Who had spent his brief life never slacking in valour. Impeccable in his service. A man who would rather die than fail in his duty.

The book was precise on this point. A man with no honour was no better than all the other dogs in the world. Better to step forward and embrace death, rather than let there be any doubt.

He picked up the bamboo sword and beckoned to Zivko, who was seated in the lounge nursing a hangover.

"Take this stick and attack me with it."

"You are not wearing any equipment."

"That does not matter."

"You want me to hit you hard?"

"As hard as you like, until I wrest it from you."

"As you wish."

They circled, Zivko holding up the stick with two hands. Marko staying out of range. Quickly, Zivko advanced and delivered a blow to his shoulder with a loud crack. Then another on his back. The pain was excruciating. Marko noted the smile of satisfaction on Zivko's face.

"Harder! Faster."

Another swing, this time to his torso. A blow that left a red gash across the hard muscles of his midriff. By degrees, the pain shifted to an exquisite joy. Marko gasped and stepped forward. Gripping the stick in mid-air; twisting it so that he caught Zivko off balance, then throwing him to the floor.

Marko stood over him while he lay on the ground. An impulse to kick the idiot in the head came over him. Suppressing it, he held out his hand and helped him up.

"You should learn to stay on your feet, Zivko. You may need them one day."

After he showered and dressed, he came to the kitchen. There, the two of them were breakfasting on pastries from a delicatessen. Soft cheese, smoked pork, polenta, yoghurt. Brewed coffee. Of the kind they usually took every morning in one of the Beograd restaurants owned by his uncle.

In answer to his inquiring look, Andrej paused.

"Near to here is a Greek cafe. There you can get the things we are used to."

"Very nice," said Marko. "Your home comforts."

Andrej said nothing. Zivko looked away and diverted himself by toasting some flat bread.

The view from the penthouse overlooked the canal,

partly obscured by damp fog. Along the towpath, a male and a female in day-glo shorts, were jogging up towards the park. In the other direction, commuters in suits headed for Mile End. High up, a drone flew over, taking pictures. He, who did not feel at home anywhere, felt strangely discontented in this gloomy city.

After they had put the breakfast things away, Marko signalled for the two of them to join him in the lounge.

"Where did you go last night?" he said.

"To a bar where they had some music," said Andrej.

"Until three in the morning?"

Andrej shrugged.

"We met some girls…"

Marko looked from one to the other. Zivko was still a kid, but Andrej should know better. Yet this was not the time to have it out with him.

He related an edited version of the Colonel's call. After he finished, Andrej spoke:

"What do we do now?"

"You are here to give me advice," snapped Marko. "Do I have to wait for you to sober up before I hear it?"

"Kill them," said Zivko.

"Kill who?"

"All of them. This other man in Spiddlefield, and Pilcher."

"Be quiet, you fool," said Marko. "Have you learnt nothing? We kill only when it is necessary. Until then we stay in the shadows."

Andrej and Zivko waited for him to finish saying whatever was on his mind.

"We are not here to have fun, but to put right a dangerous situation. Here in London, we have a lot of money at risk. Our firm is small, and we cannot afford to lose it. Nor can we risk a war with our bigger partners.

Therefore, we must be unwavering in our determination to succeed."

He was not used to speeches; before too long, the words tired him. Already he felt them emptying into the void. He got up and went to the window. Below, on the patio, were three gleaming motorbikes, in red, blue, and black. The fresh ones they had hired when they moved out of the hotel, after they had pushed the American off the boat. For it was easier to get around the city that way. Their rental, like the penthouse they were in now, ended on Monday. This business would have to be completed by that day.

Getting rid of the artist had been straightforward. It wasn't hard to get rid of a drunk who took a lot of drugs. Zivko and Andrej had watched him driving around in his Audi, going back and forwards between his boat and the university. Seen him walking around the marina and going into the hotel with his friends. Followed him when he went up the hills to draw pictures of the sky all by himself. It was easy to trail him along the high road that looked down on the valley. Creeping up on him while he sat with his back on a tree and his eyes on the heavens. Stringing him up until he choked.

He had assumed that killing the artist would be enough. But the meddling American had gone back to the police, and they had posed more questions. So he, too, had to disappear. That, also, had proved easy: pushing him off the river ferry when no one was looking. Despite himself, he had enjoyed watching the bastard struggling to stay afloat in the slipstream in his heavy overcoat, before disappearing beneath the water for good.

Now there was this other man making trouble, the one to whom the artist had given his books. He had ordered Pilcher to buy them back, but the man had failed at that, as he had everything else Marko had given him to do. Still another problem for him to solve. So much grief over these cursed paintings.

"You will go to the house of this man, Gereon, today," he said. "Zivko, you have your tools?"

"They are in the bedroom."

Zivko was a housebreaker and a locksmith. The firm used him for exactly this kind of job.

"I want you to go over to Spitalfields and take these sketchbooks. Find this doll. Andrej, you go with him."

"What if these people are inside the house?" asked Zivko. "If you don't want them killed…"

"I didn't say that I don't want them killed. I said only that it must be a necessary execution. Do what you have to do. Where are the guns?"

"Up there. In the luggage room."

"Bring me my gun and clean the others."

Later, when he was reassembling the Glock after oiling the parts, Andrej came and sat beside him.

"Are you alright?" he asked.

"Zivko gets on my nerves sometimes."

"Maybe it is your nerves that are the problem?"

"There is nothing wrong with my nerves. The thing that is wrong is that we are not achieving what we came here to do."

"Patience is necessary, too," said Andrej. "You remember that first job we did together?"

That had been eighteen years before, when they were seventeen. They had been told to eliminate a rival the Colonel wanted out of the way; it had been their initiation task. Marko and Andrej had followed him around for weeks on their motorbikes. Watching him while he went in and out of the hotels and bars he frequented, observing that late at night he liked to walk back to his apartment along the Danube embankment, with his driver following him in the BMW.

On the chosen night, Andrej had driven up alongside and shot the driver through the window. Marko had been waiting further up the embankment, and once the driver was out of the way, he walked up and shot the man twice through the head. Throwing his CZ pistol in the river, getting back on his motorbike, and rejoining Andrej and their friends in the nightclub. No one had seen them leaving, thus the alibi was perfect. Afterwards, his uncle threw a party to welcome them into the Pumas. Spoke about how proud his father would have been to see his son grow into a soldier. Then they stood in salute and sang the words to the para-military marching song of the Delije.

"I remember it. What of it?"

"We both had patience then."

"We have patience now. The difference is that the job is not simple. There are too many factors we cannot control. Now time is running out, for we must leave this place."

"We can rent somewhere else."

"No. I don't want to do that. The longer we stay in London, the easier it will become to trace us."

"Hurry breeds mistakes."

"Was it a mistake to get drunk and have sex with strangers, do you think?"

Andrej held up his hands.

"It was a mistake. I apologise."

"Andrej. Listen to me. You and I started out as children living in a one-room apartment without enough food to eat. Earning a few dinars selling cannabis at school. The Pumas have given us everything. That could all disappear in a few weeks unless we do something."

"Surely things are not as bad as that? Everyone in Serbia knows who we are."

"That is true so long as we have money and guns and are in favour with the government. If we lose our prestige, there are plenty of other kids on the estates waiting to take over."

To his satisfaction Marko saw that, for the first time, Andrej looked worried.

"Go now," said Marko. "We will meet back here this afternoon."

"Where do you go?"

"I'm going to find Pilcher," he said, pulling back the safety catch on the Glock. "He is not answering my calls."

31

Funeral Games

After Wilf's memorial service Michael, Peggy, and Sophie got into the old Volvo and drove back across the river to Kennington. They crossed by the Vauxhall Bridge. On the right, visible over the red barrier rail, a pleasure boat was motoring up towards Chelsea. On the left, in what looked like a yellowing Aztec temple, were the headquarters of the secret police.

Sophie was still recovering from the stroke, so Peggy thought it best they sat in the back. Michael disliked driving, as he did any operation in which there was too much information coming at him at once. However, the drive was short, and he was going to drive as slowly as the law would allow. He kept one ear open on the sounds coming out of the back seat. For Sophie was weeping quietly, while Peggy sniffled and held her hand.

James had badgered Sophie into having a mass said for Wilf in the Cathedral, promising to get a dispensation from the Cardinal, whom he described as a personal friend. Sophie had been too ill to put up much protest, whereupon James invited two hundred mourners, most unknown to the family. Critics, artists, writers, and rock musicians were there, one of whom had played the guitar and sung *Stairway to Heaven*, on the grounds that it was Wilf's favourite. A throng of sleek-looking City types had walked in with James and Cicely. Several Old Laudians were in attendance, including Perry Winter, sitting next to Cosima and her daughter in the front row. Finally, there were two from the School of Art: the Principal, a saturnine woman who glared throughout the service, and Karen Highet, the woman he had met that day he found Wilf on the boat.

Inside, the vast interior was cold and damp. Black soot hung off the undecorated vault. Up at the front, ranged before the baldachin, seats were sealed off from the public. But the service, except for the rock interval, had been strangely moving, with incense and prayers for the dead.

Hail Mary, full of grace...

Holy Mary, Mother of God

Pray for us sinners now and at the hour of our death.

James read the memorial in a high, crackling voice. To do him credit, he had been more respectful than the newspapers. If he hadn't known him better, Michael might have believed that James was actually mourning his brother.

Cicely wanted the reception in Walton-on-Thames. Either there, or at the hotel James used during the week, when he was working at his ethical investment fund in Threadneedle Street. But Peggy had put her foot down about that, saying that Sophie was too ill to travel and that it would have to be a quieter affair.

Turning left after the railway bridge, he drove up the long, straight road towards Kennington Tube station. After a mile or so, he drew up in the bus lane outside the old family home. He got out and fetched the wheelchair from the boot. Then he and Peggy helped Sophie out of the

door and into her chair. She pressed down heavily on their
arms, for her right leg was partly immobile.

"I'll park the car," he told them. "You go on ahead."

Up the road was a church with a car park, where
Sophie had received permission for guests to park. After
several attempts, he placed the car between two others,
leaving enough room to open the door. Getting out, he
looked at the yellow sign beside the padlocked rear door of
the church.

*These premises are under constant CCTV surveillance. Images
are being recorded in the interests of public safety.*

He shivered and lit a cigarette. Took out his mobile
phone: no messages. May no new thing happen, he
thought; an old mediterranean expression for good luck.
He hoped Isa was safe. On that wish, he walked back. But,
before he did so he took another morphine tablet as a
precaution against what might lie ahead.

On entering the family house the first thing he noticed
was how crowded the place was. People were camped in
the hall and up the stairs, forming twos and threes, champagne glasses in their hands, raising a clamour that rose to
the upper floors.

To the right, they had cleared the old parlour. In it, a
table covered in crisp, white linen laid with hor d'oeuvres,
sparkling wine, orange juice and bottles of water. Two
servers in black dresses stood waiting by the window, chatting to each other in the subdued tones people adopted at
funerals.

He went down the narrow passage to the rear. There, a
crowd stood around Sophie at the back. Peggy was
standing to one side of her wheelchair, while on the other
sat a retired priest in an old tweed jacket and a clerical
collar, whispering to Sophie: Father Kevin, who had
baptised all three of her children.

James was holding forth on the memorial service to the man on his right, who looked like a business crony. On the lapel of his steel-grey suit, James wore his MBE. For services to the environment, Michael recalled. Investing money in batteries for electric cars, wind turbines and solar panels. Making a fortune out of all of it.

"A great pity the Minister could not join us," he said. "I am given to understand that he is with the Cabinet this evening. Naturally, he would have preferred to be with us on a day like this."

His wife, Cicely, was standing behind her husband, talking to a woman he did not recognise. On the table in the corner was the macaw, flapping and growling, while two boys stared into its cage.

Going over to Peggy, he took her hand.

"You okay, honey?" she murmured.

"Will we be here long?" he asked.

She smiled at the floor, keeping her voice low.

"It won't hurt you to mix with some other creatures for a while."

She put her other hand on her mother's shoulder and bent down to whisper something in her ear. Sophie turned to her with a vacant look. She blinked her eyes twice before turning back to Father Kevin, hunched over his stool, speaking words of consolation to her.

Cicely, a woman with bobbed hair, wearing a black dress shaped like a small wigwam, was poking the wreaths laid out on the table, talking to the other woman, who Michael realised, must be James' daughter by his first marriage.

"Look at these yellow freesias, Denise," she said. "Who sends flowers like that to a funeral?"

She picked up a card and held it out.

"Mark McCallum," she read. "Isn't he one of your

analysts?" she asked, talking to her husband's back, who turned and gave her a frozen smile, before turning back to the man beside him.

"I really don't think an employee should send anything to a private funeral. I expect he's after a promotion."

Denise picked up an outsized wreath and showed it to Cicely.

Wilf. Forever in Our Hearts.

Whose Genius Will Never Die.

"O my god," said Cicely. "Just look at that. Isn't it amazing?"

"Hold it there," said Denise, taking a photograph on her mobile. "That needs to go on Facebook."

One boy chased the other around the room, knocking into Peggy, who spilt her drink over her dress. Michael seized the brat by the arm as Cicely strode over. Ignoring him, she stood over her errant son.

"Now Barnaby, you behave now," she said.

Bending over, she prised Michael's fingers from the child's arm without acknowledgement and tried to drag him away.

"Won't," said the child, getting down on the floor. "Don't want to."

"James, I need you to spend some time with that boy. I've got my hands full organising this funeral."

"One moment, darling. I'm in the middle of something important with Alec."

Cicely stared at her husband open-mouthed, while the child rolled about, beating the floor with his fists.

"I need you to do it now," she said. "Don't you know where you are? You can talk business with Alec another time."

James shrugged at his friend and placed his glass on the

table. Holding his medal close to his lapel, he looked down at his son.

"Look here, Barnie, be a good chap. Do get up."

The child howled still louder.

The macaw flapped and clicked its tongue.

"Ba-bah, Ba-bah," it announced.

Michael wandered over to inspect a picture on the wall. It was one of Wilf's, another Mediterranean scene. It showed a woman, possibly Ariadne, with her arms over her knees on a lone shore, her head down, weeping. Before her, the tide was going out, beating back to the surf in the distance. To the left of the canvas, dawn was rising. Entitled: *Return of the Native*. He had not looked at it properly in years. He wondered how much it would be worth now, for it pained him how recherché the theme was. Or perhaps that resulted from over-familiarity? At any rate, it might be another two generations before a revival of interest in art like this. If there was ever such a revival.

While he was musing on that, Father Kevin came over with his hand outstretched.

"Is it Michael? To be sure it is," he said.

Michael never knew what to call priests. Not being religious, it grated on him to call anyone 'Father'. He raised his arm in salutation instead.

"I remember you and Wilf as boys together. How long ago was that, now?"

"Twenty-eight years, five months and twenty-one days," said Michael.

Father Kevin's kindly eyes, under shaggy eyebrows, lit up.

"You have an exact figure, I see."

"I remember the day I first came to this house, that's all."

"You used to stay here a lot, I recall?"

Was there pity in that question? How much did this priest know about him at that age?

"Aunt Sophie was very kind to me. She often let me stay here… after what happened to mother."

"It wasn't just kindness. Sophie saw you were a beneficial influence on Wilf."

Michael looked back at his mother-in-law, who was staring at them both with that look of cunning that people with brain damage often had.

"She did?"

"Oh yes. He was going wild at that time. He was angry with his father and upset with his mother. Getting into fights. Getting into trouble with the police. Meeting you changed all that."

"How was that?"

Father Kevin put his hand on his shoulder.

"You got him to take his talent more seriously. We all knew he had it. But it was you that gave him a shove, just when he needed it."

"I didn't know that was what I was doing. To me, it was the other way around. He was my only friend."

"Don't you remember that carving you showed him? That was where it all started."

"But there was nothing intentional about it. It was sitting around in my mother's workshop. Wilf picked it up and…"

No. That wasn't quite right. He had explained it to Wilf, trying to get him to understand the meaning of the inscription. That had been important, too.

"None of us really know the part we play in the lives of others," said Father Kevin. "Without you, Wilf might not have found the path in life meant for him."

The priest's face was now close up; his wily eyes staring deep into his. Without his dark glasses, Michael felt naked. He wanted them now as tears came into his eyes.

"It might have been better for him if he had never found it," he choked.

Even as he said it, it felt wrong. Hadn't he been shown the shining wonder of being unveiled after he recovered from his experience in the morgue? The same wonder that he and Wilf had shared as boys, and later as young men in France and Italy?

"How is your new guest?" said Father Kevin, changing the subject. "The young man you have taken into your home?"

"Isa?"

"That was a good thing you did. You changed his life."

"We haven't changed Isa's life. He's changed ours."

He remembered Isa was still back in Spitalfields, waiting for them to return. It was time to go, in case the thing he feared happened. Excusing himself, he turned back to Peggy. But where she had been standing was a vacant space.

"She took Sophie to her bedroom," said Father Kevin. "Poor Sophie's worn out. I'd better go round and see them. I'll tell Peggy you want to see her."

Father Kevin shuffled off as Michael looked around the room. People were getting tipsy and the noise in the room was rising still more. Cicely was berating a server about something or other, while James was deep in conversation with Rod Stagg, the rock musician who performed at the service. The latter had the leathery face of a stimulant addict; his nose repaired by plastic surgery, leaving him with a small bulb at the end. The two boys were back poking the macaw with a stick, while it hopped around its cage, flapping its feathers.

The morphine took a deeper hold, relaxing him still

more and restoring him to a place of greater safety. It was just enough to temper his disgust for the people around him to something like boredom.

Suddenly the bird, provoked beyond endurance, bit one of his tormentors. Dylan, the older boy, turned aside, held his finger, and screamed. His mother went over to pull him away and examine his hand, which was bleeding profusely. A gaggle of adults gathered around in consternation.

"Somebody call an ambulance," said Cicely. "That hand will need to be looked at. Barnaby, you can go and sit in the next room. I've had just about enough of you."

"Won't. Don't want to," said the boy.

While this scene was unfolding Cosima, in a wide-brimmed, black hat entered the room, shepherding Wilf's daughter, Claudia, a girl in school uniform. They made their way over to the group through the crowded room. Cosima stopped, uncertain where to turn. Just then, Cicely wheeled to her right and touched her on the arm.

"Cosima, how lovely to see you."

Cosima appraised her with a stony look.

"And you are?"

"I'm Wilf's sister-in-law. We've met before."

"Have we? Where was that, I wonder?"

She spoke in a throaty whisper that brought a hush to the room. Someone led the two boys away for attention in the next room. By now, both were blubbering, overawed by the drama they had created.

Flustered, Cicely gestured to her husband, who came round to stand beside her, a bland smile on his face, hand outstretched to take Cosima's.

"Cosima, thank you so much for coming. Can we help you in any way?"

Ignoring the hand, Cosima stared behind him, then back at him.

"It's not you I want to see. Where is Peggy? I must speak with her."

Peggy came back into the room with her coat, holding her car keys.

"What is it, Cosima?"

"Wait a moment," Cosima replied, holding up her finger and turning to her daughter.

"Claudia, darling, please find Barry and ask him to take you home. I have some matters to discuss and shall be a while. Tell Barry to come back for me once he's dropped you off."

She kissed Claudia on her cheek and waved her away.

"Peggy, my dear, is there a place we can speak? I have some things to discuss. Private matters."

She turned to Michael, without warmth.

"This concerns you, too."

Peggy turned on her heel and gesturing Cosima to follow her, threaded her way through the crowd.

They went downstairs into the basement. To the right, at the bottom, was the old dining room with its low windows, no longer used. A polished walnut table and an assortment of chairs from different periods grouped around it. Closing the door behind them, Peggy sat down at the head of the table and motioned Cosima to sit beside her. Michael sat at the other end.

Cosima put down her bag, slowly taking off her gloves, and then her hat, which she placed on the table.

Peggy waited in patience for the ritual to conclude with her hands clasped together. She looked at Michael and raised her right eyebrow in an unspoken question.

"What do you want to speak to us about, Cosima?" asked Peggy.

"It's about Wilf."

"What about him?"

"His memory."

Cosima lifted her eyes, as if contemplating Wilf's spirit hovering above her.

"He was a great man, you know. A wonderful artist. Although, of course, we weren't close at the end."

"No, you weren't," said Peggy.

"But there is Claudia to think about. As well as Wilf's legacy. I understand he left her the future royalties from his art-works."

Cosima bit her lip and reflected for a moment. Whether about her ex-husband, or about her absent feelings for him, or about their daughter, it was hard to say.

"As you know, my brother and I represented Wilf for nearly twenty years. We were privileged to do so. But recent events have forced Tristan to step back from the gallery."

"By 'events' you mean the forgery allegations?" asked Michael.

Cosima gave him a guarded stare.

"Amongst other things… at any rate, Tristan is staying in Zermatt for a bit. I am taking over the running of the gallery for now."

"I thought you always did run it," said Peggy.

Cosima gave her a rare smile.

"We mustn't let people know that," she said, with a glance at Michael. "However, it has fallen to me to clear matters up and I want to discuss the disposal of these sketchbooks."

"How do you know about the sketchbooks, Cosima?" said Michael.

"Tristan mentioned them to me."

"Cosima," he said, with mock-weariness. "I really, truly,

hope you are encouraging your brother to go to the police and tell them what he knows about those forgeries."

"I will pass your suggestion on," she said. "But can we get back to the point I want to make?"

"What point is that?" asked Peggy.

"It is in all our interests to draw a line under this matter. Yours and Wilf's, Claudia's, and my own too. Getting rid of the sketches will clear Wilf's name."

"Letting you and Tristan off the hook?" asked Michael.

"That too," she said. "We are also the innocent parties here."

Her thin lips knitted together, her jaw tight. As if the injustice of the thing was intolerable.

"We can't help you with your request," said Michael.

"Why ever not?"

"Because the police impounded those sketches yesterday. Seems they want them to build a case against your brother and Carlo Casiraghi."

He let that sink in. It pleased him to goad her.

"At any rate, the sketches are irrelevant," he said.

"How so?"

"Because the paintings *are* Wilf's. It's only Casiraghi's signatures that were forged. By Carlo. And by what you've just told us, Tristan must have known that before he ran for it."

"Aren't you rather missing the point?" said Cosima.

"Suppose you tell us what is the point," said Peggy.

"It's this. I have been moving heaven and earth to keep this out of the newspapers. But soon, some unsavoury reports are going to appear."

"What reports?" asked Peggy.

"That Wilf killed himself because he was about to be exposed."

"But he didn't kill himself," said Michael.

"How do you mean?"

"He was murdered, Cosima. By the same people your brother did business with. The police told us the results of the autopsy yesterday, but they're not releasing that information just yet. Your friends in the media will just have to print some other fake news."

Peggy stood up.

"I think we're about done here," she said. "Nice of you to drop by, Cosima."

"Wait," said Cosima, putting her hand on Peggy's sleeve. "This can't continue."

"Why can't it continue, sweety?" said Peggy, looking down at her.

"Because I won't allow it to."

Cosima looked up at Peggy, then at Michael. A look of threat, with a question in her eyes. Receiving no answer, she shook her head and put on her gloves.

"Have a care," she said. "This doesn't end here."

"So sorry for your loss," said Michael, on the way out.

32

Sister Morphine

Peggy gunned the engine and taking a right outside the church, she drove up to the Elephant & Castle. All the while thinking about the change in Michael, who was staring out the front window as if he were watching a movie, so down in his seat that his face was barely over the dashboard. She had always thought his humour dry and pedantic until she heard him baiting Cosima back there. 'So sorry for your loss,' she repeated to herself. Then a second time. She laughed.

Michael turned his head.

"What's funny?"

"What you said to her."

Michael settled deeper into his seat, half-somnolent from the morphine.

"It's easy to play with someone who takes herself as seriously as Cosima," said Michael.

"That's funny too."

Peggy was still laughing when they joined a queue of traffic heading up to London Bridge. After a while, she realised there was something overwrought about her giggles. Time to slow down, she thought. Slow down and take stock.

"What do you think was going on back there?" she asked.

"Back there? It's Cosima doing what she does best. Controlling things from behind the scenes. Bending people to her will."

"First time I've seen Cosima look frightened."

"She has a lot to be frightened about. This business could bring down the gallery. If Tristan had listened to me, none of this would have happened."

"What did you tell him?"

"What I was *going* to tell him before he put the phone down was to co-operate with the police. Acknowledge that those paintings were Wilf's and reimburse the buyers."

"But then everyone will think Wilf was a forger."

"The paintings Wilf created are some of the best things he ever did. He took over Casiraghi's style, but he made something original out of it. Someday I'd like to bring those pictures together and display them in a gallery. Minus the signatures Carlo added to them."

"I like you when you're like this," said Peggy, when they came to a halt at some traffic lights.

"Like what?"

"Funny, passionate, caring. Reminds me of the man I married all those years ago."

Michael put his hand on her leg and looked up at her.

"I owe you an apology."

"For what?"

"For going absent the last two years. Must have been hell for you."

Peggy thought for a moment.

"How did you get out of it?" she asked.

"Get out of what?"

"That morbid state you've been in all this time."

He knew Peggy disliked philosophy, so he left out his reali-sation on the train back from the morgue that his theory that people were marionettes wasn't the whole truth. That, beyond the random cause-and-effect and chaos of human existence was all that was the case. To which nothing could be added and nothing taken away. Something that could be contem-plated, but never explained. A place of wonder and beauty.

"I just woke up, that's all."

Putting the gear in neutral, Peggy placed her hand on his. Leaned over and kissed him. Sitting up, he took her face in his hands and kissed her back, hard. She felt the ardour in him, at once yearning and self-contained. Sepa-rate, and not separate.

The traffic edged forward. Ahead of them was the river. Soon they would be home.

"I've been thinking," said Michael. "You should move back to Blackwater."

"Why? Do you want me to go?"

"No, I don't want you to go. But it's time you got on with making ceramics. Stopped looking after other people and focused on yourself for a while."

"I can't leave Mom."

"She could go with you?"

"I doubt she'd leave Kennington."

"We can work something out. But you should go. It'd be good for you."

"What about Isa?"

"Isa doesn't need looking after. He's stronger than the two of us put together."

The traffic cleared and they gathered speed over the bridge. It was past sunset and the streetlamps were coming on. To the right, two hundred feet high, stood the Monument with its golden ball of fire as a reminder of half-forgotten disasters. Peggy took a right up Gracechurch Street and headed for Aldgate.

"What about dinner tonight?" said Michael. "Do you want to go out?"

"I'm too tired for that. Let's get something in."

"All right. Drop me off at the market and I'll order from the Thai stall."

Peggy watched her husband get out and walk through the archway. He had lost that vague way of walking about that used to irritate her. Now he looked as if he knew where he was going. She wondered at it. He hadn't been the same since the night he identified Wilf's body. She made a note to ask him more about it, for it concerned their future together. Whether here or in Blackwater, she hadn't decided.

A few minutes later, she drew up outside the darkened house. The shutters on the ground-floor windows were closed. It looked eery and silent within. Feeling nervous, she got out and let herself in. Switched on the hall light and looked up the stairs.

"Isa?" she shouted up.

A muffled groan came from one room upstairs. Most likely the door on the bathroom, which swung whenever there was a draught. She fought down a panic and went into the room on the left. The walls unpapered and the floor unfinished; just the fire-place Michael and Isa had been working on. She looked down. There, in the dust, were footprints: the beetle shapes of expensive trainers. Her heart beat like a drum. Going out again, she looked at the door of the workroom next to it, and saw one of the panels had splintered.

Unable to bear any more, she ran out and got in the

car. Turned the ignition and locked the doors. Switched on the car radio and got out her phone.

A few minutes later, Michael's face appeared at her side window. He handed over a bag filled with takeaway cartons.

"Stay there," he said. "I'll be out in a few minutes."

She watched him go in. He didn't seem surprised at the burglary. Rather, that he expected it. If that was true, then he had been holding something back from her. Something he had learned from that policeman who came yesterday.

Ten minutes later, he came out again, beckoning her inside. Handing over the parcels to him, she followed him down to the kitchen. On the table was the carving and a plastic bag Michael had removed from the disused lavatory. A place he had always tried to keep secret. In the bag was his passport, cheque books, foreign bank notes, watches, a set of spare keys, and blister packs of morphine.

"Burglars?" asked Peggy.

"They didn't find what they were looking for," he said, gesturing to the carving.

"You knew they would come?"

"I suspected they might try. So, I took some precautions."

"Why are they looking for that fucking thing?"

"For the same reason they want the sketchbooks."

"Why don't you just let them take it?"

It was his turn to look angry. Shaking his head in confusion.

"But that would mean giving up."

"Well. Give. It. Up."

"Maybe this isn't the right time to talk about this. When you're this upset."

"Don't patronise me."

Michael held out his hands in supplication. There was

something about the way he was trying to mollify her that made her explode. Whether over the danger they were in, or her own helplessness, or Michael's otherworldliness, she couldn't have said.

"This is so your fault," she moaned. "You and that fucking statue."

Now she was shouting as her frustration unloaded.

"You knew! And you left Isa here to deal with it on his own. You should have been here yourself."

She spat out the final syllable, her hands on the sink, her back to him.

"Peggy, this isn't helping."

"Help? You talk to me about help? Wilf's dead, my Mom's paralysed, the house has been burgled, and now Isa's gone missing. Maybe dead. While you're running around worrying about whether your toys are safe."

She held up the morphine pack.

"Is this what you really wanted? This shit?"

"That's not fair, Peggy."

"No. It isn't fair. So why don't you clean your shit up? Then you go find Isa."

She made to knock him out of the way but stopped dead and looked up. There was someone standing at the top of the stairs, looking down at her.

Slowly, Isa descended. Halting at the step one from the bottom, he stared at each of them, shaking his head. A stern yet composed look on his face.

"Peggy, Michael," he said. "You must not fight. It does no good."

She ran over to him, and putting her arms around him, she wept.

33

The Underground Railway

On the afternoon of the funeral, Isaias was planing down some more wood on the bench when the men broke in.

He rejoiced in using the skills his father had taught him around the family home in Asmara. A low, ramshackle building hit by a shell in the Ethiopian war, it housed accommodation, a general store, and a workshop. In it, he and his father repaired things their neighbours brought them. All the while restoring their home to the state it might have been in decades before. In that way he had learnt to build a wall, make a door, frame a window, and repair a roof. Along the way, learning the ways of commerce in the store his mother ran. He might have been there now, were it not for the gangsters who persecuted his family and drove them out.

It was his first time alone in this house, a place he had come to think of as a resting place on the long journey ahead. He sang as he worked, an old Tigre lament his father had taught him on the kraar. A call followed by a response which changed key at the end of each line:

Who is that so far from home?

The hunter coming down from the hill.
What does he bring so far from home?
He comes bearing gifts for thee.

He and Yonah, with whom he escaped from prison, had often sung that song together at nights while they huddled, wretched and hungry in the enormous hangar in Tripoli, waiting for their boat to arrive. Endless days, waiting for the smugglers to come for them. But when they did, it was always more money they wanted. One thing he had learnt on the long journey from Eritrea was how little pity there was in the world. How easy it was to become an unwanted dog whom others treated with contempt. It was a lesson he would not forget.

When first he met the Doctor, that night he knocked on the door in the rain, he had seen the shadow on his face, his eyes turned inwards on some private trouble. There had been no pity in that look. Yet, he had also seen that the Doctor was not a wicked man, but an unhappy one. So, he prayed for him and earlier in the week, after the Doctor came home from seeing his dead friend, the light had come back into his eyes and Isa rejoiced.

He saw that the Doctor and Peggy were not happy together. When first he met them, he had thought he was the cause of their trouble; he had heard them arguing about him upstairs that first night. But it was not so: they had been unhappy before they met him.

He wondered that so many people here were sad. In the village where he lived as a child, before his father moved them all to the capital, there had been little work, little food, and they had fetched water from a well two kilo-metres away. Many had not even a pair of shoes. Yet every evening, the villagers gathered to share what food they had and to talk and sing. Here in the West people had more possessions than they knew what to do with, yet were miserable.

A noise from the back of the house disturbed his reverie. He heard the basement door open and, after a pause, the heavy tread of more than one man coming up from the kitchen. The door rattled from the next room, and the men went in. He counted the footfalls: there were two. Heavy men, he thought, big men. Or at least one of them was. They were not speaking English, but a language with long vowels and hard consonants.

He stood still by the door and listened some more. Heard the men come back out into the passage, then one of them tried the handle of the door. The other issued a command and there was a loud bang as they kicked the door. Then again: a louder bang as one of them threw his weight against it, splitting a panel. He ducked down out of sight.

After some argument, he heard the men going up the stairs. He put his eye to the gap in the panel and watched. Two men, both white, wearing leather jackets. One of them with a leaping puma tattooed on his throat; the other, a man with a shaven head and a gun in his belt. Shortly afterwards, he heard them inspecting each room upstairs, one by one. Soon, no doubt, they would find the box he had left for them.

What to do now? The Doctor had warned him these men were killers and to absent himself from the house. But curiosity had prevailed. That, and a refusal to be afraid. He had met men like this many times in his exile. Pitiless, barbaric men like those who had taken money from himself and Yonah, then pushed them out to sea in a rubber dinghy with thirty other people to drown. They, too, had laughed. Waving their hands in farewell and in mockery.

He sat down on the floor and, after what seemed a long time, he heard them coming back down the stairs, this time more slowly than they had gone up. One of them was singing in a discordant voice. He put his eye back to the gap in the door. The singer was in front, carrying a plastic bag. The one behind had the box, which he was carrying under his arm like a trophy. He had on thick, leather motor-cycle gloves.

He was not exactly frightened. Rather, his nerves were strung up in expectation, as they had been when the secret police came to arrest him, taking him away while his mother screamed and tried to drag him back through the door. One of the soldiers knocked her out, then his sister, with a rifle butt. At that moment he had steeled himself to survive and bear witness. To test himself against evil, never giving way to fear. Even so, he prayed. He prayed for himself and his benefactors, for his mother and sister. For Yonah and his father, whose souls were now with God. He prayed for the souls of the men in the house; that they would receive the light and turn away from evil.

Hearing the front door slam, he counted to ten, then unlocked his own door. Taking a deep breath, he pulled up his hoodie and peeped out into the street. The men were twenty metres up on the right. Closing the door behind him, he followed them up the road.

By now, he knew his way around fairly well. Peggy had told him that this area had always been an immigrants' quarter, which explained the French street names, the Jewish synagogue, and the Bengali shops. But it was easy to lose direction in the narrow streets, so he concentrated hard and tried to guess where the men were going.

They turned right up the next street towards Bangla Town, so he crossed over to the other side. After a few minutes, the men abruptly crossed the road and headed back, running to avoid a truck that was bearing down on them. He heard the driver swear out of the window. Now both of them were hurrying back towards him, blocking the pavement. The older man, the one with the shaven head, was staring at him hard.

Isa pulled down his hood and, holding out his hands, he begged for coins as the younger one barged him aside, and they continued up the street.

His legs turned to jelly, and he steadied himself, one hand on the wall. His heart beat fast. He took some more breaths to calm himself and turned his head. The men seemed to know where they were going now: back towards the city. Staying well back, he followed them for two kilometres down the Commercial Road until they came to a vast crossroads with a Tube station entrance on the corner. The men went down the steps and Isa followed, watching them go through the ticket barrier. He had a ten-pound note on him, which Michael had given him to buy lunch, but he did not know how to use the ticket machine. He queued at the office. In front of him were three tourists who did not speak English well and were taking an age to make themselves understood. At that moment, Isa realised that he would have a similar problem, for he did not know his destination.

Looking over, he saw the ticket attendant had wandered over to the far side to assist a foul-mouthed man with a refused ticket. Instantly, Isa walked through the open gate and took the escalator down. At the bottom were two platforms: eastbound to the right, westbound to the left. He went to the left and came out onto the platform. They were not there. He ran round to the other platform. A train was just moving off and inside one carriage the men were holding straps that hung down from the roof.

The younger one staring vacantly out of the window; the older one holding the box.

He sat down and thought. He did not know how the tube system worked. Was it worth waiting for the next train, hoping he could catch up? He thought not. Yet he would have to try.

Just as he was puzzling it out another train came in. On impulse, he jumped on.

The train rumbled and creaked through a dark tunnel. Moments later, they came out into the open air at the next station. *Whitechapel*, he read. The doors opened and he peered out. People were getting off and heading for the stairs at the end of the platform. Others were getting on the train. The men were nowhere to be seen. He gave himself up to providence and waited for the doors to close.

A few minutes later, they reached the second station. *Stepney Green.* This time, the platform was deserted. Taking that as an omen, he stayed on.

It took longer to get to the third station. How vast was the city! At one end of the map over the carriage doors was Heathrow. That, he knew, had an airport. At the other end were places he had never heard of, but which he guessed were close to the docks. For the river ran through it all.

The train slowed, coming into *Mile End.* It crept along the platform, as if reluctant to stop. Then he saw the two men arguing with a police officer in a yellow vest and a ticket collector in a blue uniform. He wondered what the punishment was for having no ticket. He hoped they wouldn't put the men in a cell. Then he recalled he had no ticket himself.

Alighting, he sat down on a seat and pretended to wait for another train. Now and then glancing back at the group further along. The police officer was writing out a notice, while the inspector complained about the men. She seemed to be angry at something they had said to her, jabbing one of them in the chest with her finger.

At length, the group dispersed. The officer handed over a notice, which the shaven man pocketed in his jeans. Then the two of them walked off to the exit, accompanied by further volleys from the woman behind them. Isa counted to ten and followed them out. He entered an empty hall where there were two moving stairs: one going up, the other coming down. On the floor was a pink ticket with *London Underground* printed at the top. It had today's date. He picked it up and hoped for the best.

Just as he reached the top of the escalator, he saw the men going out through the street entrance. A couple in front were putting their tickets into a metal slot which opened the barrier for them to step through. He did the same, praying for success. But it did not open. From the corner of his eye, he saw another inspector coming towards him from the left: an untidy man with a ticket machine on his stomach. Isa turned to him, doing his best to look like someone unused to underground railways. The man pulled the ticket from the metal slot and inspected it. Isa swallowed.

"That bloody machine don't work," said the man.

Producing another ticket, he placed it in the slot. The barrier sprang open, and he stepped back to let Isa through.

"Enjoy your day, sir," added the man, waving him off.

"Blessings upon your head," said Isa.

He came out onto a busy crossroads. The men were a hundred metres away on the left, entering the road to their right. He sensed the men were close to home. Not wishing to follow too closely, he stopped at the newsagents outside the station and bought a packet of chocolate caramels. He sucked one slowly as he went over the pedestrian crossing after the men.

About six hundred metres down a long road which led under a railway bridge, the men went down a passageway alongside a penthouse block. Isa watched as the men entered the building.

Isa retreated to the canal path on the left, from which he could see a long apartment window on the first floor. The two men entered the room to be greeted by a third, a man wearing a kimono, who took the box from them and opened it. Taking out the marionette, he held it up and examined it. Put it down and took out the child's drawings from the box and inspected those. Then he began shouting at the other two.

Isa laughed as three gleaming motorbikes caught his eye in the parking lot. Taking a pencil from his pocket, he wrote the plate numbers on the back of the sweet paper. Adding the number of the block and the name of the road. That, and his descriptions of the men, would be sufficient.

He laughed again. God had not been idle today. Jumping down over the wall, he ambled back to the Tube station. He had been careful to note the cost of a ticket back to Aldgate. Making sure there was enough change left over from the purchase of the caramels. And there were still four left to enjoy on the journey back.

34

A Mist of Error

Marko, Andrej and Zivko drove up the City Road on their motorbikes towards Bonfire Street, passing through a CCTV camera to the left which surveyed them as they moved up the road. Just past the Artillery Barracks they turned off and parked their vehicles. After locking them, Marko signed to the others to follow him. Forty metres back around the corner was a Starbucks cafe and in they went.

"Order us three espressos," he said, as Zivko joined the queue. "We are going over there."

He pointed towards some empty tables in an alcove at the back.

A few minutes later, Zivko brought over a tray. Marko checked no one was eavesdropping and spoke in a fast, low voice.

"In a few days, we are going home. It's good, no?"

"Yes, good," said Andrej.

"First, there is some business to take care of. The Colonel wants it."

The others leaned forward, paying close attention to

their orders. Marko placed both hands together on the table and looked from one to the other.

"First, we have to clear up this mess. Two things."

He held up one finger.

"First, we find this man Pilcher, who has been hiding from us. We will visit him and make sure he understands he must pay us the money straight away."

He paused for emphasis.

"Quickly," he added. "Am I understood?"

"You mean, to frighten him?" asked Zivko.

"Yes. Frighten him. As much as possible."

Andrej shrugged.

"Of course, we will do whatever is necessary."

"What is the second thing?" asked Zivko.

"Our next task is to pay this joker back. The one who gave us this puppet. The puppet you two idiots took away with you when you visited his house."

"How were we to know what this thing looked like?" said Andrej. "You told us it was a carving. And that was what we found in the box."

"Pinocchio?" snapped Marko. "Is that what you thought I wanted? And a book full of pictures by a five-year-old?"

Andrej flapped his hand in exasperation. He knew better than to say anything more.

"So, we will teach this man a lesson, also," continued Marko. "Then we will take the carving and the sketches with it."

Zivko leered.

"Yes, we will teach him a few things. Him and his nice wife."

Marko glared at him.

"You will restrain yourself. Until I tell you otherwise."

"I don't understand," interjected Andrej. "What need have we for the documents if we kill them?"

"It would be better to have the documents," said Marko. "Without them, no one can trace the forgeries."

As an afterthought, he added:

"But we can kill them both, too. It is perhaps simpler that way."

Marko got up and clapped them both on the shoulders.

"But now we work. Follow me."

Outside, they put on their crash helmets. Five minutes later they walked into the office block in Bonfire Street. Marko and Andrej headed for the lift and pressed the button, then both of them turned to watch as Zivko pulled out a gun and summoned the guard with his fingers to come towards him. Made him sit on the sofa by the window, then stood guard over him. Satisfied, Marko got in the lift and went up.

On the third floor, they turned left and went into Pilcher's suite. Marko motioned to Andrej to stay where he was, while he went in to the first office. He moved fast for maximum effect. Walked around the desk where a woman in retro glasses was working on a computer screen. Yanked her off her feet by her arm and held up a finger to his lips. Then, dragging her to the door, he pointed at her bag and coat hanging beside the door.

"Bag, coat, go," he said.

The woman stared into his helmet shield with her mouth open. She looked bewildered. Lifting off her coat from the peg, he flung it at her. Then he picked up her bag and slapped it down on the coat she was holding in her arms. Turned her about and marched her to the door.

"Don't come back," he whispered. "There is no longer work for you here."

He pushed her out and checked her departure through

the door window. After a brief, confused, pause the woman fled to the lift in a lop-sided run.

He took off his helmet and went on to the end berth, followed by Andrej.

There was Pilcher, checking some figures on his desk with the aid of a calculator. Marko sat down in the chair opposite, while Andrej closed the door and aimed his gun at Pilcher's head.

Pilcher lifted his eyes, wide with alarm, and stuttered.

"What? You?"

"You think you can hide from us?" said Marko. "We are here for our money, *Mister* Pilcher."

"What, all of it?"

"All."

Marko produced a piece of paper with a Swiss bank account number written on it in pencil.

"Four million, one hundred thousand euros. Pay it now."

Pilcher shook his head, his mouth open.

"You can't be serious? Where am I going to find that kind of money in one afternoon?"

"Not my problem."

"Look, let me explain."

Marko glared at him, putting on a sinister smile.

"I mean, let me explain the problem to you," said Pilcher. "You have over three million invested in kiosks, pay-day loans, antiques and used cars. There's another nine hundred thousand invested in loans to an art gallery. I can transfer one million and three hundred thousand euros today. For the rest, I will need time to retrieve the loans and sell on the articles. Unless you want to take the painting with you?"

Marko slammed his fist on the desk.

"No! You do not explain things to me. I explain them

to you, funny man."

Pilcher jumped in his chair, quaking. His face had gone white. Marko had nothing but contempt for a man like this. A greedy man who drove around in a Mercedes, paid for by his family's money. A man who thought he could patronise them. Another corrupt Englishman.

"When you work for us, you do as we say."

"Dragan, be reasonable," he pleaded. "It's not the way this business works."

Andrej came out from behind and jammed his CZ hard against Pilcher's head. Marko waved his hand down. Andrej lowered the gun.

"It is very simple. You transfer the money to us, now, or…"

Marko looked across at Andrej, and back to Pilcher again.

"I can't, I can't do that," moaned Pilcher.

Pilcher put his head in his hands. He was shaking uncontrollably.

"I can't transfer money that isn't there. Please give me some time."

"Very well, show me," said Marko.

"Show you what?"

"Show me what you have in the account. The one in the Caymans."

Pilcher reached over, pulled the keyboard towards him, and typed. When he had finished, Marko turned the screen around to look at the statement.

"It says here, two million and one hundred thousand dollars."

"Yes, but not all that money is yours."

Marko shrugged and tapped the paper on the desk.

"Too bad. Transfer all of it."

Pilcher swallowed hard and typed again, looking at the

paper on the desk. Marko waited for the transaction to complete and turned back the screen in Pilcher's direction.

"Very well," he said, getting up. "You have three days to transfer the rest. I see now, one million, six hundred thousand euros. You agree?"

Pilcher said nothing.

"Plus, another two hundred thousand in interest."

The man sank his head further into his hands.

"You will transfer it all by Monday night, understand? Now get up."

Pilcher got to his feet, his hands in the air. Going round the desk, Marko took the carving knife from his jacket and held it to his face. Holding the jaw, Marko drew it down from the man's right eyebrow, all the way to the jaw. The blade was sharp and, at first, only a wafer-thin scar appeared. Then bubbles of blood appeared along the line of the scar, increasing until the blood ran in torrents onto Pilcher's suit and his white shirt.

"A reminder," said Marko, "of what we will do to you if you do not pay the money you owe us on time."

They turned for the exit. Disdaining the lift, they ran down the stairs. On the ground floor, Zivko was standing over the security guard and Pilcher's assistant who were sitting, subdued, on the sofa. As Marko hurried out, he motioned him to follow. Startled, Zivko put the gun back in his bag and, with a warning glance at the two hostages, he followed them out.

There was no one about in the street. Slowing to a fast walk, they marched towards the place where they had parked the bikes. Marko remembered it: they were on the street to the left that led to the barracks on the City Road. He had before wondered what it was doing there, for he had once seen soldiers coming in and out, yet London did not seem to be a city under siege.

They turned the corner. There were three police officers in the street, standing over the bikes. One was speaking into a radio. A police car was parked alongside, its blue light flashing.

Marko froze in confusion. Then he remembered they had not paid at the machine. It was strange that the English police would send a car all the way out here to check for parking tickets, but there were a lot of things about their country that made no sense.

He took off his helmet. The sergeant, a burly man in an indigo jacket and cap, caught sight of him and watched as they walked up. Marko hissed to the others.

"Remain silent."

Putting on a craven expression, he approached the officer who was standing in the middle of the road.

"Molim te sta nije u redu."

He gaped at the man, doing his best to look like a tourist.

The sergeant beckoned over the other two officers, who stood beside him on either side, watching them all with suspicion.

"These your bikes?" he said, glancing back at the parked vehicles.

The one on the left was speaking still faster into the radio below his chin. At that moment, Marko realised that something had gone terribly wrong. These men were not here about parking tickets.

"Answer me please, sir," the officer repeated. "Do these motor-cycles belong to you?"

Marko could hear the other two breathing hard behind him. Time slowed to a halt. What to do?

Marko broke and ran, knocking over Zivko as he did so. Who, recovering his feet, hared after him. Andrej had anticipated them both and was running on ahead. Marko threw away his helmet, which bounced off the wall, and rolled back down the street. Concentrating hard, he sprinted, overtaking Andrej. From behind he heard the police officers get into the car, which sped up behind them. Over his shoulder, the other two were still running hard, but falling behind.

He ran back into the long, narrow street, partly blocked by scaffolding. The police car could not follow them there. As he ran past Bonfire Street on the left, he heard the car screech to a halt behind them.

He turned to look. Zivko was on the ground holding his leg, the car having swerved in front of him. He looked like he had broken his ankle. Two officers were getting out to arrest him. The other was on the radio in the driver's seat, staring straight at him.

Andrej ran past, his fists pumping the air. Putting his head down, Marko sprinted on after him.

Two hundred metres up, they came to Moorgate and stopped, panting for breath. Ahead was the Tube station. Andrej gestured to it and bent over to catch his breath, waiting for Marko to decide. Just then a second police car, with its siren on, drove past on the other side. It was too risky to stay on the main road. Just as he was bracing himself to head back into the warren from which they had emerged, a black cab stopped at the pavement. A woman got out and paid the driver.

"Come," he said to Andrej.

They got in and flopped on the back seat. Another police car came by, this time with an ambulance behind it. Poor Zivko, he thought. Things would go hard with him.

"Where to, mate?" said the driver, looking at him in his rear mirror.

"Spitalfields," said Marko. "Hurry."

35

A Night At The Opera

The performance drew to a close in The Bleachers' Hall, close to Spitalfields to the east, and the Bank of England to the west. A charity fund-raising dinner on behalf of *The Artists' Support Fund*, sponsored by the Wuhan Bank. The men in black ties, the women in gowns, they sat at dinner tables in a domed hall held up by marble columns. On the walls were standing portraits of kings & queens of recent history; bloated, dowdy figures who stared down in disapproval. That night were excerpts from *L'Orfeo*, performed by opera singers in a variety of masks. Orpheus with his lyre; Eurydice, his wife waiting to be brought back from the dead; Pluto, god of the underworld.

Mournful voices accompanied by harps, violas, and harmoniums wafted up to the gallery where sat more spectators, less expensively dressed. Their faces lit up by the glare from the spotlights below.

Cosima Bayes sat at the principal table placed before the performers. On her left sat the Head of the Bank, on her right the Master of the Worshipful Company of Bleachers. Opposite, with his back to the ensemble, sat

Perry Winter, Secretary of State for Justice and Guest of Honour, whom, she noticed, was nodding off. He was too far away for her to kick. She hoped he wouldn't disgrace them both.

Her mind was not on the stately, melancholy music, pleasing though that was. Instead, she thought about the task ahead of her. For tonight she was going to have to ask Perry a great favour; one that might save Tristan yet.

It was only the week before that Cosima had got the entire story. That the Italian police had arrested Carlo Casiraghi on suspicion of forgery; that Pilcher's loans were laundered money, and Tristan had lied when he told her he was using Angus and Lou's money to pay them off. All this she had been told from the chalet in Zermatt, where Tristan was holding a party. She could hear his noisy guests in the background.

Fate had set her over her brother in a bond of love that no disaster could break, beginning with their parents' divorce when he was just eight years old. She, who had been fourteen then, had felt pity for him, alone and neglected in their father's house in Chelsea. She had vowed in that moment to protect him, no matter what.

Yet the hard, clear, rational side of her mind saw that Tristan was no good. In fact, he was hopeless. As a boy he was thoughtless, wild, accident prone. As he grew up, it had fallen to her lot to become his guardian. For their mother had early seen that Cosima alone could control him, where no nanny, or tutor, or parent ever could. Just the other day, Mummy had come to Onslow Gardens to plead with her to 'do something' about Tristan. Behind them stood a long trail of transgressions: expulsions from school, job dismissals, unpaid gambling debts and parking fines, paternity suits, a conviction for cocaine possession, a spell in the Priory. She had settled with angry creditors, ex-girlfriends holding babies, and a string of magistrates. Found him another job and set him back on his feet again. Setting up the Gallery had been her idea; she had made him use his trust fund money to do it. Now that, too, looked like sinking. But she could not give him up, no matter how clearly she saw his faults. He was still the child who adored and depended upon her. Besides, managing people - especially men - was her forte.

The final aria drew to a close. Voices and music rising to a crescendo of sorrow, before gradually muting.

The assembly stood up to clap. Some from relief, others from appreciation. The singers put aside their masks, joined hands and bowed three times. The ceiling lights came on. A few guests headed for the lobby, while others lingered at their tables, hoping to squeeze more joy from the evening. Cosima waited for Perry to shake hands with the Master. When he turned for the exit, she picked up a fold in her gown and followed closely behind. For everything was timed to the second on the departure of a minister of the Crown. An aide joined them in the lobby, holding their coats, falling in as they headed for the black Jaguar XJ parked outside the front door, its rear door held open by another aide. Cameras flashed as Peter waited for her to be seated, then got in beside her. The other aide got in the front passenger seat and slammed the door shut. Two police officers on motorcycles held back the traffic as the car sped away towards St. Paul's.

"I'm glad that's over," said Winter, settling down into the cream leather seat. "Rather long, wasn't it?"

"When we were children, my father used to make us go with him when he had a box at Covent Garden. He was a huge Wagner fan."

Winter looked puzzled.

"Richard Wagner," she repeated. "Most of his operas are over four hours long. One of them is six hours."

"Are they really?"

"After a while, you get used to their being so long. It adds to their beauty."

"I prefer Gilbert & Sullivan myself. Some wonderful tunes in those."

He took her hand and stared out of the darkened window at the fog. The car purred smoothly on past the Cathedral, along Fleet Street and the Strand, then under Admiralty Arch and up the Mall, where Buckingham Palace was lit up before them in a misty, golden glow. A few minutes later, the car drew up outside Perry's flat in Eaton Place.

The aide came round and held up an umbrella against the drizzle for her. Winter let them in with his key into a narrow hall, from which stairs ascended to the apartment. Dismissing the aide, he followed her up the steps.

"Pour me a drink, will you?" she said, going into the bedroom along the corridor.

She took off her dress and hung it up carefully on a hanger. Unfastening her bra, but keeping on her white stockings, she went into the adjoining bathroom. Standing before the wide mirror above the marble counter, she examined her face. Her wide, grey eyes stared back at her, cool and impassive. She knew they intrigued people, and she had trained herself to hold their stare without blinking.

She put on a white silk dressing gown and checked the fit, standing sideways to the mirror. Breast enlargements were vulgar, she thought, although she knew some in her circle who'd had them done. But it was what you wore that was important and the silk she was wearing now would emphasise their shape, as well as her long legs.

She looked closer at her face. It was much too pale: like

275

that of a corpse. Reaching for the foundation, she massaged some into her cheeks and re-applied her lipstick. That would have to do for now.

A small camera twinkled above the mirror. She wondered whether Perry was watching on the screen he kept in his office. All the better if he was.

Perry's flat had three bedrooms, a sitting room, a second reception room, a dining room, a kitchen, and a sizeable bathroom. Furnished throughout in cream, white and grey. She knew that, for she had found it for him. As she had the paintings placed on the walls and the abstract sculptures on the tables. In the dining room was a Casiraghi over the chimney piece. She had selected it partly to match the decor, for it showed a young woman in a lavender robe, holding up an urn before a sun setting below purple hills.

Winter was waiting for her in the sitting room, minus his black tie, his white dinner shirt open at the chest. He held out a small Armagnac. She sipped it, and sat down on the sofa, facing a mantle in white marble, below which an electric fire burned. Winter sat beside her and contemplated it.

"Perry, I must speak to you about Tristan."

"O Lord, must you?"

"Yes, I must."

"What's he done now?"

She told him about the events of the past few days. The thuggish police officer who had come to the gallery to question Tristan; his allegations of forgery and money-laundering; the impending freeze on the bank account; the threat to confiscate the gallery's assets.

"Did Tristan know about the forgeries?"

"Not in the least. He is entirely innocent."

"What about the money leant to him by this man, Pilcher? Did he know where that came from?"

"He says not."

"Do you believe him?"

"I know Tristan has been foolish. But he's not a criminal."

"What's he doing in Zermatt?"

"Skiing. We have a chalet there."

"In December?"

"There's no law against going early in the season. Or are you thinking of drafting one?"

Her eyes rested on his, half in challenge, half in mockery. Winter grunted.

"What do you want me to do?"

"I want you to suspend the police investigation into the forgery allegations."

"For what purpose? If Tristan is innocent, the investigation will prove that."

"If this investigation continues, Tristan's reputation will be ruined, and the police will close the gallery. They will drag my name into it. Yours, too. Where is the justice in that?"

Winter held up his hand for her to stop. Sat back, thinking, staring at the ceiling.

"You have a point," he muttered after a pause.

"Perry, the police will capture the men who did this when they follow up the money-laundering trail. The killers of my ex-husband, too. Justice will be served that way, without harming innocent people."

"All right," he said. "I'll make a couple of telephone calls in the morning. But I can't promise anything."

"Thank you."

"Now there is something I want to ask you."

"What is it?"

He placed his glass on a side-table and turned to her. His cheeks, red from the lurid glow of the fire contrasted with his fierce, blue eyes.

"I've been thinking it's time we got married. What do you think about that?"

Cosima had hoped that question wouldn't arise. For she had foreseen that the favour asked would presuppose a closer union. Even now, she didn't know what her answer could be.

"Why do you want to marry me?"

"Let me get you another drink."

She held up her glass and watched him take it over to the tray. He had a stiff walk she hadn't noticed before, as if the weight of his torso was too much for his hips. His sandy hair was greying, too. Still, he was a distinguished-looking man with a set jaw, a man used to exercising power. Not one who would take 'no' for an answer easily.

"You know, I've been divorced a few years now," he said, returning to the sofa. "A man in my position really needs someone beside him."

"But..."

Winter held up his palm for silence.

"Let me finish."

He took a large swallow of whiskey.

"There will be a cabinet reshuffle soon. I gather my name is in the hat for Chancellor. That's only one step away from Number Ten. I want you beside me if, or rather when, that happens."

"I see."

"I have grown rather fond of you," he added, slipping her a shy smile. "I think we get on rather well. Of course, neither of us are young anymore. So, ours would be a mature union. One based on mutual respect and experience of the world. What do you say?"

"Can I think about it?"

"Of course," said Winter. "Take as much time as you like. And now…"

He put down his glass and looked hard at her breasts, which were half uncovered. His lips apart, his eyes aflame with desire.

"I think it's also time we went to bed," he said.

He lunged forward and seized her by the shoulders. Kissed her hard until she was breathless. She realised in that moment what her answer would have to be. Hitching up her gown, she turned to the bedroom, her back straight, her finger beckoning him forward.

36

Final Call

Peace had descended on himself and Peggy. Helped along when he threw away the morphine packs, vowing to buy no more. Helped, also, by Isa explaining the decision to trail the men was his alone, then telling her a funny story about picking up a used ticket on the Underground in order to follow the men out of the station. That had made her laugh. Afterwards, Michael had taken him up to Liverpool Street to get him a new phone. Explaining to Peggy that he didn't want him running around after any more criminals without some means of contacting them. After that, Isa had disappeared for the afternoon. First calling his mother in the Sudan where she was now in a refugee camp, then to arrange a meeting with some other Eritreans he had befriended, who were living and working up Dartford way.

Now they were in bed together. In his bedroom, the one with the flowering cherry trees.

"That was nice," he said, stroking her face.

"Mmm."

"It's been a long time."

She snuggled up closer to him so that he could feel her breath on his chest.

"All good things are worth waiting for," she said, putting up her lips for him to kiss.

"Stay there and we could do it again in a while."

"That's a middle-aged thing to say."

"Aren't we middle-aged now?"

"You might be. I'm not."

"We could talk instead," said Michael.

"What about?"

"Us, of course."

He felt her breathing harder.

"Let's not," she said, eventually.

"Will you go to Blackwater?"

"I'm still going."

"I've had an idea about that. Why don't we sell this house?"

"You'd sell this house? Why?"

"Because we've outgrown it. Besides, you've never been happy here."

"Where would we go?"

"Anywhere you like. Some place with a workshop for you. Room for your mother and Isa to stay."

"In London?"

"No. Somewhere they aren't 'redeveloping'. Except it would have to be near a train line. Suffolk maybe, or Essex."

"Why do you need a train service?"

"Commuting back to the University three days a week. I decided to accepted Julia's offer."

"How did you change your mind?"

"Because I realised that I'm never going to stop reflecting on existence. I might as well do that at a university and get paid for it. Besides, the experiences of the past few weeks have given me some fresh material to think about."

"Such as what?"

"Do you really want me to talk about philosophy?"

She slapped his chest, hard.

"No. I don't. Just tell me what experiences you mean."

"Over the past few days, I felt a connection to something greater than me, that I never had before. Something that lives in me, and through me."

"You mean, Fate?"

"No, not fate. Something more like a universal consciousness."

"Does the feeling make you happy?"

"No. But it's made me understand that personal choice wasn't as important as I thought it was; it's participation in events that is the important thing, even when you don't understand them. That's what I want to explore."

It had always been a quiet room, for behind them was the garden and beyond that the disused churchyard. But the silence grew deeper as he waited for Peggy to make her mind up.

"Let's do it," she said.

They drew closer. It was perhaps the closest to happiness he would ever come.

A few minutes later he heard the mobile buzzing beside him, and he picked it up.

"Who is that?" she asked.

"It's Gredic. I'd better take it."

He put on a gown and went next door to stand by the window. By now there was a thick fog outside in the street. Like a grey gas seeping into the windows, doors, and chimneys of the darkened houses opposite. Blotting out what was left of the sunset.

"What's up, Gary?"

"We found the three motor-bikes Isaias identified on the City Road this afternoon and arrested one of the men. The other two got away."

"Are they the killers?"

"Could be. We're looking for them now."

Michael digested the information.

"Thing is, Mike, I'm going to ask one of my men to look after you. His name's Jack Painter. A sound bloke. He'll be around to see you in about an hour. Here's his number."

"Are things that bad?"

Gredic sighed.

"We don't know. But if these are the men the Dorset police are looking for, then it's best to play safe."

"You say they're still in London?"

"We don't know where they are. But two men matching our descriptions were seen getting into a cab in Moorgate. That's what? A mile and a half from you?"

"Do you think we should leave the house?"

"Yes. Do it."

There came the sound of a commotion from behind Gredic in the office. An urgent voice, telling him about some fresh development. He caught the name 'Pilcher'. Then Gredic's voice came back on.

"I'll have to go now, something's come up."

Abruptly, the line went dead. He turned to see Peggy waiting for him in the doorway.

"I overheard that," she said.

"It's just for a few days," said Michael. "This house won't be safe until we change the door and window locks. Maybe not even then, if these people really want to get at us."

"But what are the police doing about catching these men?"

"They're out looking for them now. Gredic's sending someone over to keep watch on the place."

"I can't leave Mom."

"I know. We'd better go over there and persuade her to come with us."

"Come where?"

"Blackwater. They won't find us there."

"The cottage is too small for the four of us."

"We'll work something out. But we have to get going. I'll help you pack."

They showered and got to work. Michael packed a suitcase for himself and Isa, leaving Peggy to hers. Then Peggy went downstairs to get linen from the laundry.

Michael called Isa. No pick up, so he texted instead.

We are leaving London. Call me when you get this.

Michael set about collating the things he didn't want to leave behind. The plastic bag with the valuables, minus the morphine packs, was still on his desk, as was the carving on the table. The yellow light from the street lamp outside the window lit up the room in mournful splendour.

Looking at the sculpture, he was reminded of how it had all started, nineteen months before, when he had contemplated it in his mother's old workshop, before it was converted to a kitchen. Where he packed it up for Wilf, who took it to Italy hoping to revive his art. A search that would lead instead to a crime, chaos, and death. Yet also a new beginning and an enlightenment. Of sorts.

He looked again at the inscription on the urn.

Never at any time was I not, nor thou.

He looked up and seemed to see his mother standing by the window. She was wearing the same kaftan she always wore; the one made of calico. She was staring down into the street, around which the fog swirled. Slowly, she turned and held his gaze. She was not smiling as she had been when she saw him off to school for the last time on the doorstep. Rather, she looked thoughtful, as if seeing complications ahead which would have to be addressed in time. Then the phantom disappeared.

He got up and went out onto the landing. Stared over the banister and down the stairs towards the front door. There was a brooding hush of the kind that descended on a theatre audience, just as the curtain lifted on the final act.

Then he heard a scuffle far below. The sound of a chair knocked over. Followed by the tread of steps coming up from the kitchen. He ducked down below the coverlet Peggy had draped over the balustrade and watched.

Two men, one of them pushing Peggy, went into the front room. Stealing away, keeping his head down, he went back into the office. Groped for his phone and dialled the number Gredic had given him. It rang and rang without answer. Then he heard more steps coming up to the landing below. He hid the phone away beneath a cushion and picked up a book.

37

A Stitch Up

Gredic and Painter were halfway through their interview with Ronny Pilcher, his solicitor sitting beside him. Over the left side of his face was a white bandage with bloody patches, held on by surgical tape. His lips quivered, and he stared wildly around the interview room.

"I've told you all I know," said Pilcher. "You can't ask for more than that."

"You admit to investing money on behalf of the Puma syndicate?" asked Painter.

Pilcher looked at his lawyer, a balding, bespectacled man in a pinstriped suit, who nodded to him to continue.

"I didn't know the money was crime money. And I'd never heard of this syndicate."

"That being five years ago?" asked Painter.

"That's right."

"Who was it approached you?" asked Gredic.

"He called himself the Colonel."

"Dmitrijevic?"

"That's him."

"Where did you meet him?"

"In Vienna. I can't remember the name of the hotel."

"Try harder."

"It was on the same street as the Opera House. Built like a palace."

"Was he staying there?"

"He told me he was."

"Describe him to us."

After Painter had finished writing, Gredic took over.

"What did this Dmitrijevic tell you he was?"

"A businessman from Belgrade. Construction, financial services, retail, all sorts."

"And he offered you two million euros to invest on his behalf?"

"Initially, yes."

"Why you? Why London?"

"He said he needed a safe pair of hands. London, because they wanted their money in sterling."

"Did you check any of this information before you invested on his behalf?"

"He seemed like a respectable man. I didn't think it was necessary."

"Is this the man?" asked Painter, putting a photograph on the table. An old snapshot of a bald man shaped like a beer barrel, wearing a tracksuit and a baseball cap.

Pilcher put on his glasses and scrutinised the picture.

"I can't be sure," he replied. "But it might be."

"When did you realise Dmitrijevic was a criminal?" asked Gredic.

Pilcher bent his head forward while his lawyer whispered something in his ear.

"No comment," said Pilcher.

"I thought you were going to tell us all you knew?" said Painter.

"My client has the right not to offer comment on leading observations of that sort," said the lawyer.

"What is your purpose in coming here today, Ronny?" said Gredic.

"To help the police with their inquiries."

"Is that all?"

Pilcher's eyes narrowed in cunning.

"Now that I'm a key witness, I'll need police protection. I mean, you won't want to have me killed now."

He put his hand to his cheek, as if checking for fresh blood leaks.

"You're not a key witness yet, Ronny."

"Why not?"

Gredic sighed.

"Let's start again with the question you refused to answer. When did you realise the identity of the people giving you this money to invest?"

Pilcher looked first at his lawyer, then at Gredic, then at the table.

"I suspected it a couple of years ago. Will that do?"

"You knew Dmitrijevic was the head of the Puma syndicate?"

"I came to realise it, yes."

"You continued to receive money from these people, knowing that it might come from the proceeds of crime?"

There was a long pause.

"Yes."

Gredic turned to Painter, who acknowledged what Pilcher had disclosed. The solicitor breathed out slowly and stared at the ceiling. Pilcher himself gazed at Gredic, waiting for him to speak.

"These men that did this to you," said Gredic, "Who are they?"

"There's three of them, all Serbian."

Pilcher gave him some descriptions, which matched those that Mike had given Gredic the week before last, and that of the man they had arrested, now languishing in a hospital ward under guard. Gredic wondered at Mike's intuition, which he had doubted before.

"I was never told their names," added Pilcher, "apart from the leader. His name is Dragan."

"That's not his real name," said Painter. "That's probably just the one in his passport."

Pilcher's mouth gaped in outrage.

"You mean he could be anybody?"

Gredic smiled at the irony. It wasn't the first time he had noticed that criminals who spent years flouting the law, turned self-righteous when others broke the rules.

"It ain't playing straight," added Pilcher, fingering his bandage. "It's about time he was locked up."

"Must be the first time we've agreed on anything, Ronny," said Gredic. "Any idea where they are staying?"

Pilcher shook his head.

"For all I know, they might be staying with the Salvation Army."

Gredic turned to Painter and nodded for him to turn off the sound recorder.

"Ronald," said Gredic. "I am going to ask you to wait in here while I speak to my superior officer. You are not under arrest, but it is in your interest to stay here until I come back. You understand?"

If he had been capable of pity for the criminals he met, Gredic might have felt it for Pilcher now. Despair written over his face, like a man told he had months to live. Getting up, he left the room, signing to the constable in the corner that she was to remain there.

Back in the office, Gredic and Painter conferred.

"What do you think, Skipper?"

"We've got enough to charge him," Gredic replied. "But there's still a long way to go before we have a solid case. What we need is a proper audit trail. One that traces the money back to this syndicate in Belgrade."

"That could take months," said Painter. "He's been using shell companies with different bank accounts to disguise that trail."

"I know, but if we offer him protection, he might cooperate. We can make a start by freezing Pilcher's company assets, and the assets of that gallery."

"You want me to get going on that?"

"No. Wait until I've spoken to Gallop. There's something else I want you to do this evening."

"What's that?"

"This 'Dragan' is still on the loose. We need to find him. I want you to go to an address in Foulard Street and sit in with the other witness. His name's Michael Gereon. If he's there, stay with him until I come over. Otherwise, sit outside. If you see any sign of these men, call for reinforcements."

"Will do, Skip," said Painter, putting on his jacket.

"Anyone know where Gilly is?" Gredic called out to the room.

"She's next door with the DI, sir," said Janet, the Administrator, looking over her screen.

"What's she doing in there?"

"No idea, sir. She's been in there nearly an hour."

Gredic picked up the case file and went round to knock on the door.

"Yes?" shouted Gallop.

When Gredic went in, Gallop was leaning back in his recliner, his hands together on his chest, laughing at something Halliday was telling him. Silence descended. Halliday adjusted her skirt without looking round. Gallop turned to him with a look of inquiry.

"What is it, Sergeant?"

"It's about the Gallery case. You have a minute?"

"Come in. Sit down. Let's see what you've got for us today."

"In private?" asked Gredic, looking down at Halliday.

"I'd like Detective Halliday to sit with us. She has been assisting you with this investigation, has she not?"

"As you say," said Gredic.

He briefed Gallop on the interview with Pilcher, ending with his confession.

Gallop leaned back still more, listening as if he had his mind on something else. A complacent grin on his face.

"If it's all right with you," concluded Gredic, "I'm going to caution Ronald Pilcher and get a court order to seize these assets."

"No," said Gallop.

"No, what?"

"You will not do that. There have been some developments and I'm taking you off the case."

"What developments?"

"The investigation into the forgery allegation is suspended. Pending further inquiries. I have that from upstairs. You will take no further action in that quarter."

"The Commissioner gave that order?"

Gallop pointed up with his finger above his head, as if referring to a spirit in the sky.

"Higher than that. All the way up to the top."

"What about the money laundering investigation?"

"That is not your case, Sergeant. Your brief was to investigate the forgery allegation. The National Crime Agency advises we should leave investigations into organised crime involving foreign nationals to them. I have assigned Detective Halliday to liaise with them on the evidence we have collected so far."

Halliday turned to look at Gredic. A smile of triumph on her face. Be careful what you wish for, thought Gredic.

"And what about these other witnesses, the Gereons?" asked Gredic. "We still have two killers on the loose. Who's protecting them?"

"As I understand it," replied Gallop, looking at Halliday, "the men threatening these witnesses are also prime suspects in a murder inquiry being carried out by the Dorset Police. I think we can leave it to them to find these men, don't you? Which brings me to another matter."

Gallop slid down from his recliner and leaned over his desk.

"Halliday here tells me you have compromised yourself with Doctor Gereon. I believe he is actually a friend of yours?"

"That's immaterial," said Gredic. "I didn't know who he was until I went round to question him about the Schoenman allegation."

"Do you usually take witnesses to the pub while you are questioning them, Sergeant?"

"I was off duty."

"Listen to me, Sergeant. I've said it before and I'll say it again. You are a loose cannon in this station. I've warned you before about your casual disregard for the rules. This will be my final warning. Any more rule-breaking from you and I will have you suspended."

"You finished? Sir?" said Gredic, mustering as much contempt as he could.

"No," said Gallop. "You are to have no further contact with Dr. Gereon, or his wife. That is a direct order."

Gallop looked up and folded his arms. Waiting, Gredic thought, for him to lose his temper.

He got up, looking down with disgust at the pair of them

"I'll leave you two to carry on with your little chat then," he said, before heading for the exit.

"Stupid twats," he muttered, in a voice just loud enough to be heard, as he closed the door.

38

End Game

As Peggy came out of the laundry the two men were waiting for her in the conservatory, into which they had stolen once more from the garden. Andrej stepped forward and seized her by the neck. Forced her into the kitchen with the gun to her head. Then up the stairs into the unfinished library.

Marko caught sight of the carving standing on the table and picked it up. It was smaller than he had imagined, no longer than the length of his forearm. A yellow knick-knack of a woman offering up something in her hands, as if she were sacrificing to the gods. A superstitious object you could find in any flea market, it filled him with distaste. Yet it was a necessary find. He would retrieve it later, for he had other business to complete first.

Going up the stairs and out into the hall, he stopped to listen. All was quiet. In the front room, Andrej was holding his gun to the woman's head. Whose mouth was open in terror, her arms covering her chest.

"Where is your husband?" he asked.

Peggy pointed up.

"He's upstairs?"

She swayed, as if she were going to faint.

"Stay with her," he ordered Andrej.

He turned to Peggy and put a finger to his lips.

"If you make a sound, he will shoot."

Slowly, he went up the stairs. On the landing were three doors, all closed. Looking up, he saw a movement in one of the upper rooms. A figure in blue. Still more slowly, he ascended the next flight. On the wall next to one door was a portrait of a woman in a red hat. Looking at it made him feel sick. He promised himself he would never look at another painting or a statue, so long as he lived.

There, in the middle room, was the man he was looking for, reading a book.

Pretending surprise at the intrusion, but with his heart thumping in his chest, Michael turned to look at the man in the grey overcoat at the corner of the stair. The man he had seen in the hotel lift two weeks before. He was more graceful than he remembered. He didn't look much like a gangster; more like a martial arts teacher. Like a younger version of Patrick, in fact. The association hardened his resolve. Throwing the book down, he made to get up.

"What are you doing here?"

Marko raised his gun.

"Sit down and shut up."

Pushing himself up the handrail on the stair, Marko came around, keeping the weapon trained on Michael. Motioning Michael to sit back on his chair, he checked the room. Gesturing to Michael to stay where he was, he sat down on the sofa next to the paperback copy of the *Bhagavad Gita* Michael had thrown there.

"Where is my wife?" said Michael.

"One of my men is keeping her quiet downstairs."

"I want to see her."

"You will. When I have finished speaking to you."

"What do you want?" repeated Michael.

"I want to know why you think you can insult me."

"You mean with the marionette I substituted for the carving?"

Marko waited for him to continue.

"That wasn't really an insult. More like a deception. I didn't want you to have it."

"Why is it so important that you risk your life for it?"

"Because it was my mother's. She was killed in this very house by someone just like you."

"And what is it you think I am?"

"A murderer. Isn't that what you are?"

Marko got up and punched him, hard.

"You should keep your mouth shut," said Marko. "You speak of things you do not understand. You and your meddling friends."

Michael's head spun from the force of the blow, which had broken his cheekbone. A throbbing numbness was there, and he lost the focus in his eyes. For a moment there seemed to be two men standing over him, shouting in his ear. When his vision cleared, he felt sick, but he forced himself to stay calm, for Peggy's sake.

"You know the carving is no use to you anymore?" said Michael.

"What do you say?"

"The police have been here and taken away the sketchbooks. That is all the proof they need about those forgeries. Taking the carving away won't make any difference."

"You are lying."

"You can see for yourself. I have a receipt."

"Show it to me."

"It's down in the kitchen. In the drawer behind the carving."

"If you are stalling me, it will be the worse for you and your wife."

Marko trained the gun on him once more. Motioning him out of the chair with the fingers of his left hand.

"Walk out of the door, but slowly. Then, turn around. Go down the stairs and don't do anything stupid."

When they got to the bottom of the stairs, Michael could see through the open door where the shaven-headed thug was standing over Peggy, who was staring at the livid welt under Michael's eye. She made to embrace him, but the man stayed her with his hand and looked at Marko, who was right behind Michael.

"Andrej," said Marko. "We are going down into the basement. We will go first. You will follow us with the woman."

In that moment, Michael knew these men were going to kill them. For why else would the man call Andrej by his name, unless he knew there could be no witnesses?

Michael turned to look at the nameless man, who returned his gaze. On his face was a cold smile of contempt as he raised his gun to beckon him out of the room.

He had always wondered how he would face the moment of death when it appeared directly. Strange, now, to discover that rage was boiling up inside. He, who had spent most of his life in indifference to human affairs. Too late, he saw now that he had been mistaken. Beneath his disconnection was a terrible hurt, something that had been there before his mother was killed. Something to do with always being treated like a puppet freak, whose happiness was of no importance to anyone; whose life could be snuffed out as casually as boiling a lobster for dinner. In that moment, too, he realised he was going to have to kill the man facing him with a gun. His own life was not important anymore. For it was better that Peggy lived rather than himself. Hadn't she given him the only love he had ever had since his mother departed?

As he walked out of the door, he turned back to Peggy, who was staring after him, looking as if she might cry.

"I love you," he said.

Before she could reply, Andrej prodded her in the back with his gun.

"No talking."

He made his way to the kitchen. Switching on the light by the door, he descended the steps. By now the numbness in his cheek had faded and his eye-socket was electric with pain. Halfway down, he caught sight of the carving standing on the table close to the edge. In the flickering light, it reminded him of the woman he used to see wandering about at night with her blown-out candle. At that moment he was filled with anguish at the thought that death was coming to this room, and that he was helpless to stave it off.

Then he caught sight of Isa crouching, half hidden beneath the wooden steps, holding a spade and waiting for the two men to come down. Casting his eyes away, he walked over and stood by the table. Waited for them to come out to the floor, first the leader, then Peggy, then Andrej, who lowered his head to negotiate past the sloped ceiling. Now that he saw their oncoming nemesis, his agitation gave way to a strange feeling of exaltation.

Everything that followed happened in slow motion, as he waited for the fore-ordained moment to arrive. Watched as Isa tripped Andrej with the spade, a vicious shoving moment into the back of the man's knees. As Andrej crashed down the steps, the gun flew out of his hand. Seizing the carving, Michael brought it down on Andrej's head as he crouched on the floor. The skull broke with a slow crunch as the carving shattered. Berserk, he swung round and jabbed the stump as hard as he could into Marko's face, breaking his nose.

Startled, Marko stepped back, ignoring the blood streaming over his mouth. Time slowed down still more as he raised his gun, just as Isa crept out from below stairs and made ready to throw himself at him. Michael reached down for the gun on the floor. Taking careful aim, Marko shot Michael in the chest as he made to pick it up. Peggy screamed.

As Marko aimed the second shot Gredic appeared at the top of the stairs, with Painter close behind. Taking aim with his own Glock, he shot Marko twice. The first bullet went through his cheek and out through his nose, breaking it again. The second, which proved to be fatal, went through the left temple, knocking him unconscious and spinning him to the floor.

Michael lay on the floor in a dream state. The bullet had entered his chest and exited at the back, but there was no pain. Only muffled voices and the sensation of waiting for something to come and take him away. Then he thought he was staring down at his body on the floor of the kitchen. Blood spreading out on the floor underneath his back. Peggy hunched over him on her knees; Isa on the other side, praying for him. Gredic was taking his throat pulse, while Painter called for an ambulance.

From behind him, further up, a tunnel opened and he drifted towards it. He felt he wanted very much to go through it and explore what might be on the other side. Somewhere beyond, his mother was surely waiting.

Yet it was intolerable to leave now, while Peggy was crying so hard.

Then the tunnel closed up and he lost consciousness.

39

Escape From The Plague

"How are you in yourself?" asked Gredic.

They were in Michael's ward on the thirteenth floor of the Whitechapel Hospital during the afternoon visiting slot. Michael's bed was by the window. Outside, snow was falling; the first of the New Year.

"I'm bored. But the doctors keep saying they want to do more tests before they send me home."

"You're lucky to be alive. Good job the bullet went through your lung, and not your heart."

Michael grimaced. The bullet had collapsed a lung, but surgery had led to septicaemia, and he almost died a second time in the hospital. He was still feeling weak from the infection.

"I've bought you some nuts. You allowed those?"

"Give me some."

Gredic shook some on his hand, then handed over the bag.

"What's new?" asked Michael.

"I've handed in my notice."

"Don't you want to wait until the inquiry is over?"

The City of London police had suspended Gredic from duty, pending the investigation into the shooting of Marko Dmitrijevic. But Gallop had made it known that he wouldn't be welcome back in SECU, now that Gillie Halliday was taking over.

"No. Bollocks to 'em."

"Going into the security business?"

"Next month. My own office in Cornhill. A black Mercedes. And double the money I was getting before."

"Hope it makes you happy."

"It's made Debbie happy. She's already planning a cruise in the Caribbean."

"Are you still in touch with the department?"

Gredic gave him a pitying look, as he used to do when Michael said something naff while they were out with the Wall Street Gang.

"You don't stop being a copper when you leave the force. Jack Painter keeps me up to date with what goes on."

"What happened to the Bayes Gallery?"

"It closed down for a while. Now it's reopening under that bird that's marrying the Chancellor of the Exchequer."

"What about Tristan Bayes?"

"Charges dismissed. His brief made it look like he was an innocent victim of deception. He's in Dubai now, setting up another art gallery."

"Isn't *anyone* going to be convicted?"

"Ronnie Pilcher will probably get three years. The others are all dead or awaiting deportation."

"Doesn't sound much like justice," said Michael, thinking of Schoenman's mourning widow, and Wilf's body still lying in the mortuary, awaiting the coroner's final verdict.

Gredic tossed his head in disgust but said nothing.

Stared out of the window at the snow, falling more thickly on the block of flats over the road.

"What are you going to do now, Mike?" he asked.

"Peggy and I want to make a fresh start. We're moving out."

"Where to?"

"Suffolk. My mother-in-law owns a cottage there, and we're going to have a look around for another place to live."

"What will you do there?"

"Not much, for a while. The doctors say it will take me a few months to recover. But I'm hoping to be well enough to start back at the university in the spring."

"Why not recover in Spitalfields?"

"Peggy's never liked that house so we're putting it on the market. Besides, it's best we get out of London now this plague from China is on its way over."

"Isaias going with you?"

"No. He's going into business with some friends in Dartford. He's coming over to say goodbye this afternoon."

"You will stay in touch?" said Gredic, after a pause.

Michael had never thanked Gredic for saving his life and he wasn't going to start now. He knew him well enough to know that he disliked effusions.

"One of the few good things to come out of this mess was you, Gary. When I'm on my feet, I want you to come and explore the pubs in Blackwater with me. Bring your family over, too."

"Bring it on," said Gredic.

Just then, Peggy's head passed by the window on her way to the ward entrance. Followed by Isa's.

"Here's my wife," said Michael.

"I'd better be going. You must have a lot to talk about."

Gredic put on his mac once more. Michael held out his hand.

"With Peggy and me, we always have a lot to talk about. You could say our marriage is one long argument."

A few minutes later, Peggy came in and the door opened onto the next chapter of Michael's life. It had been a long and troubled journey so far, yet he lived in hope that, one day, events would conspire to dispel the shadow of the marionette. An aspiration helped along by the fact his mother's carving now rested in fragments in a holdall Peggy had thrown onto a tip.

Acknowledgments.

Thanks to Hugh Barker and Gary Gibson for editorial comment on earlier drafts of this story, and Nicole Boccelli for copy-editing the final draft. Thanks, also, to Julia Lampshire, Russell Gardner, Yvonne Eaton, Thomas DeBrun and Mark McGuinness for critical commentary on the novel in progress.

About the Author

John Surdus is a consultant psychologist based in London, with a long standing interest in abnormal psychology, existential philosophy, and crime.

You can find out more information on his interests on his website: www.johnsurdus.com

Lightning Source UK Ltd.
Milton Keynes UK
UKHW041204210222
398997UK00001B/35